M000222882

Waxen Wings

이 상 묵님께

하 성란림

2011. 11

평화 …

Waxen Wings

THE **ACTA KOREANA** ANTHOLOGY
OF SHORT FICTION FROM KOREA

KORYO
PRESS

St. Paul,
Minnesota

Edited by
Bruce Fulton

Waxen Wings

The *Acta Koreana* Anthology of Short Fiction from Korea

Koryo Press
St. Paul, Minnesota
koryopress.com

© 2011 Koryo Press

All rights reserved. No part of this book may be reproduced, scanned, or distributed in any printed or electronic form without permission. Please do not participate in or encourage piracy of copyrighted materials in violation of the authors' rights.

The publication of this book would not have been possible without the generous support of the Korea Research Foundation and Keimyung University.

Cover art: JooYoung Choi
Cover and book design: Ann Delgehausen, Trio Bookworks

Cataloging-in-Publication data is on file at the Library of Congress, http://catalog.loc.gov/.

ISBN: 978-1-59743-203-0

Printed in Canada
16   15   14   13   12   11   1   2   3   4   5

This book is printed on acid-free paper.

Contents

PREFACE

Thanks to a generational change among the producers and publishers of literary fiction in South Korea, a more vibrant and productive community of literary translators, and generous support from Korean foundations, modern Korean fiction enjoys more visibility in the English-speaking world than ever before. How then to justify a new anthology of modern Korean short fiction? One answer, suggested in the introduction to this volume, is the range and diversity of modern literature in Korea. To this might be added the prominence earned by Korean popular culture on the international stage in recent decades, a movement that has brought Korean film, television dramas, break dancing, punk rock, installation art, graphic novels, and (finally), cuisine to the attention of the rest of the world. Where does literature fit into this Korean cultural wave? Increasingly it seems to lag behind these other art forms—because of the language barrier, some would say, or because of the forbiddingly elite tradition from which written literature was born, according to others. Whatever the reason, in an age when the image threatens to overpower the written word among consumers of art and culture, it could be argued that literature has never been more necessary.

This necessity has been acknowledged since the outset by the publishers of *Acta Koreana*, in which the nine stories contained in this volume were originally published. The existence of this anthology owes primarily to the generous support of the Korea Research Foundation and to Keimyung University, the publisher of *Acta Koreana*. Keimyung University, located in the city of Taegu, was founded shortly after the conclusion of the Korean War with the mission of bringing light to a spiritually dark and physically shattered landscape. *Acta Koreana*, an English-language academic journal of Korean Studies that began publication in the late 1990s, is alone among journals in its field in consistently bringing to readers a selection of Korean fiction in translation.

Literary anthologies result from a confluence of creative forces, and this volume is no exception. Scholars Kim Tschung-Sun and Michael Finch of Keimyung University, respectively the editor-in-chief and editor of *Acta Koreana*, are the prime movers of the anthology, and modesty alone prevents them from being acknowledged in print as co-editors of the volume. Kim Tschung-Sun has performed invaluable service as liaison with the authors (an increasingly delicate matter at a time when Korean fiction writers are increasingly being represented by international literary agencies), and Michael Finch, in spite of an astonishing work load, has done admirable duty with the traffic control that lies at the heart of editorial production.

I wish to acknowledge in addition the role played by my colleagues and students at the University of British Columbia. Ross King, Professor of Korean in our Department of Asian Studies, created the multi-media course in Korean-to-English literary translation that I now teach as the gateway course in our Department of Asian Studies' literary translation program. The fruits of that course and this program are reflected in this volume, the majority of the translators represented herein being UBC students past and present. I want to emphasize that several of these translators have already developed a fruitful relationship with the authors whose stories appear in the volume—Young-Ji Kang with Yi Hyosŏk, Janet Hong with Ha Sŏngnan, Cindy Chen with P'yŏn Hyeyŏng, Dafna Zur with Kim Yŏngha. This development, reflecting a long-term creative partnership between translator and author, is especially salutary at a time when Korean-to-English literary translation, especially for the commercial market, bears more and more obvious signs of a work-for-hire enterprise. In this respect a special thank-you is owed our publisher, Brian Boyd, who on a shoestring budget and a large measure of goodwill has undertaken publication of the anthology. As editor of the volume, I alone am responsible for shortcomings or omissions.

The translation of "Prison of the Heart" was undertaken in 2001 with the generous support of a Korea Research Foundation Grant.

Introduction

The short story has been the genre of choice for writers of literary fiction in modern Korea. Appearing in its present form in the late 1910s, the Korean short story reached an early pinnacle of development in the mid-1930s and continues to thrive in the new millennium. Along the way, it has diversified immensely, its producers no longer merely the descendants of the elite male scholar-bureaucrat class of Chosŏn times but now including writers from a variety of backgrounds—urban and rural, university and factory. Since the mid-1990s women have played a leading role. *The* Acta Koreana *Anthology of Short Fiction from Korea* embodies this diversity, beginning with stories from two of the early masters of modern Korean fiction (Yi Hyosŏk and Ch'ae Manshik) and ending with short fiction by four of the most imaginative of contemporary Korean fiction writers (Kim Yŏngha, Ha Sŏngnan, P'yŏn Hyeyŏng, and Kim Chunghyŏk). In between are the two writers who are primarily responsible for the visibility enjoyed by Korean women fiction writers today (O Chŏnghŭi and Pak Wansŏ), and a writer, Kim Wŏnil, who has made it his lifework to address the territorial division of the Korean peninsula. The title of the anthology, from Ha Sŏngnan's 1999 story, suggests both the transcendental qualities of the finest Korean short fiction as well as the continuing struggle of Korean literature to stake a claim for itself on the international literary map.

Though commonly considered a Western import by the *mundan*—the power structure of modern Korean literature, consisting not only of the writers themselves but those who teach, research, critique, and publish the literature—the short story has recognizable antecedents in early Chosŏn times (1392–late 1590s), in the form of Kim Shisŭp's tales of the supernatural, written in classical Chinese. Chosŏn writers, almost all of them male, seem to have turned to fictional narratives, writing them either in classical Chinese (as with Kim's tales) or in Korean, as a respite from the formal demands of writing in classical Chinese, a mastery of which was essential in their careers as scholar-bureaucrats. Also evident in some of these Chosŏn fictional narratives is the didactic propensity that lingers even today in Korean literature, reflecting the desire of that minuscule percentage of the Korean population that was literate to instruct the masses in neo-Confucian orthodoxy, which had become the official ideology of the Chosŏn court. By the early 1900s, fictional narratives were sufficiently popular that several Seoul newspapers had hired writers specifically to serialize works of fiction of varying lengths—the *shin sosŏl*, or "new fiction," many examples of which were written in response to the Enlightenment movement sweeping East Asia and to Korea's struggle to remain a sovereign state at a time when powers East and West were competing for influence on the Korean peninsula.

In spite of the links between the modern Korean short story and the fictional narratives of earlier times, striking differences between them can be seen in the short fiction of the late teens and early 1920s, fiction that, together with the newspaper serialization of Yi Kwangsu's novel *Mujŏng* (Heartlessness) in 1917 and the appearance of *shinch'e shi*, "new-style poetry," marks the advent of a modern literature in Korea. Signal characteristics of modern Korean fiction include its increased psychological sophistication, evident in the use of irony and in the increased complexity of the characters; attention to physical detail, especially important in the realist sketches of the 1920s and the modernist narratives of the 1930s, both types of stories often unfolding against the backdrop of the colonial metropolises of Seoul and Pyongyang; and liveliness of dialog (ironic in itself, in reflecting the influence of the undervalued Korean oral tradition).

Contributing also to the distinctiveness of the new short fiction was the exposure of its producers to Western models, commonly by way of Japan. Several of the fiction writers who blossomed in the colonial period attended Western-style preparatory schools in Korea before continuing on to university in Japan (Ch'ae Manshik studied at Waseda University in Tokyo) or Seoul (Yi Hyosŏk graduated from the Department of Law, Kyŏngsŏng Imperial University, established by the Japanese in the colonial metropolis of Seoul, or Kyŏngsŏng). In the course of their higher education writers were exposed to contemporary developments in Western literature, usually through the medium of Japanese translations. Scholars see in the late work of Yi Hyosŏk, for example, the influence of D. H. Lawrence.

Short fiction of the colonial period (1910–1945), like the short fiction that followed, is a complex tapestry in which one of the few constant strands is the masculine gender of the great majority of the writers. Realism and its more deterministic and concentrated cousin, naturalism, were preferred styles early on, adopted not only by art-for-art's sake practitioners but also by proletarian writers. Literary modernism is evident in stories from the 1930s, modernist writers sometimes using the literary equivalent of a camera eye to capture the new urban lifestyle of colonial Seoul. After the proletarian literature movement was silenced by pressure from the Japanese Government-General in the mid-1930s several writers, Yi Hyosŏk included, moved from the city to the countryside for inspiration for their work. His story "In the Mountains" reminds us of the solace that people have always sought in the natural environment when the demands of human society become onerous, and reflects the continuation of a tradition of rustification proudly adopted by centuries of Chosŏn worthies.

The short fiction of the post-Liberation "space"—the period between Liberation from Japanese colonial rule in 1945 and (depending on your definition) the establishment of separate regimes, North and South, on the Korean peninsula in 1948, or the outbreak of the Korean War in 1950—mirrors the economic, political, and cultural ferment that took place during those years. For the first time in years, Koreans could now publish freely in their own language, and many writers took up the brush and resumed careers dating back, in the case of Ch'ae Manshik, to the 1920s. Writers such as Ch'ae who had lived most of their lives during the colonial period were confronted with a heavy burden upon Liberation: how to explain their literary success when so many of their fellow Koreans had suffered under the Japanese. This question vexed Ch'ae until his death from tuberculosis in 1950. His answers were several, and they feature a variety of voices, each protagonist searching his soul for an explanation of how he responded to the realities of colonial occupation: a writer ("Public Offender" [Minjok ŭi choein, 1948–49]), a landowner ("Once Upon a Paddy" [Non iyagi, 1946]), a schoolteacher ("The Wife and Children" [Ch'ŏja, 1948]), and a policeman ("Constable Maeng" [Maeng sunsa, 1946]). Anticipating the gaps of silence in the official historical narrative of the Republic of Korea, the tone of some of these narratives is strikingly muted in contrast with the brashness of much of Ch'ae's work from the colonial period.

By now the story is well known of how the demarcation of the Korean peninsula by the Allied powers in the summer of 1945 led to the establishment of separate regimes north and south and to a state of war between them that, in the absence of a formal peace treaty, continues to this day. The territorial and resulting spiritual division of Korea looms so large in post-Liberation Korean history that literature in South Korea may be seen largely as a literature of national division. Kim Wŏnil, born in Kyŏngsang Province in the

southeast, is one of the most prominent voices of division literature.
He is among the small but influential group of writers who through
the themes of their stories and through political activism resulting
in jail sentences have collectively become the authorial conscience
of their nation.

Short fiction from the 1970s is notable for giving voice to the little people on whose backs the Korean economic miracle was made
possible, as well as to the millions of Koreans who were affected
by the fateful decision by Allied forces to divide the peninsula in
August 1945 in order to disarm Japanese forces; the division was
cemented by the July 1953 armistice that was meant to bring an
end to Korean War hostilities. The 1970s are also notable for the
addition of two distinctive female voices to the predominantly
male chorus of fiction writers to date. The younger of the two, O
Chŏnghŭi, was the first to debut, with a precocious story of paren-
tal abandonment, sibling death, and same-sex desire, "The Toyshop
Woman" (Wan'gujŏm yŏin, 1968). Intensely interested in the frac-
tures in contemporary Korean society and family life, O has been
particularly successful in conveying the trauma experienced by
victims of civil war and a rigid and merciless social structure. An
ingeniously intertextual writer, O in "Weaver Woman" (Chingnyŏ,
1970) adopts the herder boy and the weaving girl of one of Korea's
best-known folktales, who are separated forever for neglecting their
duties, and recasts them as a barren wife and her wandering husband, who are separated by her inability to produce the all-impor-
tant male offspring who must continue the family line and oversee
the ancestral rites.

Pak Wansŏ for her part raised a family before launching a writing career with the publication of *The Naked Tree* (Na'mok) in 1970.
As fearless as O in confronting the social, cultural, and political conflict in post-1945 Korea, she is strikingly different in her narrative
approach. Whereas O has favored interior narratives whose tension
often owes, especially in her earlier stories, to the employment of a

nameless first-person narrator, Pak's narrators often comes across as voluble storytellers, "neighborhood aunties" who have seen all and done all and are uncannily attuned to similar experiences of their listeners. As important as the engaging quality of her narratives are the uses to which she puts them. Since her earliest stories in the 1970s, such as "In the Realm of the Buddha" (Puch'ŏnim kŭnch'ŏ, 1973), Pak has explored narrative fiction as a trauma-healing device. In this story the narrator speaks of her and her mother's traumatic loss of family members during the Korean War as an undigested lump of experience that desperately needs purging. Although the character's initial creative efforts at catharsis are unsatisfactory, they represent a start to the healing process, and in Pak's case, that process has extended to a series of autobiographical novels, of which *Who Ate Up All the Shinga?* (Kŭ mantŏn shinga nŭn nu ka ta mŏgŏssŭlkka, 2008) is an excellent example.

A second use to which Pak puts her narratives is the socialization of a younger generation of readers to the societal, cultural, and geopolitical transformation of the Korean peninsula. Readers of "Winter Outing" (Kyŏul nadŭri, 1975), for example, will learn what it feels like to be the spouse of someone who has a family in North Korea. Readers of "Identical Apartments" (Talmŭn pang tŭl, 1974) will experience the shock of moving from a traditional living space in a freestanding home, be it ever so modest, to the beehive cluster that is the modern apartment complex. Readers of "Thus Ended My Days of Watching Over the House" (Chippogi nŭn kŭrŏke kŭnnatta, 1978) will feel the narrator's double sense of betrayal as her scholar husband is taken away by the authorities for some unmentioned offense—not only *How could they do this to him?* but ultimately more bothersome to her, *How could he leave me like this?*

A third function of Pak's narratives is to expose hypocrisy wherever she sees it. There is nothing new about these approaches to fiction in post-Liberation Korea. What is distinctive about Pak's approach, though, is that for the most part her stories avoid the

didactic tendentiousness of the works of some of her contemporaries.
This accomplishment owes not only to her facility for engaging her
readers but also to her use of narrators who themselves share the
foibles, petty jealousies, and status-driven scheming of the other
characters, narrators who are quick to acknowledge their own
shortcomings rather than conveniently saving face.

The mid-1990s were a watershed in modern Korean short fiction, for two main reasons. First, the pioneering work of writers such
as O Chŏnghŭi and Pak Wansŏ continued to blossom in a body of
prize-winning fiction by women such as Ch'oe Yun, Kong Chiyŏng,
Shin Kyŏngsuk, Ŭn Hŭigyŏng, Ha Sŏngnan, Cho Kyŏngnan, Yi
Hyegyŏng, Kim Insuk, and Han Kang. Gender imbalance, still evident in Korean poetry at the dawn of the new millennium, in the
case of fiction became a thing of the past. The second transformation taking place in the mid-1990s was the advent of a more reader-
friendly culture of literary fiction. Production values were enhanced
by the major publishers of literary fiction: Munhak kwa chisŏng sa
(Munji for short), Minŭm sa, Ch'angjak kwa pip'yŏng sa (Ch'angbi),
and, most significantly, Munhak tongne. The printed page became
less cluttered and dense, the covers more colorful, the photos of
authors more engaging. The fiction itself was more reader-respectful
if not necessarily more accessible. The literary journals (each of the
aforementioned publishers issued one) likewise embodied a generational change in the writers they published, the critics who evalu-
ated those writers and their works, and the outlook they represented.

Kim Yŏngha and Ha Sŏngnan debuted in the 1990s, P'yŏn
Hyeyŏng and Kim Chunghyŏk in the new millennium. All four
exhibit a lighter touch than their elders—a facility with subject matter such as sex and death, a focus on the exterior as well as the interior landscape, a relatively straightforward prose style, a sense of
humor, and a somewhat cynical world-view. Kim Yŏngha hit the literary stage running (the Korean term for "literary debut," *tŭngdan*,
literally means "take the stage") with his novel *I Have the Right to*

Destroy Myself (Na nŭn na rŭl p'agoehal kwŏlli ka itta, 1996), about a writer who takes inspiration from the life stories of clients who consult him wishing to take their own lives. But rather than allowing himself to be typecast as an enfant terrible, Kim has continually diversified, writing stories about vampires, murders, a club of lightning-struck people, and a home invasion by a renegade soldier, as well as novels that are intertextual (*What's the Matter with Arang?* [Arang ŭn wae, 2001]), that investigate the Korean diaspora (*Black Flowers* [Kŏmŭn kkot, 2003]), that involve North Korea (*Your Republic is Calling You* [Pit ŭi cheguk, 2006]), and that portray young South Koreans in cyberspace (*Quiz Show* [K'wijŭ shyo, 2007]). What makes Kim's narratives especially effective is the ease with which he presents subject matter such as suicide and sexual promiscuity. Tapping into the subconscious of his readers, he makes the grotesque sound somehow familiar. Kim is also well read and well traveled, giving him valuable insights into the changes taking place among Koreans and their society within the context of global development.

Ha Sŏngnan's works alternate between reflections on social issues, as seen in "Star-Shaped Stain" (Pyŏl moyang ŭi ŏlluk, 2001) based on a conflagration that took the lives of twenty-three children at a recreation center in 1999, and sardonic, surreal sketches of individuals who are out of place and time, as for example, in "Flies" (P'ari, 1999). Frequent in her narratives are portraits of the inner workings of a solitary individual seeking meaning in the increasingly fragmented and alienated society of present-day urban South Korea—the garbage explorer in Ha's prize-winning "Blooms of Mold" (Komp'angi kkot, 1998), the scaler of utility poles in "Banner" (Kitpal, 1999), and the transcendental protagonist of "Waxen Wings" (Ch'onnong nalgae, 1999).

P'yŏn Hyeyŏng, in her two story collections and one novel to date, has crafted a formidable body of fiction that subverts male privilege in a traditional patriarchal society. Males in her stories are subject to forces beyond their control—a pandemic, as in the title story of her first collection, *Mallow Gardens* (Aoi kadŏn, 2003) and in her novel *Ash and Red* (Chae wa ppalgan, 2010); fascination with murder victims, as in the story translated here and in "Who Killed the All-American Girl?" (Nu ka ol amerik'an kŏl ŭl chugyŏnna, 2002); and runaway urban renewal and materialism ("The First Anniversary" [Ch'ŏtpŏntchae ki'nyŏm'il], 2006). Increasingly evident in her work is a mordant wit that is focused on the lives of urban denizens today, as in the unsettling title story of her second collection, *To the Kennels* (Sayukchang tchogŭro, 2006), and in stories such as "The Death Throes of a Modern-Day Rabbit" (T'okki ŭi myo, 2009) and "The Canning Factory" (T'ongjorim kongjang, 2010). Her fictional works complement those of Ha Sŏngnan—hers are more outward-looking whereas Ha's tend to be more introspective—and in combination with the stories of contemporaries such as Kim Aeran, Yun Sŏnghŭi, Ch'ŏn Unyŏng, Kim Sum, and Han Yuju they offer us a panorama of the lives of a new generation of women in urban South Korea.

Kim Chunghyŏk is a nimble writer whose brash outlook is reminiscent of two earlier masters of Korean short fiction—Ch'oe Manshik, whose signature story, "A Ready-Made Life" (Redimeidŭ insaeng, 1934), featured a similar set of unemployed intellectuals, and Kim Sŭngok, who with Ch'oe Inho brought a vigorous, youthful energy to Korean fiction in the 1960s and 1970s. In Kim's stories, as in Kim Yŏngha's *I Have the Right to Destroy Myself*, life becomes art—and what better way to respond to the oppression brought upon citizens by traditional neo-Confucian society and the anomie of contemporary urban culture?

If the stories of these four younger writers are any indication, the future of short fiction in Korea is promising. These writers and their contemporaries are increasingly stretching the boundaries of realist narrative, experimenting with multiple narrative points of view, positioning their characters in environments, domestic or foreign, unfamiliar to an earlier generation of readers, and giving their characters unprecedented freedom of choice. At the same

time, through the Internet and an increasingly reader-friendly literary culture, readers in South Korea and abroad have unprecedented
access to their authors. It remains to be seen how this access, how
the changing demographics of South Korean society, and how the
ever-uncertain future of North Korea will influence the writing and
the reception of Korean short fiction.

IN THE MOUNTAINS

Yi Hyosŏk

Translated by Young-Ji Kang

Yi Hyosŏk (1907–1942) is one of the major fiction writers of the colonial period, an author who left a surprisingly large and varied body of work in his short lifetime. Like several of his contemporaries, Yi began publishing at a remarkably young age: his first story appeared in print before he was eighteen. But the story that first brought him recognition in the Korean literary world was "City and Specter" (1928, Toshi wa yuryŏng). Evident in this story is the author's sympathy for the working poor of Seoul and his representation of the city as vicious and destructive. Yi's interest in international socialism is reflected in stories such as "Along the Russian Coast" (1931, Noryŏng kŭnhae), which takes place aboard a vessel bound for the Soviet maritime region. Five short years later, with the suppression of the proletarian literature movement by the Japanese authorities, writers such as Yi who supported the ideals of socialism but were not themselves hard-line ideologues turned elsewhere for inspiration for their works. In 1933 Yi together with some of the most distinctive stylists of modern Korean literature—including fiction writers Yi T'aejun and Yi Muyŏng, poets Kim Kirim and Chŏng Chiyong, and the playwright Yu Ch'ijin—formed the Kuinhoe (Circle of Nine). Thereafter, like several of his Kuinhoe colleagues, and in particular the poets, he began to focus more on language, mood, and imagery. For the background of some of his best-known stories he utilized the Kangwŏn-Ch'ungch'ŏng border area where he was born. His canonical story "When the Buckwheat Blooms" (1936, Memil kkot p'il muryŏp) is flawlessly structured, timeless in its rural market-day setting, and rich in native Korean vocabulary. Also dating from 1936 (when it appeared in the journal Samch'ŏlli), "San," the story translated here, has a touch of back-to-nature mysticism that not only looks back to native Korean spiritualism but foreshadows what some scholars see as a Lawrencian eroticism appearing in Yi's works from the late 1930s on, such as the novel Flower Dust (1939, Hwabun). Yi's premature death from meningitis deprived us of an important writer whose best work might still have been ahead of him.

Chungshil searched the branches of the hazelnut tree he had just cut down. In no time he had himself a handful of nuts. They were in season, as ripe as ripe can be, and they cracked in two between his teeth.

The sky in autumn is as blue as the back of a fish—if you threw a rock up there, that crystal sky might crack open as easily as a hazelnut. High overhead is a curious cluster of clouds huddled like broken clamshells scattered along the beach. You'd expect the sky to be close here on the spine of the mountain, but it's no closer than it is when you see it from down in the village—we're talking thousands of miles distance, after all. From the valley, you'd think the sky would be within reach once you gain the foot of the mountain, but as soon as you're partway up, the autumn sky beats a hasty retreat—thousands of miles of distance.

Except for the gentle pulsing of their breath, the morning hours in these woods are still as a dozing beast. That ridge looks like the back of a sleeping bull, and in the windless quaking of the aspen leaves you can hear the mountain breathing. Look, the beauty queen of the mountains, the birch all in white. No matter how fancied up a person is, could her skin ever be as white as the birch's? The trees are more numerous than the villagers, more varied than their family names. Hushed and calm, they grow thick and carefree. The alders, the various oaks, the birches, linden and bush clover, and in the valleys maple, crab apple, buckthorn, lacquer tree, and thorny ash. The woods with their mix of fragrant evergreens on the backbone of the mountain—pines, firs, and junipers—they too grow thick and carefree, a beautiful world where tranquility and commotion jointly abide.

The aroma of fruit that's fresh and alive, the scent of trees, the smells of soil and sky—these fragrances are not to be found in the village.

Nestled in the fallen leaves and cracking open hazelnuts one at a time, Chungshil was scarcely aware of these fragrances, the sight of the trees, the sky above—for they had all pervaded him, and he felt them even before he was aware of it. He and the mountain were one.

And before he knew it, his eyes were tinted with the blue of the sky, and his skin was redolent of the forest scent. Burying himself chest deep in a cushion of hazelnut and oak leaves, softer even than a bed of straw, made his body feel just like a tree that had sprung from the ground—a tree amidst a throng of pines and oaks. His feet were the roots, his arms the branches. If he were cut, resin would flow instead of blood. A tree like them, he could pretty much guess the tacit words they exchanged, the gestures of their branches, and the earthly desires whispered by their leaves. He could easily unlock the ways and secrets of the trees, their enjoyment as they basked in the sun, their wantonness when the wind blew, and their wry faces on a cloudy day. His body was a tree.

A surge of energy sent Chungshil jumping to his feet. The energy coursed through his outstretched limbs, and he felt as if the next moment he would rise up into the sky. His only outlet for this flood of energy was to open his mouth wide and shout to the high heavens. His voice rang with the pure energy pulsating through this mountain.

The mountain answered, the trees nodding in agreement. Also responding to his call was a pair of pheasants, pounding the air from across the valley. The cock-pheasant flew with the fat hen's tail in his beak, his iridescent plumage shining brilliantly against the clear sky.

At the sight of the fat pheasant, Chungshil realized he was hungry. His thoughts turned to the venison and the comb honey in its oak-leaf wrappings that he had cached beside the stream, and he took up his sickle. He would have to gather a full load of brush before his first rest break if he wanted to arrive at the village before the market closed, sell his brush, and return to the mountain before dark. Now that he had rested awhile, his arms were plenty strong. The rustling of the leaves stirred his bosom and a shot of pure energy coursed through him. It's a million times better to live up in the mountains than down in the village! Chungshil told himself. It was a good thing he had moved up here.

There's no job in this world less profitable than working as a farm-hand.

It's not that Chungshil had wanted to argue; it was more like Old Kim wanted to pick a fight. Now that Chungshil thought about it, Old Kim must certainly have meant to get rid of him all along. After nearly eight years of work as a farmhand, he had been driven empty-handed from his home. He felt resentful and chagrined, but he didn't spend time bemoaning it.

Never had he received his yearly farmhand wage on time. Not once was he given a decent set of clothes. On festival days, he didn't have a copper to his name—he was hungry as a dog on First Lunar Full Moon Day. Old Kim would find him a wife, he would buy him a house, he would help him get settled—empty promises, all of them. Old Kim's claim that Chungshil had fiddled with his concubine was bullshit, something he'd schemed from the outset. Why, laying hands on that plug-ugly back-scratcher was the furthest thing from Chungshil's mind. Just because he'd bumped into her outside the village and they'd returned home in close proximity, she with her pile of laundry and he with his stack of brush, was no reason for him to be the object of suspicion. In fact, it was some shady reprobate that the concubine was fooling around with, and yet poor Chungshil became the victim when Old Kim decided to vent his anger. Even so, Chung-shil felt pity for this old man who suffered from his unrestrained con-cubine's brazen behavior. He was better off leaving, because he knew that things would only get messier.

Where beneath these broad skies was Chungshil to go? The place where he had always felt most comfortable was the mountain where he gathered firewood. The thick pile of leaves, softer than a bed of straw, came to mind. He was in a world of his own up there—a world that wouldn't betray him. And so, into the woods he went, his empty back-rack his only possession. The test would be just how long he could last there.

The place he arrived at was a deep valley about a mile in from Pakchung Hollow, cut off from village and folk. Gently sloping on either side, the south slope bathed in sun, it cupped a stream, beside which fruits and berries grew in abundance. Many were the times he had dozed on that sunny slope. And it was there beside the stream that he would make a fire and roast the ears of corn he had picked along the way, full though he was with akebi, wrinkled crab apples, and hawthorn berries. And for a bed of gathered leaves it wasn't that chilly a place to sleep.

The following day, he happened upon a beehive hanging within reach from a honey locust. Lighting some tobacco leaves, he smoked out the bees and managed to extract the core. It was brimming with clear honey—ready for consumption. Just a little bit took the edge off his hunger. The honey and the comb sustained him for several days.

The honey still hadn't run out two nights earlier when he noticed a fire burning across the valley. The flames, bright red as a crape myrtle, shot up into the dark sky, all the more noticeable now that it was night. The charred trees looked like mulberry leaves reduced to skeletons by silkworms, and among them pockets of fire remained. Weren't they beautiful, those flames flickering like the tongue of a hungry devil! More strikingly beautiful than flowers peeking out from a brushwood fence, more beautiful than the gleaming texture of silk, the colors of a rainbow, the brilliance of a cockscomb.

Chungshil grabbed a stick and ran off over the ridge and across the valley, drawn to the fire. He couldn't have explained the excitement he felt. The flames had seemed close by but in fact were quite far off. The fire jumped the ridge and spread down the valley. Chungshil sweltered in the throbbing waves of heat, the scorching temperature keeping him at a distance. Flaming roots crackled and the earth rumbled. The slender birches erupted in flames, their burning branches resembling coral. What a waste! All Chungshil could do was to circle the fire and flail impotently at the flames. The fire was more than a match for him.

It was near daybreak, the fire nearly burned out, when Chungshil found the deer. Trapped by the flames, it had gone around in circles until the fire claimed it. He felt terribly sorry for the poor beast, but now it was meat rather than animal, and so Chungshil slung the carcass over his shoulders and returned to his place. Best simply to consider it as the mountain's grace. This source of food sated him for days. One thing alone he longed for—salt. People he could do without, but the taste of salt, he needed that. And this thought in turn made him long for the village.

Chungshil arrived, spent, at the market with his load of brush. The prospect of trekking nonstop for four or five miles had made him sweat even more. The load of brush had reeled and lurched as he tramped along.

It was just before closing. Never had he been so glad to sell his brush. Never had he been so glad to buy things with the proceeds. Especially the one thing he needed the most.

And so it was salt that he bought, and along with it a sack of potatoes, a measure of millet, and a pot. These would sustain him during his solitary life in the woods, he told himself as he set off back to the mountains. He wouldn't have seafood—but that wouldn't kill him. His back-rack was more manageable now. What he saw about him here in the village was no different from before—noisy and squalid as ever. If nothing was worse, then nothing was better either.

And there were still the rowdy fights in the back rooms of the drinking places.

Strange as it seems, this kind of village life did not appeal to him in the least. Nor did he miss the haggard faces of the villagers much.

What was it that made him miss the mountains so? He wondered briefly if he was eccentric, but no, that didn't make much sense. It was just that he liked to be out in the sun, his eyes were drawn to the white birches, and the oak leaves charmed him. Perhaps he had been born to live out his life in the mountains.

One day, Chungshil encountered Pak Sŏbang in the village and heard news of Old Kim—not that he had felt compelled to learn what had become of him.

It turned out that Old Kim's lousy back-scratcher of a concubine had sneaked off at last with a clerk by the name of Ch'oe. A search was under way but there was no clue as to their whereabouts.

Chungshil could picture pathetic Old Kim, all by himself in the master's quarters, grumbling to himself as he tried to fall asleep. And he could imagine the old man blaming himself for driving his faithful farmhand away. But he had no intention of returning to Old Kim and the idea of trying to comfort him was not to his liking.

What this latest news did was make life in the village seem even messier.

He felt all the more relieved as he followed the path up into the mountains that evening.

It was well into the night when Chungshil was done with the dinner he had thrown together over the fire beside the stream. Stars studded the heavens; a branch was caught between the horns of the crescent moon. The birds were at roost, the wind at rest—the stream alone murmured and breathed. The dark ridge resembled a sleeping bull.

The waning fire still crackled and the savory smell of burning leaves enveloped him. He felt pleasantly warm hunched up in front of the fire as he smoked. He couldn't have asked for more.

And yet there remained one desire, welling up within him.

Hardworking fellows like Chungshil were meant to be tilling the fields and gathering wood, not cooking. And who better to do the cooking than Yongnyŏ, the girl who lived next door to Old Kim?

The only thing for it was to marry her and let her take over the responsibilities.

Just the thought of her tickled him. One by one, things were sorting themselves out in his mind.

I'll cut down some big old trees, chop them into logs, bark and all, find myself a nice sunny spot and build a snug little one-room hut. I'll clear the hillside where it flattens out and plant potatoes and oats come spring. I'll make a pen and get myself some goats and pigs and chickens. Then, if I go out in the woods and get my hands on a deer, I'll have a place to keep it. I'll be outside plowing the fields and gathering wood and Yongnyŏ will be taking care of things inside. We'll have a baby boy and it'll grow up strong as an ox and solid as a mountain. I'm going to go down to the village in the middle of the night, and if Yongnyŏ won't come along on her own, then I'll carry her back. Once I've got her up here, that's that. . . .

The embers of the fire gradually cooled, and the murmurs of the stream grew clearer.

The sky was a dizzying cluster of stars.

The moon had caught another branch.

He tamped out the remaining coals with his foot and the valley grew all the more lonesome.

What time was it? Here in the mountains, you couldn't tell. Was it too early to sleep? Too late? Off he went toward his sleeping place beneath the tree. He buried himself inside the haystack-thick pile of leaves, only his face peeking out. He felt warm, comfortable, snug.

The stars seemed to draw near, go away, draw near, go away. . . . And when they drew near, it was almost as if they were about to shower down upon him.

"One star in me. Two stars in me. Three stars in me. . . ."

Before he knew it, Chungshil was counting the stars. And when he lost count, his eyelids heavy and his tongue twisted, he started all over again, his voice louder.

"One star in me. Two stars in me. Three stars in me. . . ."

And as he counted, Chungshil felt himself turning into a star.

CONSTABLE MAENG

Ch'ae Manshik

Translated by Joel Stevenson

Ch'ae Manshik was born in a coastal village in North Chŏlla Province in 1902. Like many of the intellectuals of his generation, he studied in Japan before returning to colonial Korea to work at various writing and editorial jobs. He died of tuberculosis in 1950. ▥ Whether he was writing fiction, plays, essays, or criticism, Ch'ae was one of the great talents of modern Korean literature. His command of idiom, realistic dialogue, and keen wit produced a fictional style all his own. The immediacy of his narratives, the sense of the storyteller speaking directly to the listener, reminds many readers of the traditional oral narrative, *p'ansori*, which had flourished in Ch'ae's native Chŏlla region since Chosŏn times. ▥ Ch'ae is often thought of as a satirist, but he was much more than that.

Before satirical sketches such as "My Innocent Uncle" (1938, Ch'isuk), about an opportunistic young man and his socialist uncle, and "Mister Pang" (1946, Mistŭ'ŏ Pang), set during the 1945–1948 American military occupation of what would become South Korea, Ch'ae had written "Age of Transition" (1923, Kwadogi), an autobiographical novella about Korean students in Japan testing the currents of modernization that swept urban East Asia in the early 1900s. In other early works, such as "In Three Directions" (1924, Segillo) and "Sandungi" (1930, Sandungi), he dealt with the class differences that are so distinct in Korean society past and present. In these earlier stories Ch'ae is concerned as well with the plight of the unemployed intelligentsia who thronged the colonial metropolis of Seoul. Impecunious young intellectuals making the rounds of publishing houses and pawnshops are portrayed with devastating accuracy in "A Ready-Made Life" (1934, Redimeidŭ insaeng). In the late 1930s Ch'ae wrote two of the most ambitious novels of the colonial period, *Muddy Currents* (1937–38, T'angnyu), about grain speculation, and *Peace Under Heaven* (1938, T'aep'yŏng ch'ŏnha), which skewers those who thrived materially but wasted spiritually during the Japanese occupation. ■ Ch'ae's works from the post-Liberation period are more muted. "Public Offender" (1948–49, Minjok ŭi choein), for example, is a semi-autobiographical response to the post-Liberation trials of those accused of collaborating with the Japanese. In these stories, the author's wit is tempered by the spiritual turmoil of having to come to grips with the role of the artist in a colonized society. "Once Upon a Paddy" (1946, Non iyagi), and "The Wife and Children" (1948, Ch'ŏja) are pessimistic accounts of post-Liberation society. ■ "Maeng sunsa," translated here, was first published in 1946 in *Paeng-min.* Tackling the delicate issue of the constituency of post-Liberation security forces under the American military government, it also features one of Ch'ae's recurring themes—the war between the sexes—as well as revealing glimpses of a traditional status-based society.

W as Constable Maeng a direct descendant of the great sage Mencius, known to us as Maengja? No one seems to know. Nor was it known for sure how many generations separated the noted prime minister Maeng Kobul and the Chinese scholar-official Maeng Chŏngsŭng.

"You're such a bumbling fool—ten years a constable and you've never once given me a silk dress. What do you have to say for yourself?"

It used to be that the wives of constables had three distinguishing characteristics. To wit, they were cunning, they looked down on others, and they dressed lavishly. In fact, it was on account of the vanity of women like this that constables were all the more stubborn and stern in the execution of their "duties." Sŏbun was the wife of Constable Maeng, and we can say with certainty that in terms of eloquence and brains (or should we say conceitedness) she took a back seat to no one. Only when it came to clothing was she unable to hold her head high. She became the wife of this "great" constable and what a shame it was that she couldn't dress extravagantly. It was indeed a pity the way she lamented this fact.

But this wife of a constable was most certainly not at fault for her purported lack of confidence with respect to extravagant dressing—

incompetent she was not. The fact was, during the eight years her husband was a constable (she had exaggerated when she told him ten), never had he provided her a silk dress. You see the constable wasn't too savvy and he had no talent for obtaining the goods they needed.

Immediately following Liberation Constable Maeng found himself out of a job. By then his life as a constable had become like a dream to him. But still he would have to contend with this simple woman and her one-track mind. She would cling to her lost opportunities even to the point of death. Why, only just this morning she had started up her bitching about the silk dress and the constable's bumbling nature.

"Suppose I gave you a wardrobe full of clothes. What would you do with them? You put them on and you take them off. Is there more to it than that? I can't figure you women."

The constable said this rather softly. Exactly to the contrary, Sŏbun replied in a loud, bitchy voice, "What do you mean, put 'em on and take 'em off? What have you ever given me to put on and take off anyway? Where are all these clothes you're talking about?"

"Oh, I'm not saying you, in particular, have a lot of clothes. I'm talking about women in general."

"You are such a jerk. If you had a mouth as big as a wicker basket there's nothing you could say for yourself. It's no use. No matter what I say you don't get it. You're a fool! A bum! A moron!"

"You mean you don't like your good-for-nothing husband?"

"Is there anything good about you?"

"Well, should we split up?"

"Oh, puhleeze!"

"So!"

"I'm so sick and tired."

"Well whatever, I'm signing up to be a constable again."

"What's a man good for if his wife doesn't have clothes to go out in?"

"All right. When I'm a constable again I'll get you that silk dress and a black camel-hair overcoat and a satin jacket and a platinum watch to go with it . . ."

"Oh no you won't, not a two-bit constable like you. Maybe a constable with a lot more smarts than you've got. Anyway, I've given up on the silk dress. I'd settle for a plain one."

"Ha! Don't you remember that song 'We're so poor, but we have each other and a little bit to eat, and that's all right by me'?"

"Yes, I remember . . . but so what? . . . We've never even had a few coppers to spare. How am I supposed to run this household on nothing? Day after tomorrow we'll be out of rice and firewood."

"I worry about this too, you know!"

With that, Constable Maeng stubbed out his after-dinner smoke, eased himself up, and prepared to go out. A light autumn rain had begun.

This year Sŏbun was twenty-five and in the prime of young womanhood. At seventeen she had wed Constable Maeng, who was then thirty. The constable had lost his first wife the year before.

Sŏbun was as tall and slender as her tongue was sharp. She was a high-maintenance sort of woman, and the knowledge that she was her husband's second wife, with all that this entailed, made it seem worthwhile for her to play on his affections by pestering him terribly and behaving badly. Constable Maeng spoiled her by indulging her behavior. He was thirty-eight and his wife, thirteen years younger, was like a daughter to him. This made him all the more infatuated with her. Daughter or wife, it didn't matter; his infatuation blinded him to her faults, which he thought were simply adorable.

Constable Maeng would soon be forty. A person who turns forty has seen it all. The rough edges get rounded off and he begins to mellow. Besides this softening brought on by age, Constable Maeng was of an easy-going disposition. Most things wouldn't get him riled. He never forced his opinion on anyone, nor was he overly stubborn. It was against his nature, and besides, he considered such behavior distasteful and unnecessary. Rare indeed were the times he argued or feuded with others. To put it nicely, he sort of went with the flow. But, in fact, there were those who called him dim-witted and foolish, who said he lacked ambition and talent.

Realizing the kind of man he was, Sŏbun knew that no matter how poorly she comported herself, no matter how harshly she pestered him, he would seldom stand up to her or fight back. Try as she might to pick a fight, all he would ever do was respond with the same gentle voice.

As he eased himself up and gazed out at the rain falling in the yard, he drove the point home to his wife,

"It's a good thing I'm an upright man. You've heard about the others, haven't you? Some were beaten to death, some had their houses burned down, some had their arms and legs broken."

But to Sŏbun these were empty words—the same old lame excuses.

"Hmph! Mr. Kanamoto got promoted to inspector even though he's as crooked as they come."

"How long do you think that will last?"

"Well if that's the way you see things, then you must be smug. Mr. Kinoshita and his family moved back from Yŏju and now he's rolling in dough. They have two Injang brand sewing machines and a bunch of furniture and his wife's clothes fill fifteen trunks. Now that he's back in Seoul, do you think he feels guilty? He bought a gristmill and now he's making good money and living the easy life. Nobody was killed, nobody got his limbs broken. You're wrong!"

"The things people do . . . Well, isn't it all just thievery?"

"So, even when your belly is rumbling with hunger are you going to keep yapping about how upright you are?"

"You bet I am. No matter how poor you are, as long as you're upright, you've got nothing to fear."

Finally, Constable Maeng made his way over to the wardrobe. His face twitched at the sight of it. Back when he had been a guard at the jail, there had been a furniture maker among the prisoners. Sŏbun had pestered Constable Maeng to pass on a slip of paper to the man. The constable put up a feeble show of resistance to the idea but ended up presenting the note to the prisoner. When a wardrobe arrived at his door two days later, Constable Maeng asked no questions.

The wrinkled hemp uniform hanging in the wardrobe caused the face of this upright constable to prickle even more than the wardrobe itself. The suit had been custom-made early last fall at a tailor shop across from the police station, about which there were some nasty rumors flying around. The suit bore a price of 32 *wŏn* and change. When the constable went to pick it up he had only 3 *wŏn* in his wallet. Reaching for his wallet, he asked, "How much is it?" The owner said, "Don't mention it," and ushered him out the door in possession of the suit.

The wardrobe and the suit were just two examples. During his eight years of making the rounds as a constable there was a three-year interval in which he supplemented his meager salary through bribery. Thirty *wŏn* here, 100 *wŏn* there. He couldn't refuse—this was how he rationalized it to himself. Far be it for him to know how much he had collected over the years. Apart from what people volunteered, when he was lacking something he'd go looking for a likely victim and say something like, "I'll pay you back soon—can you lend me just a hundred *wŏn*?" Here was a frequent source of spending money.

He was treated to countless rounds of drinks. And not to be missed were rice, firewood, meat, fish, liquor, and the like. They all flowed in. There was no shortage at home, and many were the times he was invited out. Even though the constable's wife complained to the high heavens that he never gave her anything, he had in fact procured fabric for her several times. But for some strange reason, when it came to the silk dress, he just couldn't produce. And then Liberation, August 15, caught him by surprise.

Inconsequential though these incidents were, still they consti-
tuted bribery. Even so, Constable Maeng felt pretty confident in his
uprightness. It was no sin to accept a suit of clothes, a few *wŏn* here
or a hundred *wŏn* there, or the rice or the firewood or the groceri-
ies or the bottles of liquor. It was a common practice and anyone
would have done the same. Therefore, it counted neither as corruption nor as an abuse of his position. Rather, corruption or crime was
something that involved tens of thousands of *wŏn*—hitting the jackpot and changing one's life-style. Only then did it become a problem.
Constable Maeng had never taken more than a hundred *wŏn* at any
one time. For that reason he considered himself upright.

But look at the people he had worked with: Nine out of ten raked
in conspicuous sums—talk about being in fat city! Some bought ten-
thousand-*wŏn* homes, some bought productive farmland in Yangju,
and some of them retired as shareholders in trading companies.

*If only I could grab onto a chance like that . . . a chance to get a
house. . . .* Constable Maeng was always on an anxious lookout for
his big chance. But for some reason, opportunity never visited him.
So he ended up out of a job in his "upright" way, with nothing but
small-time pickings to show for it.

It is true he had desired and expected a bigger piece of the pie,
but that wasn't the problem. To Constable Maeng's way of thinking
uprightness went something like this: *Since I wasn't a big player, and I
didn't get rich, I am upright.*

His umbrella fending off the drizzle, Constable Maeng headed
off for the police academy at military headquarters. The application
and resume he'd been carting around were tucked into the breast
pocket of his coat.

Immediately following Liberation Constable Maeng had come
down with a bad case of fear—the fear of being beaten with a club
at any time or stabbed with a cold steel blade in some dark alley.
Now what do you suppose the good constable did to protect himself
from those who would do this kind of thing? Why, he unbuckled his

sword and retired. But now that he was without a job, he had to face all these perplexing problems day after day. His wife did not have to tell him that they were scraping the bottom of the barrel, but it was unclear to him how they would buy rice and firewood.

It seemed that the world was full of money and that there were plenty of jobs and an abundance of goods to be had. But no other kind of work presented itself to our Constable Maeng, who had never known anything else.

"Since that's the only kind of thievery I know, what can I do? Times are different now," he tsk-tsked. "What's a guy to do?"

So in the end, he reluctantly gave in and decided to go back to being a constable again.

The cap, uniform, and saber were the same as before. And now with the addition of an armband, Constable Maeng was a new constable of liberated Korea. He walked to a police box on east Chongno. With his eight years' experience and a simple test to prove his qualifications, he had been appointed on the spot and assigned to a police station. As he was finishing his shift on the second day, he was reassigned to another branch station. This was his destination now.

Although Constable Maeng was decked out as always, for some unknown reason he felt no sense of dignity or excitement in his work. The people he met showed none of the caution of old and barely gave him a second glance as they went by. Some passersby actually dared to glare at him with animosity and disdain.

Now that constables didn't willfully arrest people or threaten them—and of course they weren't allowed to rough anyone up anymore—he just couldn't fathom why the citizenry didn't feel more at ease around them.

He walked along wrapped up in thought:

Maybe we acted terribly in the past. . . .

That must be the reason.

I guess we did treat innocent people badly and wrongly accused others.

So now if people are rude, there's not much I can do.

But, what goes around, comes around. I guess it's true what they say, that all good things must come to an end. We had a good thing going, and now it's time to pay for it.

Unconsciously, he sighed.

Finally he arrived at the police box, and there he discovered another reason people despised constables.

The junior officer suddenly awakened, his head jerking up from the table at the sound of Maeng's clumping footsteps.

"Hey . . . sleeping on the job?" yelled Constable Maeng from habit. He looked the junior officer up and down. It was Noma. Constable Maeng wouldn't have recognized him if it weren't for the red spot on his face.

Noma, the tenant's son.

Until this year, when he moved to his current house in Hongp'a-dong, Constable Maeng had lived for six years in Sajik-dong. Noma's family were already renting there when Constable Maeng had moved in. Noma, with the red spot on the left side of his face, was twelve then. He attended a neighborhood school but never took it seriously and dropped out after a year. He would hang out in front of the Umi Theater carrying advertising banners and handing out flyers for movies. When he came home he was often whipped by his parents.

Once Noma was a little older, he joined the Umi cinema gang and roamed the streets at night making trouble. Constable Maeng had even had him released several times after he was brought in for some offense or other.

Noma wore an embarrassed sort of smile. He was glad to see Constable Maeng.

"Hard to imagine isn't it, sir? I look forward to working with you, sir."

"Since when do colleagues go around calling each other 'sir'?"

It must have been age that made him say this, and Constable Maeng laughed with Noma without showing what he was really thinking.

But silently he told himself, *If a guy like that can be a constable then it serves us right to be scorned.*

It annoyed Constable Maeng that he would have to do all the reports and paperwork for Noma, the kid was so ignorant. On the other hand, he could send Noma out on patrol and have the kid run errands for him while he kicked back and took it easy.

After about a week of treating Noma as a manservant, Constable Maeng was feeling rather at ease. And then Constable Noma was transferred to a different police box. A new recruit was scheduled to replace the kid.

I wonder who it'll be? I sure had it good when Noma was here.

Constable Maeng was sitting reading the newspaper and thinking thoughts like these when he heard the distinctive rattle of a saber at the door.

"Top of the morning to you!"

In marched a burly brute of a man.

Constable Maeng looked up, gasped, and nearly fell over. His hair stood on end, and he felt cold sweat trickle down his back.

The new replacement recognized Constable Maeng even better. With an evil grin he said, "Well, well, well, I've got you where I want you!"

Constable Maeng was speechless.

"What's the matter, cat got your tongue? Going to sit there and blink, or are you going to say hello? The least you can do is greet a police officer of the new Korea."

"Uh, hi."

"So, still plugging away as a constable, huh?"

It was Kang Pongse . . . convicted murderer and robber, sentenced to life in prison . . . Kang Pongse.

The year before last when Constable Maeng had been a guard at a holding cell, Kang Pongse had been brought in; the charges were robbery and murder. Constable Maeng had guarded him for half a year or so. This is how they had become so well acquainted.

Once Kang had made a scene about some cigarettes, and in the process caused a big ruckus. Because of this the day-shift guard didn't feed him lunch or dinner. That night when Constable Maeng came on shift, Kang Pongse pestered him continuously for dinner and then went off on the constable grinding his teeth and cursing: "You wait and see, if I get off with a life sentence and ever make it out of here, I'll slice you wide open. Who's going to stop me from running you through?"

And here he was, that very same murdering robber, Kang Pongse.

So can you forgive Constable Maeng for feeling as if at any second Kang would yell, "Hey, sucker!" pull out a long knife, and stab him in the guts? Constable Maeng was scared to death the whole day. He couldn't wait for his shift to end. Those few hours were practically an eternity.

Arriving home breathless that afternoon, Constable Maeng bundled up his uniform, his cap, and his sword and wrote his letter of resignation.

"So soon?" Sŏbun started in on him.

"You have no idea. You should be thankful you're not a widow," he said, to which Sŏbun had no reply.

"I thought only dissidents and political prisoners were supposed to be released. But they've gone and let all the dangerous felons and murderers loose too. Is that bloody-minded or what? With that kind of thinking it's no wonder they lost the war!"

"A murdering robber was let out?"

"It's not just that he got out, he marched right in."

"What do you mean?"

"He marched right in the branch station . . . with a sword and a uniform and a hat."

"An imposter, right?"

"Are you kidding? He was a constable all right. He even had a letter of appointment and all. A proud graduate of the academy."

"No way! You mean now we have to watch ourselves around constables too?"

"Come to think of it, was there ever really a difference between constables and murderers? All we ever did was extort goods and kill innocent people. Yes, whether we were constables or murderers it was all the same."

WEAVER WOMAN

O Chŏnghŭi
Translated by Miseli Jeon

O Chŏnghŭi was born in Seoul in 1947 and studied creative writing at Sŏrabŏl College of Fine Arts. She made her literary debut in 1968 with "The Toyshop Woman" (Wangujŏm yŏin), an original and remarkably mature story that she began writing as a teenager. She subsequently received the Yi Sang Literature Award in 1979 for "Evening Game" (Chŏnyŏk ŭi keim) and the Tongin Literature Award in 1982 for "The Bronze Mirror" (Tonggyŏng). ▨ In both technique and subject matter, O is one of the most challenging of contemporary Korean writers. She uses flashbacks, stream-of-consciousness technique, and a variety of narrative viewpoints to good effect. Her most accomplished stories are powerful, sensitive, carefully crafted portrayals of family relationships strained by unspoken emotions and unseen external forces. In these works, O probes beneath the surface of seemingly quotidian lives to expose nightmarish family configurations warped by divorce, desertion, insanity, abuse, and death. Darkness is a physical presence in many of O's stories, reflecting the holes in the fabric of the family. ■ O is also noted for coming-of-age stories such as "Chinatown" (Chunggugin kŏri, 1979), "The Garden of Childhood" (Yunyŏn ŭi ttŭl, 1980), and *The Bird* (*Sae*, 1995) and for intertextual stories such as "Weaver Woman," which echoes the folktale of the herder boy and the weaver girl; "A Portrait of Magnolias" (Mongnyŏnch'o, 1975), which includes a retelling of the Ch'ŏyong legend, and "Fireworks" (Pullori, 1987), which begins with a recounting of the Koguryŏ foundation myth. In the latter stories O, like several other contemporary Korean fiction writers, connects strongly with Korean tradition, investing her stories with archetypes found in myth, legend, and folktale. ■ "Weaver Woman" (Chingnyŏ) first appeared in 1970 in *Wŏlgan munhak* and was reprinted in O's first story collection, *River of Fire* (Pul ŭi kang, 1977). Remarkable in this collection is the author's use of a nameless first-person narrator in each of the stories, a technique that has the effect of simultaneously drawing in and distancing the reader. The narrator of "Weaver Woman" and her husband each have a physical abnormality: the narrator is barren and the husband is a *yuksoni*, one whose hand has six fingers. Miseli Jeon, translator of this story, argues convincingly that the hand with the extra finger represents an extra set of norms within neo-Confucian ideology, an extra set of laws designed specifically to control women and their sexuality. Incapable of performing her role of producing

a son, the narrator is separated from her husband, just
as the weaver girl and herder boy of the folktale are separated forever for neglecting their respective duties.

I open my window and below me at a sharp angle I see the stream.
I focus on the dark knot on the skewed plank that crosses the
stream, tracing a line from there to where my chest touches the
window sill, and then back to my eyes. Myriad motes of glittering
dust drift inside this triangle. The stream runs dark and deep, and
the plank above it seems so narrow and flimsy. The original bridge
must have been swept away during the rainy season, or maybe there
never was a bridge—after all there aren't any remains.

If you stretch your arms wide once, twice, three times, and add
a few handspans more, you have the width of the stream. The plank,
probably appropriated from a house going up nearby, sits unsup-
ported at either end, barely spanning the stream; the careless place-
ment carries with it the delight of the impromptu, seems to harbor
a lack of purpose, even a daring abandonment, if you will. So, the
over-cautiousness of the man now crossing the bridge has always
struck me as deliberate.

I couldn't tell the exact time this man crosses the bridge. Still,
when I get up in the morning and beat the dust from the quilt, and
when I open the window near sunset to welcome you home, the
hunched-over figure of the man creeping across the bridge never
fails to catch my eye.

The sun is most crimson when it's about to touch the horizon.
This is when you come home. I fuss with my make-up and keep looking for the bus. The man is almost across. He lifts his right leg high
and hops off. That's the way he does it, always jumping that last step.
As if he's embarrassed at his timidity, or thinks someone is watching him every step of the way, he seems to excuse his playfulness as

something we all used to do as children. Once he lands, he makes sure that the manila envelope is still there under his arm. His arms and legs are unusually long. He strides out of the triangular space I have created, now swarming with yellow motes of dust, and proceeds toward the Public Housing Complex—a part of the national affordable-housing plan—its buildings all seemingly cut from the same mold, television antennas hovering above their slanted roofs of red or green slate like a white cluster of dragonflies. The sameness of the windows, the window-bars, and the chin-high cinder-block walls takes on a curious beauty against the backdrop of twilight spreading slowly across the sky. I follow the man until he turns down a ruler-straight alley, and once he is lost to view, I turn my eyes away.

The surface of the stream reflects the sun with the brilliance of fish scales. I look up to watch the road. Along this dirt road pass buses that leave behind clouds of dust. They come along every ten minutes on the dot. A run-down bus creaks to a halt, takes shape from out of its veil of dust, spits out a few passengers, and in no time, covered by a thicker veil, sets off again. Never more than three or four get off at a time.

I wonder if you're there; I can't make you out. Everything is blurred. I squint, trying to focus. Here comes a short man and a woman with a basket of groceries; down the alley and out of sight they go. Ten more minutes until the next bus. I close the window and walk outside.

The top of this cinder-block wall offers an open view of the road. I can have a good long look at you getting off the bus and walking toward home.

Here's the next bus. A single person alights and the bus leaves.

The stream loses its brilliance and deepens to a midnight blue. The plank is just as narrow and precarious as ever. I avert my eyes from the bridge.

The summer sunlight is lush, nightfall abrupt. I'm fixing my eyes on something and suddenly the light is gone. It's like an illusion, and darkness blocks my view, taking me into a dark, secret cave.

The bus stops. You get off. I recognize you right away—arms limp at your sides, your steps tired. But then, I lose you. Never before have I lost sight of you getting off the bus and walking toward home. Between here and the road, there used to be a desolate field overrun with stubborn weeds. Whenever I opened the window at the expected time, I would see you get off the bus and walk straight across the field along the path traced by my gaze. But now, the once-empty field is filled with houses that hide the sight of your return home. They condescend to reveal you briefly, only to snatch you out of my sight for a long stretch of time. Presently you reappear flickering in and out of view among the houses. And then your image blurs in the darkness that rises from the depths of the earth.

You no longer shade your eyes from the strong golden glint of the last sliver of sunlight reflected by our window. You merely walk, head bowed, like a shadow. By the time you enter the gate, you are already cloaked in a carapace of darkness. I never realized how abruptly night sweeps in after the sun sets. It was always before nightfall that I had you back home, the front door shut and locked.

From my perch high up on the wall, I swing my legs like a little girl. You step through the gate in silence. I hop down from the wall. If you were to ask, "What are you doing up there," I would say, "I've been watching you." You make for your room without looking at me. There's a white smudge on your back. I reach out for it, but end up brushing off the front of my top. White clothes easily get dirty. I gather my traditional skirt and jacket from the clothesline and go inside. The night has turned their white into blue. The stars are out, but the wind is sticky. I feel the rainy season coming on.

Twelve geese skim past the moon. The echelon seems confined by the narrow borders of the hanging scroll. The lead goose is poised to thread the moon. In your room, across the veranda from mine, the light is on. Sitting here in the dark of my room, I capture every last movement of the geese in the light filtering through the paper panel of my door. There on the wall, twelve exquisite lines—strings of the *kayagŭm* propped up near the door. I take the instrument, rest it in my lap, and pluck a string. The layered dust puffs out like ink on paper, followed by a slack *twing*. I pluck each string in turn. The notes dissolve, and my fingers are left with a residue. The shadow of your slumped shoulders stands motionless on the paper door. I play the highest note, making a prolonged vibrato with my left hand, and strain to listen. The note escaping the sounding board is desolate as the wind. There is no sign of movement in your room. I rest my hand on the bridge and pluck the strings from high to low and back up again, removing the dust. I listen to the hollow notes wending their way through the sounding board, but I can't link them into a melody. Snatches of "Reflections on Mt. Yŏng" go around inside my head, especially one part, "The Ballad of Mt. Seryŏng," but my hands have forgotten how to play it. These twelve notes that my fingers made don't sound right. I wonder if I tune the instrument, would that bring the melodies? I undo the strings on the head of the instrument. But the clump of strings on the floor sends a chill through me; I quickly put the strings away and place the instrument against the wall.

I open the window. It's so dark out. I can't see the stream, the bridge, or any trace of the man who was crossing it. From somewhere near the stream, frogs croak like the bubbling of a primeval swamp. Every window is bright in the apartment building across the road. I imagine a foreign cruise ship anchored on the sea, somehow festive, magnificent, and yet unreal.

I slide the window, harder than I need to. Your room is quiet. I turn on the lamp in my room. The switch clicks, and the room is bright. I notice the laundry hanging on the far wall. I ease the door open and go into the kitchen. I fill a gourd-dipper with water and tiptoe across the veranda, ever conscious of your motionless shadow. All I can see is your profile.

I spread the laundry on my lap, sprinkle water to soften the starch, and flatten each and every wrinkle. I pull the fulling-block toward me, place the neatly folded laundry on it, and catch myself just in time before using the club; no, I plug in the iron. You are someone who can't stand noise.

I remember that first summer we were married and the time you flew off the handle and threw down the box of matches. I thought it was because of the electric fan blowing out the matches when you were trying to light your cigarette. There must have been a dozen of them wasted. I looked in turn at all those matches and you, and finally I pulled out the plug of the fan. "I'll just pull the plug out," I said in a small voice. You took the cigarette out of your mouth and threw it away. I couldn't say a word, couldn't look at your face. As I collected the scattered matchsticks, I realized my hands were trembling. There was a silence, and then you said that you couldn't stand the mechanical whine of the fan and the muggy air that it produced. It was an unusually hot summer, but from that day on, I hid the fan away in the attic. For the rest of that summer, you used a folding bamboo-fan, and I played the *kayagŭm*. We share a taste for classical things and, every night, enclosed by the eight-panel folding-screen, featuring a painting by one of your ancestors, depicting a hermit and his little helper living deep in a mountain nestled in among a sinuous swirl of hazy distant peaks, we imagined ourselves back two hundred years in the past and made love. Once you started returning home after dark, my sojourns to that dim and hazy past stopped, and the serene melody of "Reflections on Mt. Yŏng" was lost.

I take the high-waisted skirt I've ironed, gather the hem, and reattach the waistband. Then, I remove my clothes. I first slip off the top and then untie the waist strings. The skirt drops to my feet. There in the mirror is the naked body of a small woman. Her breasts are round and firm like ripe fruit.

I am conscious of your gaze—the gaze of your countless eyes penetrating the fine lattice-work of the door. I ever so slowly drape my naked body with the skirt I've just put back together. The woman in the mirror has rosy cheeks. "Girls who have rosy cheeks usually have a tough life," I remember my young widowed mother saying with a sigh while she placed a pillow under my head as I was drifting away to sleep.

I shake my head, put my hands on the high-waistband, and press against my breasts beneath it. I turn back to the clothes I removed. I pull the collar free from the top, then the waistband from the skirt, roll all of it into a ball, and slide it into the corner. There in the mirror, a woman in white.

I run my hand over my belly—my flat belly. I smile into the mirror, "I am going to have your baby." Opening the door silently, I go out. The light passing through the paper panels of your door is bright as day, but the arched silhouette of your back is still.

The knob on the gate, the iron crossbar, the hollows of the cinder-block wall, the secluded alley beyond—all wear a thick glaze of darkness.

Night is always so dark and dense. Objects that were immersed in daylight quietly surface, their vague shapes hardening, each asserting its own color and significance. My night vision is poor, and I keep stumbling—the pebbles in this narrow graveled alley could be as effective an obstacle as boulders.

The iron gate to the playground is locked shut, but climbing over presents no difficulty at all. I gather up my skirt and hop over the chain-link fence. The swings, all four of them, haven't been chained to the pole. The man who looks after the playground must have forgotten. This is lucky; it's an awful chore to have to unchain them from high up on the pole.

I climb up onto one of the swings. The sky is dark. The air is pregnant with rain and so oppressive that it's all I can do to set myself in motion. I plant my feet on the plank and make myself swing.

Back and forth I go, my movement strong now. Soon I'm high enough to see the red light of your window and inside, perhaps part of your forehead. You are looking down.

When I'm almost upside down, my skirt flies up my legs, and the breeze plays soft and smooth between my thighs.

The next time up, my skirt balloons. Beneath my tightly fastened waistband, my bosom bounces and my heart pounds. The skirt keeps puffing out; it's like a parachute, covering your window and now draping the entire roof.

You just won't lift your head.

The slide has lost its day-long swarm of children and the swings, impossibly thronged, hang empty; the seesaws and monkey-bars have all been abandoned. When the sun sets on this place, children go home without a backward glance at this world they made their kingdom. Thoroughly, they lather their faces, hands, feet, the backs of their ears, and then send the thick suds swirling down the drain. Finally, they become sweet-mannered and sit down at the dinner table. Now, there is no trace of them, and the place looks lonely and even strange.

I often come to this place during the day and watch the children play. They play quietly. It takes quite a bit of squinting and staring to tell the boys from the girls playing in silence in the sunlight, moving like shadows. Every single one of them is so sweet; even the boys have long fringes over their milk-white foreheads, just like the girls.

The croaking of frogs just won't let up. Insects flit through the lush thickets.

Suddenly, a meteor plummets across the sky. Oh, I must make a wish. I almost lose my grip on the swing. Tightening my hold, I look up into the sky. A network of small ellipses creates a bridge to the sky, and far up at the zenith, seven dim stars form the shape of a dipper. I'm reminded of the seven flowers you twirled with your long fingers.

On our wedding day you removed the veil from my hair and took in your hand the seven decorative flowers. Yaśodharā's flowers, you called them. When I asked what you meant, you fell silent, contemplated, then answered that Yaśodharā's flowers symbolize the karma of married couples. You spoke softly, all the while twirling the seven flowers.

"Yaśodharā was Śakyamuni's wife. By virtue of the karma gained by her offering seven flowers to Śakyamuni in her previous life, she became his wife in the following life."

I listened, eyes downcast, thinking I would plant flowers in the garden the next day.

It becomes harder to swing. The stars look dimmer and the sky lower. I listen to the grating of the metal chains, while waiting for the swing to come to a stop. My skirt, now damp, sticks to my legs. I lean my head against one of the chains and gaze at your window. As my swing moves, so does your window.

All at once the windows of the apartment building—that bright city in the ocean—disappear into the dark. The lights much farther away in the dreamlike distance have also disappeared. It must be a blackout. The apartment building is now crouching black and eerie like a haunted ship. I look at your window. I can still see your black hair and forehead.

Your window alone is bright as day, breaking the density of darkness. As I gaze at it, I forget the stubborn, dark space between your bright room and the swing that I am on. I'll be able to fly to you like a bird. I have just leaned forward when a violent pain shoots through my belly.

In my flat belly, your son is beating a drum.

I wake up to a din. Dawn has broken. Mornings never come quietly. They arrive noisily, uttering all the sighs that have been held back from passing through the dark secret cave of the night. The light in your room pales in the light of daybreak, and the shadow of your slouched back has also faded from the paper panel of your door. Lying in bed, eyes closed, I strain to listen to your room.

I hear a rooster flap its wings; it's something I hear from your room every morning. I stretch out and pull the quilt up to my chin.

Again the flapping of the rooster, followed by a pitiable moan that escapes between clenched teeth. At dawn every day I hear this from the expanse of the bed in your room.

I pull my legs in, tuck the knees hard against my belly, and then run my hand over my belly. I am going to have your son.

I reach over the pillow to change the station on the radio. Unrecognizable, heavily nasal, the honeyed voice of a woman streams out. I listen carefully to the foreign tongue whispering softly yet incomprehensibly into my ears.

I realize it's raining. For no reason, this puts me at a loss. The patter of rain on earth admits the occasional howl of a dog from somewhere in the neighborhood. It's hard to imagine such a drawn-out howl coming from a dog whose ribs are almost showing through its thin hide; dry and urgent, it seems the sound of nature itself rather than that of one living creature.

Dawn swells with amorphous noise.

Finally, church bells start to toll. Each with its own timbre and appeal, they ring all at once as if fighting with one another, or threatening the still slumbering neighborhood at the foot of the hill. Most distinct above all the bells and chimes are hymns, "My lord, grant me peace, lead my way." Maybe it's due to the poor quality of the record, the hymn always stops at the phrase "lead my way." The needle scratching the warped disk creates a vibration that ironically adds sincerity to the imploring tone of the hymn.

The sound of the rain, the howl of a dog heard intermittently like the wind that drives the rain, and the rooster flapping in your room. I remember I heard from somewhere in the neighborhood the same blood-chilling howl of a dog in heat on the nights when you rushed away from me, deriding my infertile womb, as well as at the dawn when you were unexpectedly returned to me, shrouded by a coarse hemp cloth.

I get up to open the window. The rain poured down all night and yet refuses to ease off. The earth reveals its red flesh; down its every cleft flow torrents of muddy water. The stream has almost reached the top of the banks.

The man crosses the bridge, wearing long rain-boots, holding a vinyl-domed umbrella low over his head as if wearing it like a bamboo hat. He takes more cautious steps than ever and finally does his one-legged jump off the end of the bridge. Through the open window my eyes follow the man. Only when he disappears do I close the window, wiping from my face rainwater that I didn't even feel.

Not a child comes to the playground even at midday. The metal chains of the swings look glossy, wet in the rain. The foot-planks are slippery and any slight misstep may very well send me forward, off the swing. Standing on one of them, I look at the blue slate roofs of the Public Housing Complex in the distance, sprouting like moss in the rain. Then, I notice the water tanks, which stand erect on the rooftops of the two-story houses around the housing complex, also getting wet in the rain. Some children's clothes are hung on the balcony of the house with the steep French-style roof. Perhaps someone has forgotten to bring them in. They are flying like flags, red, blue, all in bright colors.

An airplane flies by. I turn my head up to see the plane. Even on rainy days, planes fly.

Umbrellas throng the road. Passengers from each arriving bus locate their umbrellas and quickly take shelter beneath them.

I can't spot you in the haze of the rain. I keep wiping the window with the sleeve of my blouse, but the rain hitting the pane makes it fog right up again.

If I, like the other wives who wait at the bus stop holding umbrellas, went out to meet you with your raincoat and long boots, you would get off the bus, roll up your trousers to the knees, change into the boots, and hurry under the umbrella that I held. I imagine us under our small umbrella, soaked to the skin like two little mice.

I give up wiping the fog off the window and instead open the window as wide as I can and gaze out. The stream is already overflowing its banks. The narrow plank-bridge must have been swept away by the torrent; it's nowhere to be seen and so neither is the man who crosses it.

You do not come back, not even when the windows of the housing complex are so bright against the solid darkness of the night. I tighten my waist strings and set out in search of you, only to be thwarted by the arrows of the rain, more menacing than the night, as stubborn as the pillars of an age-old temple; and by your even rows of teeth, their dull sheen appearing among the arrows like the blades of kitchen knives.

I hear the clamor of the stream overflowing its banks.

Your room is dark, the mulberry paper of the door swollen in its faint white glow.

You are walking slowly up a hill lined with tall trees. The leaves are thick and heavy on their branches and sparkle like those of silver poplars. The sunbeams coax from them a click-clack sound, just like the sound of castanets. The ground is fluffy white as if covered with cotton. Breathless I run. The hill is not all that steep and you walk slowly. Yet, I find it so hard to catch up with you. Would it feel this way if I walked through the clouds? My legs are too heavy to take another step. I call out to you, "Wait! Please, wait!" But you continue on, the bushy hair on the back of your head toward me. Leaves are waving, all together. You are getting farther away from me. "Please, wait for me," I call, my hands cupped around my mouth. Giving up hope, I cover my eyes. They are smarting in the strong sunlight. I look through the spaces between my fingers. Sunlight cascades everywhere. I spot a tree with branches bent, heavy with leaves. It could be a plane tree or a silver poplar. It hides an abundance of fruit among its castanet leaves. I spread my fingers and look more closely. I gasp and close my eyes. What I see amid the thickness of the flickering leaves is a profusion of penises, hanging heavy from the branches like a bumper crop of fruit.

Sunlight floods through the open window and finds its way into the far reaches of the room. It passes over me where I lie in my bed on the floor and prepares to scale the opposite wall. It must be around dinnertime. I try to rise. There's a wrenching pain in my head. The castanet leaves of my dream continue to click. Hands on the pillow, I manage to raise myself to a sitting position and lean back against the wall. My head aches so much I can't even turn my head away from the sunlight stinging my face. Instead I crawl on all fours toward the mirror. The face reflected in the mirror is swollen, especially the lids that hang heavily over the eyes, giving the face the look almost of a mask.

I approach the window. The days of downpour have ended and from the window everything looks clear and balmy.

The angry torrent that overflowed the stream's banks is tranquil now. The stream seems much wider without the narrow plank and unfamiliar without the man.

The occasional bus arrives in a cloud of dust, stops briefly, and departs. I pay no mind to the people getting on and off.

The corner of the cinder-block wall that I share with my neighbor has crumbled. It must have given way during the days of downpour. I can see my neighbor's garden through the opening. A tricycle with a missing wheel has been abandoned there, and above the crumbled blocks stands the trunk of a red-blossomed peach. Its great clusters of crimson flowers make the tree seem on fire. I open the door and step down into the yard. Where the wall has crumbled, I reach through the hole and strip the length of a branch of its flowers. My palm stings; I imagine blood oozing out. My eyes hurt in the sunlight. The world beyond the wall glints in the sun like a vast mirror.

Have you ever felt a shiver down your back when you see a blossom that's wide open? Awakening from a deathlike sleep one afternoon, I color my swollen eyelids blue and my lips red and leave home with seven blossoms in my hand. I step through the gate to find you there, cautiously crossing the sun-lit stream. Only now, I see the sixth finger on your hand—you're a *yuksoni*.

WE TEACH SHAME!

Pak Wansŏ
Translated by Teresa Kim

In a literary career dating from 1970, **Pak Wansŏ** has firmly established herself as the elder stateswoman of contemporary Korean literature, a household name both within Korea and in Korean communities abroad, and long respected in the *mundan* (literary world) of her country. The story of her own life is compelling—entry to Seoul National University in 1950 followed shortly by withdrawal necessitated by the outbreak of the Korean War; two decades spent raising five children; and an award-winning career in letters. From the fabric of that life Pak has woven a body of literature that gives voice as the work of no other author has to the trauma of civil war and territorial division as well as the subsequent upheavals in Korean society and culture. If there is one quality that has cemented Pak's appeal to a mass audience, it is her uncanny ability to empathize with people's lives and experiences. Her works draw a visceral, almost cathartic reaction from readers young and old who report hearing an authorial voice so clearly and directly it is almost as if they are in the physical presence of the narrator. ▉ The story translated here is from early in Pak's career. "We Teach Shame!" (Pukkŭrŏum ŭl karŭch'imnida) was first published in August 1974 in *Shindonga*. Like other of her stories from this time, such as "In the Realm of the Buddha" (Puch'ŏnim kŭnch'ŏ, 1973), "Camera and Workboots" (K'amera wa wak'ŏ, 1975), and "Winter Outing" (Kyŏul nadŭri, 1975), it is a dual narrative, juxtaposing the present with events two decades earlier during the civil war. The trauma of the war years is never far from the surface in the narrative present of "We Teach Shame!"—the narrator's displacement from Seoul during the January 1951 retreat launching her on a peripatetic lifestyle involving several locales and a succession of husbands. A central theme is the hypocrisy of individuals who purport to live successful lives but are bewitched by the trappings and status symbols of an increasingly affluent urban lifestyle.

There's not much light in this coffee shop, but once my eyes adjust I have another look around. No familiar faces yet. I take out my compact. Damn eye make-up. It doesn't make my eyes look bigger and brighter like it's supposed to but instead turns them dull by emphasizing all the little crow's-feet. And it's not just the eyes but my whole face that looks so drawn. Is this what it means to be "worn down over time"?

After we had moved to Seoul and had found temporary lodging in Karhyŏn-dong, we started looking for a house. It was a task so tiring that I was on the verge of collapse. As expected, my family in Sanggye-dong suggested we move nearby saying they had already found a number of possible places, while my in-laws in Suyu-dong assumed that since we were back in Seoul it was only natural for us to live near *them*. I couldn't refuse either side so I had to go through the motions of looking around both neighborhoods. But my husband had an entirely different plan in mind. He wanted a place that was within our price range while still being presentable, at least from the outside. He kept hinting that Hwagok-dong was just the area to find such a house, and so I was forced to look around there, too. But this meant I was roving across the heart of the city, from Karhyŏn to Sanggye, back to Suyu, and then to Hwagok, from the edges of Seoul's western-most precincts to eastern, from north to south.

I guess it was this continual back and forth that wore me down, but what amazed me was how disgustingly large Seoul really was. I felt no deep sense of home here—there probably aren't many who would consider Seoul as a hometown—and even though I had grown up in Seoul, I chose rather to think of myself as being without an ancestral home. But I still held a clear image of what Seoul as a hometown used to be, an image that prompted me often to recall the memories as if I had pulled out an old postcard and was overwhelmed with nostalgia.

Seoul, January 1951. On a wobbly pushcart, we loaded up all our belongings and my little brothers and sisters and joined in the retreat from Seoul. Taking turns with my brother who was two years younger than me, I pushed and pulled the rattling cart, constantly looking back at what remained of the city. The sky was low with a mellow overcast, snow starting to flurry around those buildings that remained standing in defiance of the destruction, their windows left sooty by the blazing flames. I thought I could hear the crackle of gunfire from the mountain pass to the north as people carrying their belongings on their backs hurriedly abandoned their homes.

Late in the morning we left our house near the Chunghak Bridge and continued through Chongno, Kwanggyo, and Ŭlchiro, all the way to the South Gate. By the time we got there, mother was worrying that if we continued at such a sluggish pace, we wouldn't even be able to cross the Han River by sunset. But before I could set my sights dead ahead and focus all my energies forward, I had to take one last look behind me—and what a striking image I saw.

The South Gate—standing undaunted amid the falling snow— was so beautiful and magnificent, as if I were seeing it for the first time. The flakes were small and sparse, and even though they weren't piling up on the streets yet, I could see them accumulating in the grooves between the columns and rows of roof tiles. The contrast between the black tiles and the white snow produced an inexpressible harmony, like the soft blurred lines of black ink on mulberry paper. But the entire picture—grand and severe as a mountain— overwhelmed my narrow field of vision. My heart began to burn with a strange surge of emotion. Suffering through this evacuation was the price one had to pay to see the South Gate at the peak of its beauty, and how could anyone resist acceptance after seeing such a beautiful sight? I knew I would never again see anything like it and was sure it was my compensation for the bitter and sorrowful sacrifice I had to make.

I gazed up at the South Gate with an almost religious piety, then turned away and continued our southward journey with a feeling of less despair.

I continued my home-away-from-home existence—my fate ever since our flight to the south—but the poignant beauty of the South Gate that I saw through the snowflakes did not fade and had become for me a stronger source of nostalgia than my mother, my siblings, our old Chunghak-dong house—or any other part of Seoul that once held memories from my youth.

We had been back in Seoul for a month or so and during my daily cross-town journeys I had had countless opportunities to see the South Gate. But time and again my eyes were so preoccupied I ended up missing it. Seoul had boomed to that extent; there were so many things to see, endless houses to look up at, so many cars and people that from my vantage point on the bus, I would lose myself in all the hustle and bustle about me. It was during this time that my interest in the South Gate started to slip away. I knew right off that the city was no longer ruled by the sentimental spirit of the South Gate, that a new order had extinguished anything the South Gate had left to offer.

As I came to realize this, I felt as if I could see through to all the hidden disorder that lay veiled behind the garish trappings of this city.

But despite everything, it was my own self that was in the most serious state of disorder. If I was in a hurry to get somewhere but saw people crossing a busy street, I would automatically follow even if it was the wrong direction. Standing at a busy intersection, waiting for the light to turn green, then walking side by side bumping shoulders within a group of people simply felt like the right thing to do—it felt rewarding. After a number of these inadvertent crossings, I'd find myself totally lost, forget everything I had planned for the day, my mind numb after I'd hopped along like a rustic who had just come down from the hills. I was left with a feeling of disconcertment, the emptiness after a rush of excitement, the confusion after awakening from a trance. I often felt this way, and not only when I was walking on the street. Just coming back to live in Seoul was like this.

My husband had tricked me and the elderly realtor into thinking we were going to buy a house, but then one morning he changed his mind and we hurriedly moved into a rental. We grew preoccupied with furnishing the house, starting with the living room furniture, a dressing table, a stationery chest, and other shiny household goods, and I forgot all about being displeased that the house was merely a rental. But even while consumed with dressing up the new house, I used to panic at the noise of the airplanes coming in and out of Kimp'o Airport, just next to Hwagok-dong. When all the windows in the house rattled and the planes roared by so low it seemed our heads would be taken off, I felt as if this house was made out of a thin sheet of glass that could shatter at any moment. After the rumbling had faded into the distance, my body would go limp, my mind numb and blurry.

My husband would roll his eyes at me. "Stop acting so retarded." He didn't understand why something like the noise from an airplane would make me go all numb. But he was wrong. It wasn't so much that the noise made me lose my mind; rather, it awakened me to our reality. In the moment of peaceful tranquility after the roar of the planes had faded and the windows had stopped rattling, I clearly saw that our life was a sham, hidden behind a façade. But these thoughts never lasted long. My husband set out to keep me busy and forced me into a state of perpetual flurry. This in fact was my husband's natural disposition, but since we had moved back to Seoul, his greed for success hit overdrive and he ran around like a madman set on making his fortune overnight. It was quite a sight. His eyes were bloodshot from his overflowing desire, and he ran around like a chicken with its head cut off. He expected, or rather demanded that I keep my hands and feet as busy as his. But I couldn't get it right. I couldn't understand why he was always so rushed. If he had an important business meeting at nine in the morning, he'd look at the clock a hundred times and say he had to hurry or he'd be late; but then he'd take the time to make seemingly unimportant phone calls, swearing when the line was busy but persistently redialing. Then when the countdown reached thirty minutes, he would start hollering at me as he got dressed. Dissatisfied with the necktie I had laid out, he would make us play a game of "You choose, I reject" with every single tie while still managing to cleverly blame me for his being late. Finally satisfied with his choice (and conveniently forgetting that the tie was the very same one I had originally laid out), he would take one last look at his watch and run out as if the house was burning down only to return five minutes later, gasping that he had forgotten an important document. "Hurry up and find it!" I couldn't just reach into the top drawer and pull it out, that would have made him even madder. Instead I had to pretend to be equally flustered, blurting out things like, "Oh my goodness! What are we going to do? Where could that file possibly be? I swear . . . if my head weren't attached," and then I had to make a show of throwing aside whatever I was doing, tread around in circles, jerk open this and that drawer, even force open drawers that were jammed, and only after a round of this foolishness could I finally produce it.

I had to play along like this every time, but I never got the hang of it. He knew this and consistently grumbled that we at least had to be on the same page to make it work! I was always tired but it wasn't the kind of nice tired that comes after a hard day's work. It was an unrewarding and empty fatigue, the type you get after forcing your body to dance to a new and discordant beat. I'd say it wasn't my body but my mind and spirit that suffered the most.

Even when my husband wasn't home he managed to keep me busy, assigning me "homework" such as going to the local administrative offices to draw up various certificates. But answering the phone, or rather answering it "correctly," was my main task. There were calls that simply required me to take down a message, calls that required me to reply according to my husband's instructions, and calls that required evasive answers. Most of these answers were lies anyway, and I was always scared that I might forget my husband's instructions or get the information mixed up. My husband's masterful boasting had acquired him the company of well-known and influential personages—I was constantly surprised at how many people he knew, people from every social standing. But all these connections did for me was create the delusion that our Hwagok-dong rental house with our rental phone was the general office of some grand business venture, a thought that wore me down. So even though in reality the only calls that came were either wrong numbers or calls from my husband asking if there were any calls for him, I spent the whole day on edge, a slave to the phone. When my husband wasn't home, the phone replaced him as my master.

I wasn't pleased with our rental house, but I hated our rental phone even more. This probably explained why I couldn't easily attach any pleasure to my new life in Seoul, even a "newlywed life" that should have been bursting with happiness. Yes, at my age I was a newlywed. I had been married twice before and now with husband number three, I guess it was only natural that I would feel this way.

But it was thanks to that rental phone that I was able to get in touch with my old classmates upon returning to Seoul after some twenty years. Or more accurately, they got in touch with me. I never gave out my number to anybody, but people started calling, asking for me.

"Oh my gosh . . . it *is* you! I heard you were back in Seoul for good. How could you come back and settle in without even so much as a peep? You sneaky little fox. I've missed you . . . I really have."

I began to receive calls from this person and that, all making a fuss as if they were absolutely dying to see me. And then a few decided to actually do so, simply informing me of the time and place. I was a bit reluctant to meet them, weary just at the thought of it, but since there was no particular reason not to I felt compelled to humor them.

I never really got the whole "dying to see somebody" thing, especially between girlfriends. So you can imagine my surprise when my husband started gushing about it.

"Hey now, that's more like it! Why don't you get out for some fresh air? Meet some new people, that's *exactly* what you need to do. You know, there's always a way to use them to your advantage, and that's the honest truth. What do you think connections are? You simply find the strings and pull them. And hell, there's no law that says your friend can't be the wife of a rich CEO or a high government official. Even the wife of a tax clerk is better than nothing." His eyes sparkled as he stabbed the air in frantic excitement. Then he added more seriously, "Whatever it takes, let's try to rake in a fat fortune and share in the good life."

Oh how repulsive. A sick feeling rose in my throat, a feeling of disgust. This was a bad sign, but what was worse, this feeling was unbearable. It was the same feeling I had had when I separated from my first husband, and again from my second. People thought my first husband had kicked me out for not being able to have kids, and my second because I was an ill-tempered, second-hand woman who couldn't cut it as a housewife. This was my "natural disposition" and so remarrying twice—even three times—was probably expected of me. Nobody understood the magnitude of the repulsion I had to live with.

Wondering whether this latest marriage will end in another divorce, I take out my compact again and look at my reflection—my way of attempting to scare myself into realizing that I'm too old to remarry. It isn't the obvious aging around my eyes but the bone-aching fatigue that makes me yearn to just live a stable and peaceful life.

As the compact clicks shut a woman walks in and looks around eagerly. She is wearing a breathtaking Korean dress; its rich orange hue seems to paint the walls of the dim coffee shop with the glow of the evening sun. It's Hŭisuk. We immediately recognize each other and make a big fuss. Yŏngmi arrives soon after. She walks right up to me and gives me a hug. This type of greeting suits Yŏngmi very well, but being a country bumpkin, I can't hide my awkwardness.

"God you're looking good!"

"I almost didn't recognize you."

The first thing that catches your eye when you meet an old friend after twenty-odd years is probably how much she's aged. But this must be the usual Seoul-style greeting, to skip the obvious and simply say, "You've gotten prettier." I don't know how to reply. I feel out of place.

"So I hear you've moved back to Seoul for good? That's great, really great. How long have you been back?"

"Let's see . . . probably about two months—"

"What? Already? You little snob. You didn't want to see me, not even once?"

Yŏngmi scowls and pinches my thigh. She and I used to be best friends. But over the years I've hardly ever thought about her, and I can't say I'm any happier to see her than I am to see Hŭisuk. The coffee shop is noisy and full of cigarette smoke. We raise our voices over the noise and start to gossip. On the wall Hŭisuk is leaning against there's a reproduction of a van Gogh. It's a nightmarish painting that shows the heavens crumbling down toward the earth while the ground storms up and pierces the sky. Hŭisuk's orange dress of fine flowing silk is made picture perfect by the diamond ring on her finger, but her cheap, worn-out undergarment is sticking out at the cuff, and her hands are coarse and unseemly. A bitter taste—here is the very image of a woman whose husband has only recently, after years of hardship, gained a foothold in the good life. Is this what I have to look forward to? Yŏngmi's Western-style dress is simple and chic enough, but she can't hide the weariness and exhaustion of a career woman well past age forty, still having to pinch pennies, plus contribute to the household income.

I feel like I've already found out everything I need to know about my classmates. Like a veteran pawn shop owner appraising and pricing merchandise, I judge them in an instant, come to the conclusion that they are no better off than I am, and stand firm in my beliefs. I participate only half-heartedly in their conversation.

This isn't to say that I lost interest because they didn't turn out like my husband had imagined: the daughters-in-law of rich families or the wives of government officials. I never expected that. I just wasn't interested in finding out any more about them than I already knew.

"By the way, what does your husband do?" is one of Hŭisuk's first questions.

"Oh, he's in business."

"Business? What kind of business?"

"A technical tie-up with a Japanese firm."

This blundered response must sound like a lie made up on the spot, but I'm pretty sure it's one of the plans my husband has in the works, or at least that's what I think he told me.

The waitress pours a drop of cream into each of our coffees. The drops remind me of a runny nose. I snivel unnecessarily and take a sip.

"Huh? That's weird. I heard your husband was a rich local farmer in Ch'ungch'ŏng Province. When did he become a businessman?" demands Yŏngmi.

"You're not the only one who's confused," Hŭisuk hisses like a viper. "I could have sworn her husband was some sort of university professor."

Both of them are hinting at the same thing and their eyes sparkle with a sly and vicious confidence. That's when I realize that both women have come here already knowing I've been married three times. I'm annoyed that I've caught on so late, but nothing to do now except brazen it out.

I let out an exaggerated laugh and clap my hands in a show of pure amusement.

"You're right! Both of you!"

"What?"

"Well, my first husband was a rich country farmer, my second was a college instructor, and my husband now is a businessman."

"You mean you actually remarried three times?"

I really hate how the word *remarried* sounds, but I don't let it get to me and instead force a bigger fake laugh.

"Not exactly. One was my first marriage, so I've only remarried twice."

I use the word *remarriage* so coolly and proudly that I swear I can see their jaws drop. I've made my point and yet I'm not pleased with myself.

"You've really changed a lot, huh?" Yŏngmi says with contempt. You used to be so modest."

She must be talking about the old days. It's not true for schoolgirls now, but back when we were growing up, bashfulness in a girl was both charming and proper. But with me, my bashfulness didn't know where to stop.

I used to hate the way my face turned bright red at the slightest mistake even before I knew I was embarrassed—I only became aware of it when I felt my face heat up. I wouldn't know what to do with myself and flushed the type of red you turn if you've committed some horrible crime. If only my embarrassment had stopped there. . . . But even if I was singled out for the top score on a math test, I wasn't proud but wanted instead to disappear into a mouse hole. I thought about how hard I had pretended not to care about studying, reading romance novels all day at school before going home and pulling all-nighters. Now the whole world would know I was a complete fraud. And if my teacher read my work out loud because I had done an exceptional job, I would be on pins and needles trying to think up excuses for where I had plagiarized this passage or where I had stolen that expression. That was the only thing on my mind and every word she read stabbed at me.

I knew for sure there had to be something wrong with my wiring—a morbid sensitivity that made me overly vulnerable to embarrassment. And because I had to protect it like an open wound that never healed, I was always seen as a gentle, low-profile, perfect student.

Before I could graduate from high school, the Korean War broke out. Just like everyone else, I went through all the hardships that summer and in the winter our family was among those that evacuated Seoul.

Saying that no one suffered as much as I did would be a gross exaggeration, but considering how large our family was, the phrase "every man for himself" seemed to apply to everyone except me. We had no father, and since there was no strong male figure to depend on, it all fell onto the oldest child—me.

Our only source of income was the room rent we collected from our large Chunghak-dong house, but because it was hard enough just trying to get everyone out alive, the house was the last thing on our minds. We didn't even have enough time to pack proper clothes, and this lack of preparation also meant that our food supply was soon eaten up.

We barely avoided starvation thanks to the intermittent distribution of free flour to the evacuees, but my brothers and sisters were at an age where they ate so much it disappeared faster than it could be replaced. They ate and ate but still were bone thin and spent their days crazed with hunger.

My mother and I would scrape the bottom of the empty pot saying, "It's so true that in times of trouble, the parents starve to death while the kids die of a burst stomach. Just look at them."

And then we'd heave a sigh of resentment.

That's when she fell into the habit of beating the kids for no reason and calling them good-for-nothing leeches. Like a hellish nightmare all too real, I still remember how she'd glare at them as if they were sworn enemies from a previous life. "Die, just die!" she'd say, and jab her finger at them while the kids wailed in fear.

Spring came and my siblings and I spent entire days like hungry beasts, grubbing the fields and mountains for food. One day we arrived at the barren expanse where the school had stood before it was burned down, and discovered a Quonset hut that looked like it was made of logs; camouflage-colored jeeps and trucks coming and going, making fantastic *vroom*ing and honking sounds. The American army had set up camp. We got all excited. Foraging for food suddenly felt foolish and demeaning.

The news that a base had been set up just over the mountain spread like wildfire through our neighborhood. It was as if we had hit the jackpot—a weird sort of energy started to pulse through this place where the evacuees outnumbered the native residents three to one. Already the children were becoming impatient if there was no smell of greasy fat when they put their noses up to sniff the dough-flake soup with mountain greens.

But the first effect of the Yankee presence wasn't the attraction of fatty and greasy food but rather the sickening lewdness of the women. As if a large ship had docked at port, spewing out toxic oil and polluting the water, an unexplainable eroticism misted from the American army base and instantly bewitched the town. Fantastic pictures started to circulate and the women would sway their hips indecently, giggling as they walked around. Even the kids would mimic the Yankees, rolling up their sleeves and babbling the one or two Yankee words they'd picked up whenever an American passed by.

Jumping on the bandwagon, uncertified hairdressers started going from house to house, coaxing the girls to get a perm. They applied a foul-smelling chemical to the hair and wrapped the locks around an iron rod heated by burning charcoal. The girl's hair would come out all curly and frizzy. This was called the "fire perm"—a definite must during that time. A singed scalp was a small price to pay.

Buildings began to appear with signs written in curvy Yankee letters, such as *Laundry* and *PX*. The idea of course was to catch the eye, but the signs mostly drew scowls of silent indignity instead. The locals sent their marriageable daughters to live with relatives where they would be safe, and the evacuees gathered up their entire family and left for elsewhere. But this was an option only available to people with money in their pockets and food in their bellies. For the have-nots, it was a matter of coming up with ways to cash in on the jackpot. All they could think about was how to lift dollars from the pockets of the big-nosed, gum-chewing Yankees cruising around in their noisy jeeps, and how to be the first to sample all the exotic, sweet-smelling goodies from the ration packs. They even fantasized about getting inside the barbed wire of the army base on the off chance of finding jobs doing domestic work for the Yankees. Whichever tack they took, these movements breathed life back into the community.

They couldn't have cared less when people with money or those who put on airs frowned at or deplored them. "Let's see how long you'd last if you had to skip a few meals," they'd snort. "Pretend all you want, but in a dog-eat-dog time like this, you'd probably eat us alive if you had to."

As more and more "Yankee girls" trickled in from other parts, our neighborhood gradually took on the appearance of an honest-to-goodness military camp town. In no time the local girls who had already fried their hair with the hot rod were also putting on makeup—powdering their faces ghostly white, painting their lips blood red, penciling in arched eyebrows, stuffing their mouths with chewing gum. But no matter how difficult their refugee lives, these girls from respectable homes didn't become GI sweethearts right off the bat. In the beginning they found jobs on the base under respectable titles such as "housegirls" and "waitresses." Even the boys seemed to be finding good work as "houseboys."

From every house came the savory smell of creamy, full-flavored food, and everyone's rough skin grew smooth and radiant. But our family remained poor. The sight of people eating would drive my little brothers and sisters crazy, and like living ghosts, they were insatiable no matter how much they ate.

My mother's temper got worse by the day. Instead of my brothers and sisters, now it was me she tormented. And one day, out of the blue, she brought home a hair-fryer and, fists trembling with hate, told me I was to have my hair permed. But as soon as she saw I wasn't going to give in, she unleashed a fury of curses, yanked loose her knot of hair, cut it right off and had what was left frizzed by the fire rods.

It was such a pitiful sight; poverty and hunger had already made her face dark and drawn but the frizzy hair nested on top made it even worse. And if that wasn't wretched enough, she started putting on make-up. She got hold of some face powder and a nub of lipstick from who knows where and set about defacing herself in front of a cracked mirror. And then this hideous monster took to walking up and down the road. It was so horrible I couldn't even feel ashamed. My poor mother! But what could I do?

Then one day, my mother exploded in a fit of tears and ripped open her blouse. It was an awful sight. Her sallow skin clung to her ribs, the nipples of her drooping breasts withered and puckered like dates left out to dry for years. Ranting and raving about how miserable her life was, my mother began to claw at her horrid chest. The nails raised white streaks on her scaly skin that turned crimson.

"Take a good look, you inconsiderate cold-hearted bitch. Look how pitiful I am. Do you think I can pass for a Yankee whore? Even a blind Yankee wouldn't go for me! No matter how much I want this to work I can't make it happen all by myself. Oh, we're all as good as dead. Listen to me, you stiff-necked spiteful little brat. It's not like anyone sticks out in a crowd anyways. You're useless!"

I was absolutely mortified. I felt as if everything inside me were crashing down. At that moment, my open wound, my every trace of sensitivity to shame was encrusted forever. Here I was, the daughter of a woman who went raving mad because she couldn't turn her daughter into a Yankee whore. I had been brought up sucking on those breasts, on those disgusting nipples. How could a person like me even think of indulging in luxurious sentiments such as shame?

Shortly thereafter I got married. I was still young, though in the old days I would already have been a mother and then some. I had no choice; no way was I going to become a Yankee whore. The old matchmaker from our town suggested that we simply get it over with, saying that it's easier to get rid of one mouth than to feed ten. My mother perked up her ears at this. I hated the idea of getting married as much as I hated any alternative, but I went along with it.

This isn't to say that marriage ranked any higher in my ethical judgment. I just didn't want to give satisfaction to a mother who became hysterical because she couldn't turn her daughter into a whore. Plus, I had no wish to support my little brothers and sisters who ate like hungry ghosts, caring only about filling their stomachs, whether their older sister ate or starved. Nobody was going to benefit at my expense.

And so I was married off as a second wife to a man in his thirties who came from a supposedly rich family in the countryside. The word that he was a wealthy farmer made it as far as Seoul, but it was only after the National Government was reinstated and my family's situation eased up that my mother confessed she had blown things up to satisfy her motherly vanity in finding a good match for her daughter. In reality he and his wife were only middle-class farmers, but they seemed to have made a small fortune through means you wouldn't have expected. They lent out money to other farmers at ridiculous interest rates, and when it came to making money they stopped at nothing and didn't give a damn what others said.

Everything in the house was glossy—the cheap worn-out kitchenware, the soy jar, the kettle cover—as if it had all been dipped in oil. Buffed to a shine, the house didn't impress but rather oppressed me in a whole different way.

My husband was arrogant and ignorant as hell—I'd never met anyone who took so much pride in his ignorance and his money. His ability to take an interest in anybody other than himself was completely stunted.

Lucky for me, he had no children from his first marriage, but all the other domestic chores, from serving his family—his grandparents, his parents, even his brothers and sisters—to the endless wiping to a shine of the household appliances, became my responsibility. But at least I wasn't hungry anymore. How wonderful not to be hungry! Knowing this enabled me to suppress the butterflies I felt whenever I was tempted by thoughts of freedom or tested by my maddening curiosity as to how other people lived. I did this for some ten years. But even though I ate my fill and was healthy, I couldn't get pregnant, and so my husband took in a concubine and I decided I had to leave. I was met with ridicule by my husband's family: "You come into our house, can't even conceive a child, and you have the gall to leave just because we bring in a concubine? Are you sure you don't have some screws loose in your head?" But I stuck to my decision.

Divorce certainly isn't something to be celebrated in the way marriage is, but I chose it nevertheless. I took pleasure in the fact that for the first time in my life I had followed through on a choice *I* had made.

I was familiar with my second husband, an instructor at a local university, even before my friend introduced us. He wrote columns for the newspaper and although I had only read a few of them, I was instantly attracted. I saw him as somebody who could deepen and give meaning to his life by finding the significance hidden within "worthless" things. Money and fame would mean nothing to him. Finally, I had found Mr. Right. On top of that, his writings were infused with romanticized descriptions of "T City," which was in reality only a shabby small town. It had been my belief that I could never look upon this place with affection because of all the pain I had suffered in the farming community nearby, but his almost lyrical professions of love for T City made me think it was a place I could call home.

But when I finally met him, a man whose face bore a look of forlorn despair, he wasn't the man I had envisioned or indeed longed for. Even so, my heart ached at the sight of this broken man. It hadn't been long since he'd lost his wife.

I fell hard. I just wanted to be happy for once in my life. I won over his motherless kids with cookies and sweets and gained his affection by offering smiles, pecks on the cheek, and a show of maternal love. By these flatteries I burrowed deep into their family nest and in the end became his wife.

But I was again forced to see that I'd been fooled. He was a scaredy-cat, a coward, and a liar. His real self hungered for fame and fortune and he was sick and tired of T City and his teaching post at its second-rate university. Consumed with the belief that his brilliance was being wasted in such a place, he held a grudge against the top universities in Seoul for not acknowledging his fame or seeking him out. His opinion of himself was laughable—he was a megalomaniac in disguise. Lazy in his studies, he had been able to make a name for himself (in the loosest sense) only by submitting scrawlings to the newspaper on topics he knew nothing about. Even more ludicrous was the bitterness with which he lashed out in his writings at the very things he loved, never hinting at his true feelings about the big city, money, and fame. He was a twisted man who was beyond salvation.

He seemed to regret ever having married me. He said that for a scholar like himself who knew only his studies, a capable wife was the only shortcut to success, and he never hesitated to whine about his "crappy luck" in not being able to find such a wife. He swore and he vented and his already wry face grew more twisted. "How come so-and-so's wife got him a promotion, and such-and-such's in-laws are carrying him up the social ladder, but here I am stuck, married again to a woman who knows nothing except how to cook. Talk about shit luck!" If this had come from a little brat nagging his mom to finagle first place for him at school because he didn't feel like studying, it would have at least been cute. But coming from a middle-aged, full-grown man, it grew old, fast.

We grew tired of each other and so we went our separate ways. I'm pretty sure it wasn't because I was acting like Western women who demanded love in a marriage. Rather, it was probably the extreme Eastern reason: I didn't have children. After my first divorce, this second one was a breeze.

My third husband was a businessman from T City who was known to have earned some money. A widower, he had lived alone some ten years, and now that his sons and daughters were all married he was looking for a wife. This was the selling point. He was the perfect candidate because from my second marriage I had already learned that raising stepchildren wasn't easy, and I didn't have the guts to raise children of my own. Like the old saying "Third time lucky," I really wanted this one to be successful. I liked the fact that he was a businessman. Since it was his job to go out and earn money, he wouldn't be a bullshit hypocrite like the university instructor. In fact, he didn't even try to hide his worship of the Almighty Dollar. "Let's earn money and have a good life!"—his always-on-the-move attitude was summed up in this one phrase.

"Kyŏnghŭi said she'd be here. I wonder what's keeping her."

Hŭisuk yawns and looks down at her watch.

"Kyŏnghŭi?"

"Come on, you remember her, don't you? The pretty girl with the snaggletooth who used to get overly embarrassed, just like you. She'd always cover her mouth when she laughed because she was ashamed of her teeth. You know, the girl who started all those rumors about herself and the teacher because she would turn red and give stupid answers whenever he asked her a question."

"I hear she hasn't changed a bit. Still fresh-faced and pretty as hell. Probably because she married well and lives a worry-free life. She's exactly the same, even still gets embarrassed easily."

I suddenly feel a violent hostility toward Kyŏnghŭi. It's an exciting feeling, something I haven't felt in a long time. I see her as the last human being on this earth who is capable of feeling shame, and I'm eager to witness it before it goes extinct.

"She should have been here by now. Could we try calling her at home?"

Yŏngmi makes the call and returns with an annoyed pout on her face.

"She said for all of us to come over to her place . . . something about not being able to go out because of an important guest. It's pretty obvious. Accepting some grease no doubt. I can see right through her. She just wants to show off her oh so perfect life. Let's go. Hey, it's a free lunch."

With a husband who is an eminent member of the elite crowd, it seems Kyŏnghŭi is the envy of all housewives. But as we get closer to her house in Hannam-dong, I get the odd sense that Hŭisuk and Yŏngmi's attitude toward me is turning hostile. They practically foam at the mouth, telling me in great detail how well off Kyŏnghŭi is, but all the while I know that they're just trying to see my reaction, to figure out my present circumstances by seeing how shocked and jealous I become at hearing this. My friends are probably most interested in knowing how well off I am, naturally, since it's the first thing you want to know when you meet friends or family. But it seems they haven't been able to figure it out yet. Then again, there's no way they can know, since I don't know myself. *How frustrating is that?* I have absolutely no idea whether my husband is rich or poor, or even if he's deep in debt.

Kyŏnghŭi's house with its landscaped garden is pretty big, but I'm not overly impressed. It's larger than my house and the layout is a bit more elaborate, but somehow it isn't all that different. With these convenient Western-style houses, after you've seen one you've seen them all. Even the furniture is the same. Granted, the mother-of-pearl stationery case in her room is probably more valuable than mine, and the Chinese porcelain on top of the case is probably not the thousand-*wŏn* knock-off we have in our house. But such house-hold items have no higher purpose than use, monetary value, or show, and since neither of us likely has any affection or taste for beauty in such things, it is all in all insignificantly the same. I'm not the least bit threatened. Kyŏnghŭi greets me with a poise that keeps within the limits of grace and friendliness. She then asks me, "So what does your husband do?" Yŏngmi jumps in with a wry grin. "I think she said something about him being in a technical tie-up with a Japanese firm." Then Hŭisuk adds, "Funny thing is, it's her third husband."

Kyŏnghŭi's cheeks flush pink as if she's just heard something indecent and unsuitable for a modest woman. "Oh, you girls," she gasps, then covers her mouth and laughs. That habit of covering her mouth started because she was ashamed of her teeth, but now it takes into account even the charm of her snaggletooth and is nothing more than a polished pose. Adding to her ladylike grace is the deep, perfectly chiseled emerald set in the ring on her softly composed, eel-like finger. Yes, it is a beautiful pose but it has nothing to do with shame. It's like something an actress does—a beautiful, carefully staged pose that is meant to produce an artistic effect. The core of shame is hollow and only the shell of the pose remains. I feel disappointed but relieved at the same time.

Kyŏnghŭi shows great interest in what my husband is said to be doing and asks if I would be interested in signing up at the Japanese language school she goes to.

"If your husband is going to associate with Japanese, then he'll probably need a lot of help from you. You know, making it big these days depends more on how good the woman is at supporting her husband. It'll be good for you to learn Japanese, that's for sure. Me, though, I'm just doing it for myself."

"As if Japanese is the only other language you know. You've learned a bit of almost every language, haven't you?" Hŭisuk laughs fawningly.

"Not really. I just memorized a few basic expressions whenever we went overseas on vacation."

I go home and give my husband a relatively detailed account of what happened. When he hears I have a classmate who's married into what he considers "the elite crowd," he becomes disgustingly happy as if he's a shaman whose prophecies were right on the money.

"Well look at that! Didn't I tell you there's no law that says you can't have the wife of a high-ranking official among your friends? This is good news, really good. . . . What? Japanese language school? Of course you should. No question about it. You can't let slip an opportunity to cozy up to a woman in such a position. That's the secret to success in life. The art of social intercourse, schmoozing, whatever you want to call it, it all comes down to stuff like this." Then in a tone both patriotic and grave he adds, "Knowledge is power. To learn is to survive. For you and no one else."

And now here I am attending the Japanese language school—not because of Kyŏnghŭi's suggestion but because I can't take any more of my husband's annoying insistence. But if there's another reason, it's probably that I consider Japanese as my fallback plan just in case I get divorced again. I can use it to help me stand on my own. Isn't Japanese tourism on the rise, after all?

I rarely run into Kyŏnghŭi at the language school. We're in different classes—she's intermediate and I'm just a beginner—but she doesn't take school that seriously and so she misses a lot of classes. When we do see each other she always warns me not to let anybody know she's the wife of Mr. High and Mighty, and goes on about how she might have to take a private tutor because she doesn't want anybody to find out who she is. And so the rift between us is widening.

My Japanese isn't getting any better. I studied some Japanese during the colonial period, and since I thought I had picked it up pretty well back then, I expected I'd catch on quickly now. But I'm so bad that even when the instructor pronounces "*Ohayo*" and "*Sayonara*" for me, I can't get the words out myself.

In addition to the Japanese language school, there are lots of cram schools in the Chongno area. It seems like every kid in Seoul attends a couple of them at least. English and math institutes, international language schools, prep classes for university and high school entrance exams, other prep exams, and mock exams, all-in-one programs, teacher training programs, the Seoul National University program—into this infinite number of schools go masses of students carrying bags full of heavy books; in they go and back out they spill. Having no experience raising kids of my own, I see them and think, *Hey, I wouldn't mind having one of those.* But unable to understand their rebellious gestures or their extreme fatigue, I get a bit scared.

Today I notice a group of Japanese tourists passing by on our street, a Korean tour guide leading the way. The guide exudes class but the tourists look cold, casual, and cunning, even obtusely boorish as if they belong back in the remote countryside. It's a sad sight to see, like casting pearls before swine. It's not just that the guide looks stylish, but her determination, liveliness, and confidence are those of an able worker whose focus is commerce and the pursuit of foreign exchange. Just then the students pour out from the various schools and mix in with the Japanese tourists on the street. The tour guide threads her way through the crowd and whispers in a voice loud enough for me to hear, "*Anō minasama, kochira atari kara suri ni go-chūi nasaimase.*" What she's saying is, "Listen up everyone. Be careful, there are pickpockets nearby."

At first I am terribly embarrassed—why did I understand everything the tour guide said? Then I start to feel hot, and an odd sensation, almost painful, comes over me. There it is again. Shame. If a paraplegic person is to regain feeling in her limbs as the result of some miraculous stimulation, she must also accept the pain before shedding tears of joy. I welcome my pain and with it a feeling of pride—I can feel shame again!

I feel flushed and hot all over, as if a fire has ignited in me.

All around me are waves of students who, dissatisfied with the normal school curriculum, seek out this and that institute to gain more knowledge. But none of these places teaches shame.

Amid the jungle of painted signs on these institutes I want to stream a flag that cries out "We teach shame! We teach shame!" No, it doesn't even have to be a flag. A handkerchief blowing in the wind will do, a handkerchief with the words "We teach shame!" Yes. This is exactly what I need to do. But I don't think I can, because my new-found shame is my own.

PRISON OF THE HEART

Kim Wŏnil

Translated by Michael Finch

Kim Wŏnil was born in the Chinhae region of South Kyŏngsang Province in 1942. At the age of seventeen he had a story published in *New Literary Arts* (*Shin munye*), a short-lived journal for high school students published by the influential Chŏngyang publishing house; his formal debut came in 1966 in a New Writers competition sponsored by the *Taegu maeil shinmun*, a daily newspaper. Kim studied creative writing at Sŏrabŏl College of Arts and obtained an M.A. in Korean language and literature from Tanguk University. Now in the sixth decade of his career he is one of Korea's most prolific writers of fiction, his stories and novels bearing witness to the years leading up to and following the Korean War, and to the territorial and psychic division of the Korean peninsula.

His name is synonymous with the division motif of contemporary Korean fiction. He first attracted widespread
attention in 1973 with his story "Spirit of Darkness"
(Ŏdum ŭi hon) and by 1990 his works were sufficiently
well known that his autobiographical novel, *House with
a Deep Yard* (*Madang k'ip'ŭn chip*, 1989), was made
into a popular TV series. Among his major novels are
Afterglow (*Noŭl*, 1977–78) and *Winter Valley* (*Kyŏul
koltchagi*, 1984–87). His many literary awards include
the sixteenth Tongin Literature Prize (1984) for "Disil-
lusion Found" (Hwanmyŏl ŭl ch'ajasŏ) and the second
Hwang Sunwŏn Literature Prize (2002) for "Accordion"
(Sonp'unggŭm). "Prison of the Heart" (Maŭm ŭi kamok)
first appeared in the journal *Hyŏndae sosŏl* in 1990 and
was honored the same year with the fourteenth Yi Sang
Literature Prize.

At the Seventh Moscow International Book Fair this year, the
Republic of Korea was present for the first time ever, exhibit-
ing some 570 books. The Korean Publishers' Association, which was
in charge of the project, advertised for personnel to form a team of
representatives to take part in the book fair and a fact-finding tour
of the Soviet Union. In response, applications were received from
twenty-two publishing companies belonging to the association. I
also applied to join this group. The book fair lasted a week and then,
with the rest of the Korean delegation, I completed a twelve-day tour
of the Soviet Union, including visits to Leningrad and Kiev, before
returning to Korea. My wife met me at Kimp'o Airport and after a
few words of greeting told me about Hyŏn'gu.

"I didn't tell you when you phoned from Leningrad because I knew it wouldn't be easy for you to make international calls, and you would have been going around worrying pointlessly, but Hyŏn'gu was admitted to North Kyŏngsang University Hospital a week ago." The order permitting Hyŏn'gu to go into hospital for an examination because of his illness must have finally come from the court. I could guess from what my wife said that my younger brother's illness had worsened so much it was now necessary for him to be kept under continual observation by a specialist. At his trial Hyŏn'gu had been sentenced to eighteen months' imprisonment, and his appeal was now pending in the high court. As the permission to go into hospital had come rather late, however, I could not interpret the court's action in an entirely favorable way.

Ten years ago, in 1979, my younger brother had contracted hepatitis just after his release from prison. His sentence had been suspended after he had served twenty months. The whites of his eyes had gone a jaundiced yellow, but he had quickly recovered after some rest at Sug'yŏng's house along with outpatient treatment at a local hospital. Although I could not say my brother had a robust constitution, he was not frail either, and so after the illness he'd gone back to his busy life without any apparent problem. After being arrested for the latest incident and being held in custody to await trial, however, he'd been unable to digest what he was fed in that charming place. He'd complain to visitors that he always had a burning feeling in his stomach, he had no energy, and it was difficult for him even to sit up.

One day in the beginning of July at the onset of the rainy season, I went down to Taegu to visit him. Even though it had only been a month since my last visit, as soon as I saw him, I noticed how emaciated he was. The color of his skin didn't look good either. His face was a dark yellow, and his cheekbones jutted out. He was obviously malnourished—as though he'd started fasting again. He looked just the same as when I'd visited him at Andong Prison five years earlier. At that time he'd fasted a week, taking only water, to protest against the prison authorities' brutal treatment of prisoners of conscience. The difference was that his face had looked pale then.

"I wasn't able to sleep, worrying about how the poor people could eat and make ends meet in this rainy season when there's no work to be had, and then I seemed to be dreaming I'd been released and was running up to some poor mountain village." As Hyŏn'gu spoke, he gave a shy smile that did not quite seem to fit his age. Among his expressions, he had a particular one when he smiled. The wrinkles around his mouth made him look just like an old man, even though at thirty-nine he was in his prime. I asked him whether he'd had a checkup, as he obviously had some problem with his stomach or liver. He answered listlessly that he'd managed to get some indigestion tablets and was taking them. He said he was in no particular pain and would soon be better.

I met Chu Yŏngjun, the lawyer who was handling his case. I asked him to apply for permission for Hyŏn'gu to be admitted to a general hospital where he could be examined and treated, as he was clearly ill. Then I returned to Seoul. By the time I'd left for the Soviet Union, however, this permission had still not been granted.

On the way home from the airport in the car, my wife told me she had gone to Taegu two days earlier and that Hyŏn'gu was undergoing a general examination. According to the doctor, the problem was with his liver rather than his stomach, and his condition was not good at all.

"They said he lost about fifteen pounds after they removed the fluid from his abdomen. I couldn't bear to see him looking so thin. He's not even able to eat rice gruel because of the medical examinations . . . I'm afraid Mother may fall ill too, taking care of him. But you know I can't go down there, because of the children. You must visit him right away, no matter how busy you are." As she spoke, she wiped her eyes with a handkerchief and added, "I almost forgot— your sister gave the lawyer one million wŏn for his expenses and to thank him for his efforts this time and last time."

I could almost feel the scorching heat of mid-August outside the car. The leaves on the roadside trees were wilting and drooping, and the apartment blocks in the distance seemed to wobble and collapse in the shimmering heat. Beyond that shimmering scene, I tried to visualize my emaciated brother's features; the face I saw looked like a shriveled leaf sinking under water. I was eight years older than my brother, so we'd never had any deep conversations, and until now we'd spent more time apart than together. We'd lived together until I graduated from high school. When he was at middle school I was at university in Seoul, when he was at high school I was doing my military service, and when he was at university in Taegu I was already working for a company in Seoul.

The next morning I left my car covered over, as it had been for two weeks, and went to work by city coach. I saw from our sales that during the two weeks I'd been away, practically everyone had left either for the sea or the mountains; not surprisingly our books, which were not exactly summer reading to begin with, hadn't been selling well. I checked on the progress of three new publications that were due out in the autumn. I also met with the professor of Russian who'd translated Anatoly Rybakov's *Children of the Arbat*, wanting him to get started on Rybakov's novel *Fear*. I had brought this book back from Moscow, where it had been published only a month earlier, its publication made possible in the climate of Mikhail Gorbachev's *perestroika* policy, and it would soon be translated into several Western languages. *Fear* was the sequel to *Children of the Arbat*, the masterpiece of this internationally renowned author's declining years. Citing the summer heat, the professor was reluctant to agree to my request to complete the translation of the roughly 300 pages of text within two months. Because I felt it was urgent to publish a translation of this novel, I briefly entertained the possibility of getting hold of a Japanese translation, as Japan was usually one step ahead of us in translating important works of international literature. We could then divide the work into several sections and ask a few people to translate them. But I'd made it one of my basic publishing principles not to do that kind of thing, and so I'd no option but to try to persuade the translator of *Arbat* to carry on with this sequel, especially since I knew his meticulous translation work to be reliable. The small-scale publishing company I ran with nine employees had published some eighty books, but since last year we'd not brought out any outstanding works and, in fact, were barely surviving—which led our business manager to quietly bemoan our policy of refusing to publish the trendy fiction that appeals to young readers. But as the international news sections of the dailies recently seemed dominated by articles on the Soviet Union's reform policies and democratization, our sales of Rybakov's *Children of the Arbat* in three volumes had risen to 90,000 copies. This had been a great help in covering our operating costs. And then as luck would have it, the international book fair had taken place in the Soviet Union, and I eagerly went abroad for the first time in order to interview Rybakov and to negotiate with the Soviet Copyright Association, an organ of the Union of Soviet Authors. I had also brought back from Moscow Varlam Shalamov's short-story collection *Kolyma Tales*. This book denounces the conditions in the concentration camps during Stalin's regime and was now being reappraised in Russia because of the cultural thaw there. Consequently, that evening I met another professor of Russian over a meal and beer to negotiate the translation of that novel.

And then, as I'd promised my wife when I'd left home that morning, I phoned her to say I was leaving and caught the night train to Taegu. When I arrived at East Taegu Station, the short summer night was over and the station plaza was bathed in the pale light of morning. With my one bag I got into a taxi and asked the middle-aged driver to take me to the University Hospital. In fact several medical schools have now appeared in Taegu, but anyone who has lived in Taegu for a long time would know I meant the North Kyŏngsang University Hospital in Samdŏk-dong. The medical college and its affiliated hospital occupied spacious grounds and stood facing each other across a narrow avenue in the city center. They were among the few remaining old Western-style brick buildings in Taegu. From East Taegu Station to the hospital by taxi it's only the base rate. When I got out of the taxi, the avenue between the medical college and the hospital was unusually peaceful in the early morning light. Thoughts of my middle school days came back to me. I used to deliver the morning edition of the *Chungang ilbo* in the area around Samdŏk-dong and Tongin-dong. The street and its surroundings hadn't changed in the slightest, and I recalled how it had seemed such a long, broad road then. Looking up at the dawn stars, I used to scurry along that deserted road where no one else was in sight. Six copies of the newspaper went to the medical college, and seven to the university hospital. After I'd pushed those copies through the gap in the door of the caretaker's booths on either side of the road, my stack of newspapers became lighter; I felt as though I'd already finished delivering half of them.

That would have been 1953. My younger brother, a war baby, would have been five years old. Our mother raised her three children by selling American-made goods in the Yankee Market, and just as it was for all the other refugees then, it was a time of real poverty for us, too.

I came to the same low brick wall over which you can look into the broad grounds of the hospital, where there is a thickly wooded enclosure. The lush *pŏjŭm* trees, wet with morning dew, came together like a roof over the road they lined. The tipsiness I'd felt when boarding the train had long since passed, but my head ached, perhaps because I'd been unable to sleep properly. My tiredness made my skin feel tighter, and I felt dizzy as I walked along. Then too I'd only had two days to get over the seven-hour time difference between Moscow and Seoul.

In the booth inside the main gate of the hospital, the uniformed caretaker, cap and all, was nodding off under a dim fluorescent light.

I'd intended to ask him which ward Hyŏn'gu had been admitted to, but decided not to bother him and walked the short distance along a paved pathway through the trees toward the somber, stolid main building, constructed during the Japanese colonial period. I breathed in the fresh morning air through my nose. My heart became heavy as I thought about seeing my brother, and despite my headache, I lit a cigarette. Somewhere among the trees, the sharp cries of a waking bird scattered the deep stillness.

According to my wife, Hyŏn'gu had been admitted to an isolated ward in a separate building that lay up against the ivy-covered rear wall of the hospital complex. It sounded as though he'd only been released from prison reluctantly, and I felt as if they'd dumped him in a psychiatric ward. Inside this single-story brick building a long, gloomy corridor confronted me. At the end of it was a door with two windows that looked like the square lenses of a pair of spectacles. I felt a cold shiver, as though I were entering one of the prisons my brother had been in and out of all his life just as though they'd been his own home. From where I'd entered the building, windows looking out onto the broad, heavily wooded grounds flanked the corridor at intervals of half a dozen steps, while the rear of the building was partitioned into wards. The building's age—it had been in existence for seventy or eighty years—showed in the plastered ceiling and walls, which were engrained with soot and dust, and in the cement floor, which was a ragged patchwork of repairs. There was that particular hospital odor of cresol mixed with a fetid, moldy smell. I looked for my brother's ward as I walked down the gloomy corridor. In spite of the occasional fluorescent light, I had to practically put my nose to the doors to read the room numbers. My footsteps sounded unusually loud. Perhaps because of the heat, one of the doors had been left half open, and from inside it came the low-pitched moans of a patient. The sound was like a desperate appeal welling up from deep in the ground and it weighed down my already heavy heart. A few of the long benches running along the wall of the corridor were occupied by patients' relatives curled up asleep without any covering. Wondering if my mother or Tongsu's mother might be among them, I looked closely at the sleeping faces. But after two of the people I'd examined in this way told me my brother was in a private ward, I realized I'd have to keep going before I'd find them.

"Well there you are, Son. It's me, your mum."

It was difficult to make out anyone's face in that gloomy grayness. Nevertheless, Mother with some special maternal sense had recognized me walking toward her from the distance. I couldn't see her face as she sat hunched up with one knee in front of her on the corridor bench but could only hear her hoarse voice.

Mother asked whether I'd had a good journey abroad, and I asked why she was sitting out in the corridor. Mother glanced toward the ward and said she couldn't bear looking at the guard on duty inside and had come out here to close her eyes for a while. As my brother was still on remand, I knew even though he'd received permission to go into hospital, there was a prison guard stationed in his room.

"Yungu, something doesn't seem right. I don't know what this special permission is all about, but some high-up from the police came and told me not to worry about the hospital and treatment fees. He said the state would pay for everything. Besides, they seem to have finished the general examination. They strap people onto a big metal plate like a cross that turns round and round as though they are torturing them. But the doctor won't say anything . . . everyone's wondering whether it's cirrhosis of the liver or sclerosis. I just don't know what to think. . . ."

Mother choked up momentarily and she couldn't continue. Nor could I bring myself to ask if it might be cancer. At this hour my brother was best off sleeping comfortably, and as I hadn't come with any particular plan of action, there was no point in waking him just now.

"Haven't you got a classmate who's a doctor at the university hospital?" Mother asked.

"Yes, the only one who didn't go up to Seoul." Out of my high school class alone, five close friends had got into the medical college of North Kyŏngsang University. Four had since gone up to Seoul as heads of departments in general hospitals or to set up their own hospital. Only Ham Kŭnjo had remained, working in this hospital for twenty years in the clinical laboratories.

"You don't say. The two of you must have known each other since you were in diapers. You have to try to see him. But then what if he says. . . ." Mother's voice faded away. Her small body seemed to become even smaller as she choked back tears of remorse. The white hair on her forehead trembled as it caught the gray light.

I thought back to the winter of 1947, just before I entered primary school. Father had opened a church mission in a village of about forty homes nestled in a mountain valley about twelve miles from Hoech'ŏn, in the backwoods of North P'yŏng'an Province. He fled south with just our immediate family for religious freedom. When war broke out three years later, like most of the other residents of Seoul, our family was unable to get away. Father was hauled off to the Office of the Interior. When Seoul was recaptured on September 29, he was taken north by the retreating People's Army, and Mother followed him northward in the wake of the South Korean troops. At that time she had two young children with her and was in the final stage of pregnancy. But before she reached Sariwŏn in Hwanghae Province, she met several people who'd been taken north along with Father but had made a daring escape and were making their way back to Seoul. One of them told her Reverend Pak had been killed along with about twenty other men in the center of Yŏnch'ŏn in Kyŏnggi Province during an attack by American warplanes. She knew then that her husband was dead. Fleeing from that place, she gave birth to a son on the earth floor of an abandoned house. That son was Hyŏn'gu. Caught up in that nightmare and not knowing how we were managing to survive as we moved south in the winter of 1950, Mother had become a young widow; she was just twenty-nine. When the Chinese communist troops entered the war, Mother even had to endure the ordeal of being caught up in the retreat of the South Korean army. Long afterward she used to say it was impossible to describe everything that had happened at that time. Coping somehow with the bitter cold of that terrible winter, she made her way alone with her three children down to the unfamiliar city of Taegu. I was a third grader at the time, and even I can remember the cold and the hunger, the endless trudging, and the stabbing pain in my toes, which felt as though they were about to drop off. Those vivid memories are with me to this day. In some situations women are said to be tougher than men, and I can still see the determined figure of my younger sister, Sug'yŏng, as she doggedly kept up without complaining.

With no other blood relations here in the South, my widowed mother had been a pillar of strength for her three children from that time until today. Now that I'm forty-seven years old, I have sufficient depth of heart to understand my widowed mother's life. I could read in her dark, wrinkled form that in her motherly heart she might as well have been standing on a precipice as she sat there dispiritedly, wondering whether among the three children she had raised, she might not have to send one of them from this earth before her. I could see the glistening of tears welling up in her eyes as she told herself that crying like this wouldn't help. I thought about how she'd brought up her three children in an unfamiliar part of the country, overcoming all the harsh dealings of this world to become a tower of strength, and yet that tower might now begin to shake from its very foundations. Nevertheless, even though she was past the age of sixty, Mother had thought nothing of putting on a headband and a sash and energetically attending citizens' protest meetings to help secure the release of my brother from prison. She used to say almost out of habit that waking or sleeping, her younger son—born after the death of his father—and her husband were joined together inside her. And in the world outside the prison, she would say, she'd prepared a prison cell in her own heart for Hyŏn'gu.

"Hyŏn'gu is twenty-nine years younger than me. Last year I thought together we'd get past the number nine which everyone says is so unlucky," my mother muttered to herself as she gazed out the window.

Mother's way of reckoning ages around the number nine was our traditional way of calculating our ages. I could read in her husky, subdued voice, sounding as though it was choking back many tears, the despondency that had flowed over her in inverse proportion to the passionate outpouring of her love. I was lost for words and could only follow my mother's gaze. Through the broad, outspread branches of a Himalayan cedar and across the wide courtyard, between the two-story brick buildings opposite, I gazed at fragments of sky. The crying of the birds scattered like rays of light in the breaking dawn. Even though one spark of life was dying out in this hospital block, there at the end of the earth, as always, the sun was rising impassively.

I took my bag and stood up without a word. There was a notice on the door of the ward: "Authorized Persons Only—No Unauthorized Entry." I went into the ward. The first thing I saw was yet another sign, this one at the foot of the bed: "Bed Rest." Hyŏn'gu's eyes were closed and the needle of an intravenous drip was sticking into his forearm. Three vinyl-covered metal chairs for visitors were arranged around a table that stood in the center of the ward. On one wall the light from a translucent lamp was becoming faint as sunlight streamed into the room.

A young man in uniform was dozing off in an armchair whose armrests he had padded with pillows. At the sound of the unexpected intruder he bolted upright and shot me a glance. A pair of handcuffs and a truncheon were attached to either side of his belt.

"I'm Hyŏn'gu's elder brother," I said in a quiet voice.

I placed my bag on one of the chairs and went up to the bed. My brother was asleep, his emaciated hook-like hands resting gently on top of the coverlet. It was as though he'd been fettered by the IV needle. I felt sorry to see his hair soaked in sweat and the uneven stubble on his face. His face looked as though it had been carved out of wood, and if any more wood were shaved off, his bones would be laid bare. Above his hospital gown his collarbone stuck out so much you could have grabbed hold of it. I felt a sense of unworldly piety in his miserable, emaciated appearance. When we used to live in a single rented room in Changgwan-dong in the center of Taegu, Hyŏn'gu and I attended the First Church Sunday school. My younger brother was in the lower class, and I was in the upper class. Once I heard the lower-class teacher marveling at how well shy Hyŏn'gu could recite and pray saying, "Our Mother, Our Mother." As a child he was attentive to Mother in a way that was quite out of keeping with his age, so he was cherished more deeply than his brother and sister. In the gathering dark, he liked to ambush Mother as she walked home from work, wanting to have supper with her. "Ah my faithful little son, you've waited until now to eat together with Mum, haven't you?" Mother would say as she took him by the hand and went in through the front door. When I saw the peaceful face of my brother as he slept, I felt how kind people seem to retain a boyish purity in their faces despite their age and recalled how he had looked as a child.

I didn't want to awaken Hyŏn'gu, so I sat down on one of the chairs. At some point Mother had come into the ward. The young man, who had cropped hair and a square face, introduced himself as Prison Officer Ch'oe. After recording my name, address, and telephone number in a visitors' register, he asked me various questions about nothing in particular. Since the questions seemed designed to alleviate his boredom, I answered them in a half-hearted sort of way.

The door to the ward opened without a sound, and a woman wearing a headscarf came in cautiously carrying a plastic water container. She was dressed in an army top with the sleeves rolled up and a pair of baggy trousers.

"Sangju-*daek*. You're up early." Mother greeted her cheerfully.

"Work starts from half past seven," the Sangju woman replied. Her skin had been browned by the sun, and she spoke in a subdued voice as though she'd committed some crime.

Sangju-*daek* set down the water container explaining it was fresh water from a spring up in the hills in back of her home. She gazed at Hyŏn'gu's sleeping form from where she stood, then sat down, deliberately clasped her hands together, and asked my mother to pray. Mother bowed her head and earnestly prayed to the Lord to save Hyŏn'gu's life. Sangju-*daek* left after about ten minutes, treading softly so as not to wake my brother. Meanwhile, the prison guard had returned from washing up outside.

"You probably remember Sangju-*daek* from Hyŏn'gu's trial," my mother explained. "This whole trouble started when the demolition gang pulled down her rented home. That's why she's going to such trouble. She has to take care of three children and a mother-in-law who can't get around very well. So she gets up at the crack of dawn to work at a building site. She walks along rickety walkways on the fourth or fifth floor carrying bricks and sand." As she spoke, Mother moved the water container under Hyŏn'gu's bed.

Hyŏn'gu awoke thirty minutes later, perhaps from the bustle of footsteps in the corridor.

"Brother, when did you get back?"

My brother's voice was subdued. He asked me about the push for democratization and reform in the Soviet Union, which was then being called the last great decision of the twentieth century. He asked about the support Gorbachev was getting for his reforms, and about the reports that he was afraid the conservative Bolsheviks, who had held power for seventy years, might undermine them. He also asked about the response of ordinary Soviet citizens to the collapse of the wall dividing East and West Germany, about the ideological turnaround of the Eastern European nations, and so on. The table next to his bed bore, along with a Bible and a telephone, several pages of a newspaper in which I imagined he'd read about these things. At the same time, he seemed interested in my own first-hand account. On the other hand, perhaps he was wondering how a member of the gray, middle-class intelligentsia like myself, who was neither a progressive nor a conservative, felt about these reports. But I felt it was too early to make an informed reply about the great popularity of Gorbachev or about the Soviet Union, which was now undergoing a bold revision as it dismantled socialism and the hegemony of an absolutist ideology. Then again, such problems were relevant to Korea and my fleeting observations might have sounded shallow to my brother, who'd been an activist for over twenty years, struggling by himself to find an answer to those problems. So I answered in a vague, roundabout way that I'd noticed the struggle to change the strong doctrinaire tendency of socialism, which was meant to improve the lives of the people. I didn't want to mention such things as the long lines of customers outside the department stores and shops in Moscow and of course Leningrad, because of the shortage of all the necessities of life. Then I would have had to elaborate in tedious fashion on the top-down bureaucratic political system, the qualitative stagnation of products due to the lack of competition in society caused by the nationalization of industry, and the listless attitude of workers toward their work. To be sure, all these things had been reported in the newspapers. My brother shook his head weakly and said he didn't know if such a thorough reform of Marxist economic theory was right—there was, after all, so much social injustice in our own country. My brother didn't seem to be in any pain as he spoke—I wondered if there was a painkiller in his IV, or if liver disease had any subjective symptoms. On the contrary, his voice was animated, his expression bright.

"There's a housing complex for the Writers' Alliance in the outskirts of Moscow. It's a model village for writers, built under Lenin in 1933 at the request of Gorky. Rybakov, the president of the Soviet Union PEN Club, lives there. The houses are like cottages surrounding a big courtyard, but they're old and built of wood with only two rooms. One room is a bedroom and one is a writing room. Rybakov's home was a little different, and we talked in a dining room cum sitting room. I could see straightaway the frugality of the house of this old master, but, of course, the homes of all families in the Soviet Union are like that. He was happy when I told him that *Children of the Arbat* is widely read in South Korea. Even though he's seventy-seven, he's a vigorous old man with a strong voice and a sparkle in his eyes. That's how he could produce a masterpiece like *Children of the Arbat* in his old age. Like other members of the intelligentsia, he's an ardent supporter of Gorbachev. That's because Gorbachev has removed all restrictions on travel and extended the right of free speech to ordinary Soviet citizens, and at the same time writers now have complete freedom of expression. Take *Children of the Arbat*—it's a denunciation of the dictatorial politics of terror under Stalin. According to Rybakov, during Stalin's twenty-two-year dictatorship more than seventy million people, including intellectuals, were either executed or exiled. He gave me a fiery speech about how they'd survived, just like the Russian people had silently endured centuries of slavery under the invading Mongols and Arabs—that's why the Slavic people are stronger than any other race. The reason he told me all this was to explain that *perestroika* is the fruition of decades of Slavic patience!"

Fresh from my travels abroad, I was going on for longer than I'd intended.

"I've read the three volumes of *Children of the Arbat* you gave me," said my brother. "The scale of Russian literature is truly something else. But according to the brief bio of Rybakov in the book, he was sentenced to three years in Siberia as a student under Stalin, but after that he adapted to the system, and he even won the Stalin Prize for literature—while Stalin was still alive! For over thirty years he never wrote anything like *Arbat*; all he did was follow his instincts for self-preservation. He only got going and launched an attack against Stalin once freedom of expression had arrived. What do you think his reputation would be like if he'd died seven years ago?"

If it were me making such a scathing attack, I could be accused of being a bourgeois, intellectual, armchair theorist. But my brother was sufficiently qualified to voice such criticisms.

"Well, that's why they say even writers adapt to the times."

Hyŏn'gu ignored my weak retort and changed the subject.

"Wasn't the ideology of socialism originally based on moral righteousness? After the success of the Bolshevik Revolution in 1917, didn't Lenin first get rid of class distinctions, in accordance with the principle of the redistribution of wealth? I thought Gorbachev was introducing economic and political pluralism through *glasnost* and *perestroika* on top of that strong socialist foundation in order to improve the people's quality of life?"

"Well, socialist economic theory made sense in 1917 after the revolution, but now it seems to be hitting some limitations. In the nationalized department stores the clerks don't even have commonplace electronic calculators—they use abacuses instead."

"What's people's daily life like?"

"From a capitalist viewpoint it's generally poor. The quality of goods in the department stores is like ours used to be in the mid-sixties. But their social welfare system seems to work well, and they don't seem to have to worry about the basics of life. As you said, the strong point of their society is that it's very pure from an ethical point of view. The people can't help but be honest and simple. I don't know about the high-ranking party officials, but there's no corruption or abuse of power there, because lies wouldn't get you anywhere in their society."

"That's exactly the problem. Even though the standard of living in the Soviet Union is thirty years behind the standard of living in advanced Western countries, they have achieved an equal quality of life for everybody, haven't they? The important thing is to build that equality step by step, even if it takes a long time. But what about our country, where a small number of monopoly capitalists and a parasitic leisure class just advance their own quality of life? Look at our reality. The haves have too much and eat and dress in style, living on their unearned incomes, while the poor have to live seven or eight people in a rented basement room. The difference is like heaven and hell, isn't it? I'm not arguing we absolutely have to put socialism into practice on this earth. Even I accept the weak points of socialist countries—they're politically totalitarian, culturally uniform, and economically backward. But when we take an objective look at our own reality, we have to rectify this vicious circle, and soon. Our society is mature enough now that we should turn a more sympathetic eye on the three-and-a-half million or so people living in poverty and social exclusion. In other words, growth and exports aren't more urgent than establishing a fair distribution of wealth. When that happens, we'll see socialism and capitalism finally come together. . . ."

Hyŏn'gu's voice changed as he became short of breath.

"That's enough now," Mother intervened. "It's not good for you to get all worked up. Hasn't everything you've said been written down more than two thousand years ago in the Bible? The Lord knows everything already. Didn't he say it's more difficult for a rich man to go to heaven than it is for a camel to pass through the eye of a needle?"

I had nothing more to say about these issues either. To someone who had lived that reality and fought with all his strength, I was a mere onlooker.

"What a time we're living in. Your very first trip abroad, and you get to go to the foremost socialist country . . ." And that was all Hyŏn'gu said for a while. He sounded exhausted.

Hyŏn'gu was well aware of the trouble I'd suffered as his elder brother. When he wasn't in prison and was on the run, I also came under investigation by the authorities, who twice had picked me up and worked me over to make me reveal my brother's whereabouts.

At university in Taegu, Hyŏn'gu first got involved in the Christian Student Alliance. This was only natural as Father had been a minister, and all three of us had been baptized and from a young age had gone to church. Whatever he was seeking, he found an answer in the Christian response to social reality known as "popular liberation theology," and he began to attend anti-government meetings and demonstrations that advocated liberating the people from oppression and poverty. He was a gentle sort and tended to be introspective, and no one around him, especially Mother, could ever have guessed such a change might come over him. At the risk of resorting to popular psychology, one might say this change was possible because of an inversion of his introspective character. After several instances of having to go underground and then being apprehended, he was forced to go into the army in his third year at university. He reported enduring harsh treatment in a special detachment deployed on the front line, before he was discharged. One year later, in 1976, just when he was about to graduate, my brother ran afoul of Emergency Measure No. 9. Once again he became a fugitive, and was arrested the following year while working as a day laborer on a construction site in Kyŏngsan. He earned a two-year prison term and a four-year ban on doing any work requiring professional certification, but was paroled after serving one year and eight months. After that he threw himself into the Taegu labor movement. He never did graduate from university and, playing down his educational background, started work as an apprentice at the Tongyŏng Dyeing and Weaving Company, located in the dyeing industrial complex in Pisan-dong in Taegu. This was the beginning of a vagabond life as a worker, a workers' night school instructor, and an activist for the poor in Taegu's Kŏmdan and Third Industrial complexes, the Pisan-dong Dyeing Complex, and the Sŏngsŏ and Wŏlbae complexes—and all during this time he never let us know where he was living. In 1980 it was my turn: I was dismissed from my job as a reporter and had to struggle to make ends meet until I started the publishing company three years later. Then and of course later, investigators were constantly barging into my home and my company office in Seoul try-

ing to find Hyŏn'gu. According to them, wherever they found Pak
Hyŏn'gu, they were also bound to find labor disputes, strikes, and
demonstrations demanding better conditions for the poor. During
that time he was imprisoned twice—these periods of enforced inac-
tivity were the only times the investigators stopped frequenting
our home. The last time he'd been imprisoned was this spring—the
result of his involvement in a dispute between demolition workers
and residents in a redevelopment project in Pisan-dong. He and his
wife were devoting themselves to the poor in that hillside shantytown. He'd been arrested and charged on suspicion of causing griev-
ous bodily harm to one demolition worker and slightly injuring
another. Although he was well known as a troublemaker by the
authorities in the Taegu area, I just couldn't believe Hyŏn'gu was
capable of the violence attributed to him. The brother I knew is the
type who looks gentle but has a strong spirit, and he was humble to
everybody. When he told me about his activism on behalf of the poor,
he always emphasized service, dedication, and love. But witnesses
had testified that he'd grabbed one of the demolition worker's crowbars and had wielded it against him, and my brother had admitted
to this in court.

Last year in mid-June, I went down to Taegu after Sug'yŏng had
twice called pleading with me to help her save face by attending her
youngest sister-in-law's wedding. My sister and also her husband
had often been called to the police station on account of Hyŏn'gu. The
only thing she could be proud of in front of her in-laws was that her
elder brother at least had the title of "company president" in Seoul
and was a model citizen. And so I had attended the wedding together
with Mother, and afterward, in accordance with her wishes, we
went to the shantytown in Pisan-dong, behind Talsŏng Park, where
Hyŏn'gu was devoting himself to the poor. It was around two in the
afternoon. Mother ridiculed my idea of taking a taxi and stubbornly

insisted on taking the bus. I bought a large cake at a Western-style bakery as a gift for my nephew Tongsu. The access to the Pisan-dong hillside area where we got off the bus was a main road crossing over a shallow stream. The pavement was so packed with stalls and street vendors that people couldn't walk along it. Our ears were assaulted by the cries of people hawking cheap clothes, fruit, hot cakes, and toys, women selling greens, and youngsters with plastic household wares spread out in front of them, as well as vendors of varied and miscellaneous articles. There were fortune tellers with copies of *The Secrets of Tojŏng* and palmistry charts spread around them, paraplegics selling toothpicks and ear-cleaners, shoulder to elbow with runny-nosed beggars lying prone with grimy palms extended. Depending on how you experienced it, you either saw a lively scene of people engaged in the competition of life, or you heard the clamor of people grieving as they tried to scrape together a meager existence. I followed Mother into an alley that ran past establishments whose signs revealed them to be an employment agency, an old-time inn, a pharmacy, and a beauty parlor, and then up the hill to the shantytown. The incline must have been a good thirty degrees, and it would have been impossible for any kind of vehicle to get up there except for a handcart or someone with an A-frame carrier on his back. All around was a dense cluster of houses roofed with tiles and corrugated cement panels, and the alleyway, just wide enough for two people to pass each other if one of them stood to the side, was lined with scrub. Outside some of the houses in the alleyway were small pots and cupboards the size of apple boxes with goodness knows what inside them, as well as the usual rubbish bins. Wandering these narrow confines in nothing but vests and underpants were skinny children, who would burst into cheerful laughter, while old people sat in the shade chatting. That moment was the first time I'd ever experienced the smell of poor people's lives—the odor of open sewers and urine combined with the acrid smell of burning hair, all of it blending in the sultry air of early summer into one repulsive stench. Although I'd gone into the shantytowns of Sanggye-dong and Sadang-dong in my days as a cub reporter for my newspaper's city section, they had become a dim memory since I'd moved into the middle-class apartment district of Kangnam five or six years earlier. Now I was faced again with an utterly alien area. The way began to bend and twist a little, and then suddenly the slope had increased to a forty-five-degree angle. How could water possibly be piped up here? What did the people do with their rubbish and sewage? What about drainage?

"Ask people around here what they do for a living," Mother said between gasps for breath, "and you'll find some are factory workers, plasterers, or carpenters. Even so they're a respectable bunch. They say about sixty percent of them are unskilled laborers, street sellers, or unemployed. Do you know what the rest are? They're invalids—they can't work because they're sick or injured. It's the same as in the Bible, isn't it? Just as there were lots of sick and handicapped people in the poor villages, so there are lots of people here who are groaning from their mental and physical suffering. But the Lord always ignores the rich and takes care of our pitiful neighbors, doesn't he?"

As Mother spoke these words she continued to clamber uphill, with each step placing her hand on her bent knee for extra support. And then she came to a stop and suggested we rest our legs by a temporary water tap at which people with water containers had formed a line fifty yards long in the scorching sunshine. They cast envying looks not so much at my smart appearance as at the large cake box I was carrying. I looked out over the shantytown spread before my eyes. Among the crowded scab-like roofs washing was hung out to dry like a string of flags on sports day at a countryside primary school. The sunlight blazed down on us.

"It's a sight to see them jostling their way down to work at dawn carrying their lunch boxes," said Mother wiping away perspiration with her handkerchief, "but it would make you cry to see them coming home from work and to see the ones going out on night-shift around sunset. . . . Well-fed people could never understand the hollow, starving eyes of these people as they climb up here clutching a bag of flour, a sack of rice, or a few coal briquettes held together with a piece of rope. All the young people who are going out on night shift, even the girls plastered in make-up going out to work in the bars, let the people gasping for breath as they go up this hill pass by first. It's a kind of courtesy among the people who live here."

When I asked my mother how far we were from Hyŏn'gu's house and the nursery school, she answered with a smile as she looked up to the top of the hill, "The poorest people on this earth are those living closest to heaven." All over the upper reaches of the hillside the houses were clustered together in layers like crab shells. Making sure we were out of the way of the women carrying water containers on their backs, dripping with sweat, Mother and I started off again. As I looked down on the houses we had passed, I saw that even though a house occupied about forty square yards, it looked much less than that from above, and the yards offered just enough space under the eaves to leave your shoes. According to Mother, the households averaged about seven people, who were divided into just three rooms. The owner would use only two rooms and rent out the third, or use one room and rent out the other two. Hyŏn'gu, as you would expect, was one of the renters and not an owner. Under the eaves of the house in which he lived was a narrow walkway with a simple cupboard and a wash pan placed to one side, and next to them a fire hole for the coal briquettes—there was no separate kitchen. Knowing nobody was home, Mother pushed open the door to my brother's rented room. The dark space contained a chest of drawers, a folded quilt on top of it, and three bags. The only other item of furniture was a low table with folding legs. The only things of any value were some books stacked up in a corner. All these belongings could have fitted into a single handcart. The floor space could have accommodated three adults lying down, no more.

"This is how Hyŏn'gu and his family live. But if he chooses to live this way, it can't be helped. Sug'yŏng offered to buy him a television, but Hyŏn'gu flat-out refused, said he wouldn't have time to watch it. He says the less he has, the more free he feels. That boy doesn't belong in this world."

Mother pulled the door shut and set off toward the nursery, saying we should hurry to see Tongsu. The nursery was at the top of the hill, among scattered pines and scrub. Ragpickers had once built huts and lived there. After they left, the area had become a dump, but two years ago the rubbish had been covered with fill and the nursery set up in a tent on top of it. Now it was a large building made of cement blocks and roofed with corrugated cement panels. Still, it looked quite neat. Even from where we were we could hear the chattering of the children. There were two classrooms of about forty square yards each and a playground of about eighty square yards. Playground and classrooms alike were packed with children, supervised by three teachers. I realized they must be the student volunteers who I'd heard took turns helping out Tongsu's mother.

Tongsu's mother came out to meet us, pleasantly surprised to see me there as well. The children on the playground arrived in a thick cloud of dust, jostling around the cake box. Mother peeped into the classroom where Tongsu's mother had been, then went in to get Tongsu. I handed the cake box to the boy when he emerged in his grandmother's embrace. According to Tongsu's mother, Hyŏn'gu at that moment was looking into insurance coverage for a local man who had lost two fingers while being trained at a "cooperative workshop"—this was also the reason he'd not been able to attend the wedding. This was some time before there was any national medical insurance, and I was reminded of what Hyŏn'gu had once said when he'd come up to Seoul intending to repay me 300,000 *wŏn*.

"Not all poor people behave ethically, you know. Sometimes you have to think of them as though they were naughty children, crotchety old folks, or mentally ill. They can be impossibly stubborn, they start fights for no reason, they tell lies, and steal into the bargain. But they do all those things out of the despair they feel over their tough lives. I could never have understood their childishness, complaining, and violence if I hadn't experienced the pain of their hard lives together with them. Unless I have the same feeling of unconditional love a mother feels even for a son who has committed murder, I couldn't live among them as one of their friends even for a day. But by starting out in a spirit of service, then realizing the satisfaction of sacrificing, you have to finally forget your own pride and adopt the humility of someone who has learned that the practice of love is an end in itself. I'm always emphasizing this to my wife. Let me tell you another story. A few days ago a woman came to me carrying her son on her back—she begged me to save her boy, said he was dying of cancer of the bone marrow. For two days I went around with his mother, carrying that boy on my back to eight different hospitals. Every single one of those hospitals turned the boy away because we didn't have enough money to pay them. Around the evening of the second day, the boy died, right there on my back. I collapsed by the side of the road together with his mother, and we bowed our heads and wept with outrage and despair. I've come to see you because there's another family in the same awful situation who've begged me to save their child. . . ."

I was looking inside the nursery school as I recalled what Hyŏn'gu had said then. The figures of the small children grew distant and tears welled up in my eyes. I could see at a glance that Tongsu's mother, and not just Hyŏn'gu, was working hard for the shantytown nursery. I looked through an open window into a temporary structure beside the nursery school. Inside were some twenty women and children sitting in rows. One group was making silk flowers and a second group was absorbed in threading beads to make cheap necklaces. Those women and children of the shantytown who didn't go out to work as day laborers, housemaids, or peddlers would make a little money by knitting sweaters, sealing envelopes, making silk flowers, or threading beads onto necklaces.

Around half past eight Tongsu's mother arrived at the hospital ward. I imagined she'd left Tongsu at the nursery school and had brought her husband some food in the cloth wrapper she carried. Her face was freckled beneath the eyes, and her straight hair was combed back and clipped tightly in place. She wore a loose cotton shirt with the sleeves rolled up. Perhaps because it was summer, she was not wearing the blue jeans I was used to seeing her in but a knee-length skirt.

She gently asked her husband if he'd slept well and if he'd been comfortable during the night and then greeted me:

"We always seem to be indebted to you, making you come all this way when you must be so busy with your work, and you haven't even had time to recover from your journey abroad. They say having a third-year high school student is exhausting for mothers, so your wife must be completely worn out with having to take care of a third-year middle school student as well."

In fact, Tongsu's mother must have been three or four times as busy as most other women, taking care of the nursery school and visiting her husband in prison. But I always found her expression bright and her movements energetic. Although it was quite harmless, her habit of chattering sometimes brought a frown to my mother's face, but she only spoke that way because of her unreserved character.

"If it wasn't for the nursery school, where could parents leave their children in that shantytown full of germs and bad smells? When the parents all go out to work, she takes in their children and washes them, feeds them, teaches them to write, and takes them to hospital when they're sick. . . . There's no one else like Tongsu's mother. And through the nursery school she was even able to set up a women's movement for the shantytown. She's running around doing everything from helping people find work to sorting out their rent problems. In my opinion she's right up there with Mother Theresa. She must be made of steel. If she ever collapses, I don't know what'll happen."

This was how my mother had spoken about her daughter-in-law when she'd come to stay with us in Seoul the year before.

My sister-in-law had gotten to know Hyŏn'gu around the time he opened a night school in the Third Industrial Complex in Nowŏn-dong in Taegu. She'd just graduated from a high school in the countryside and was working in the general affairs department of a factory that made spectacles. She used to help my brother at the night school. And so they got to know each other, in spite of the nine-year difference in their ages. I recalled the day they were married by the Reverend Wŏn Hyŏngsŏp in a church in the Sangok-dong shantytown. The well-wishers in attendance were the factory workers who attended the night school and the residents of the shantytown. Everyone feels a nervous sense of happiness on his or her wedding day, but I still remember the bride's bright expression and the smile that never left her face. Older people might find fault with a bride who smiled on her wedding day, but she simply couldn't conceal her happiness, even though her groom was well over thirty years old.

The young guard Ch'oe swapped over with an older guard, Hong, and soon afterward Hyŏn'gu's attending physician, a specialist named Min, came by on his morning rounds with a group of interns. Dr. Min was in his mid-forties and had the sleek look of a well-peeled chestnut. As he checked his patient's condition, he exchanged a few technical medical terms with the interns, and then he left the ward. I hurried out after him and asked about the tests that had been performed on Hyŏn'gu. In a gentle voice the doctor simply informed me that the results were still being compiled and analyzed. Tongsu's mother then asked him if the patient could have some mung bean porridge she had prepared at home as a snack. Dr. Min reminded us that the hospital provided all necessary nutrients, and no food could be brought in from outside. On top of that he warned us the patient could only drink barley tea, and only a moderate amount at that— nothing else, not even fruit juice. He then bustled on to the next ward with his interns in tow. A little later when the team of nurses came in on their rounds, the head nurse repeated Dr. Min's warning.

"Mother, you have to eat breakfast. Let's go out for a while."

But she refused, saying she'd been fasting in the morning for a long time now. At the prospect of going out by myself to find somewhere to eat, I made up my mind to skip breakfast, too.

Instead I went to find my high school classmate Ham Kŭnjo. He worked in the laboratories located in the next block.

Kŭnjo greeted me warmly: "Hey, if it isn't Pak Yungu! What are you doing here so early in the morning without so much as a phone call. Just because I'm trapped in this regional hospital, people think they can treat me any old way. So, how's the publishing business? Are your books selling?"

It must have been more than two years since we'd last met. We moved to a lounge connected to the main hospital building, where we sat and chatted, updating each other on our classmates; he drank ginger tea while I had milk. Coming from a prestigious local high school, well known for its connections to the TK faction,[*] many of our classmates had done very well for themselves in the business and political world. But ever since I'd been sacked as a journalist, I had given up attending the alumni meetings in Seoul. As a consequence I'd lost touch with most of my classmates, who'd gone on to make names for themselves in Seoul, so Kŭnjo was much more aware of what they were all up to. He jokingly asked me what the

---

[*] The TK (Taegu-Kyŏngsang Province) faction derives its name from the fact that Presidents Pak Chŏnghŭi, Chŏn Tuhwan, and No T'aeu, as well as a disproportionate number of the Republic of Korea's social élite, have come from the Taegu region of North Kyŏngsang Province [trans.].

heck I was doing running an insignificant publishing company—even as a sacked journalist I could be reinstated or taken on by one of the new papers. I remembered the last time I'd come down to Taegu, for some matter concerning Hyŏn'gu, and met up with some classmates. He'd said something similar then too, mentioning that dismissed journalists often joined political parties or became champions of the opposition. He'd asked me whether I had ever considered going over to the ruling party, seeing as how I'd majored in sociology, and my TK background meant I had no chance of making it as a champion of the opposition. He'd also said that if I just made up my mind, I would have many friends who'd support me. I told Kŭnjo my purpose in life was not just to satisfy a desire for fame, laughing in embarrassment like someone who's blind to the ways of the world.

It was around the time that I, the wretched sacked journalist, was attending meetings and occasionally being away from my family while participating in demonstrations, that my mother abandoned her life in Taegu and came to stay with us in Seoul. Scarcely a day would pass in which I didn't hear her imploring me to bear in mind the path Hyŏn'gu had taken in life. She begged me not to forget that she had come south as a refugee, placing all her trust in her sons, and as her eldest son I was not to take a difficult path in life myself.

"Didn't you swear to me when you went to university that if unification came in my lifetime, you'd carry me on your back and, if it was spring, take me to see the azaleas blooming in the hills of my ancestral home? As your mum, I don't expect you to earn a lot of money or get some high position like others and be envied by people under you. I just want you to have a happy married life, take good care of your children, and be healthy—nothing more. I'm always praying to God for that."

Mother said this kind of thing, too. When she went as far as to fast and pray through the night that I, her eldest son, would make a stable and secure family, I had to accept that my mother was just plain different. The conflict between my mother's love and my own situation was intense, and I struggled with that conflict, to the point that I began to drink a great deal of *soju*—and I was not a strong drinker.

The Fifth Republic had just started when Hyŏn'gu came to see me about publishing the manuscript of a book entitled "The Real Facts About the Labor Movement in the Taegu Area." I rejected it, not so much because I was embarrassed to publish a book by my brother but because I felt my company might get into trouble if we were connected with the Taegu Area Democratic Labor Union. Half the manuscript was concerned with the economic changes taking place in the Taegu area, the industrial structure, the present condition of the manufacturing sector, and the living conditions of the working class. The rest of the book recounted the tearful struggle for survival of low-paid workers and their wretched working conditions. The opposition of the authorities generally made it impossible to form labor unions. Consequently, the workers had to join together in informal societies to carry out their struggle against their employers. In diary fashion the book recorded this struggle in the different factories. When the government was carrying out its plan to take control of the media by abolishing and merging newspapers, rather than standing up to fight, I merely followed my conscience and got myself fired. On the other hand, my publishing company had published more than ten progressive books in the field of social science. Nevertheless, the book that Hyŏn'gu had written had to be published by a press that specialized in that kind of work. But I wasn't in a position to recommend any publisher to Hyŏn'gu. Referring to the generally difficult situation at that time, I strongly advised my brother to defer publication. Hyŏn'gu, hiding his true feelings, smiled politely in his shy way, apologized for taking up his busy brother's time, and left with his manuscript.

The manuscript came out as a book four months later, and Hyŏn'gu sent me a copy as if to say, "See." Just as I had predicted, the book was confiscated by the authorities. My brother and, of course, his editor and a representative of the publishing company were detained for about fifteen days.

My thoughts were interrupted by Kŭnjo: "Yungu, did you hear about Yi Chinsŏ? You know, the tubby one who worked in construction. He's dead. He had a heart attack from overwork."

Yi Chinsŏ was a close friend when I was in my third year at high school. I would never have imagined he might die like that. My thoughts went back to February 28, 1960. The authorities, wanting to keep high school students from taking part in the Democratic Party's election meetings, got the schools to persuade their students to attend school on Sunday by showing movies—it was a ridiculous ploy. High school students all over the country took to the streets for the first time to demonstrate against attending school on Sundays. At five past one in the afternoon on that February day hundreds of us ran through our main school gate led by the third-year students. Shoulder to shoulder we charged down to the main road in the direction of the Panwŏltang crossroads. We shouted out all kinds of slogans: "Support student rights! Revive democracy! No political interference in our schools! We cannot be corrupted!" Caught up in preparing for my university entrance exam, I was not one of the prime movers of the demonstrations. Nevertheless, I was as indignant as anyone at the undemocratic maneuverings of the Yi Sŭngman regime as it plotted to prolong its hold on power. Everyone felt a surge of energy as the destinies of the individual and the group became bound together. We continued to shout sporadic slogans as we dashed past the city center toward the plaza in front of the provincial administration building. The friend whose arm was around my shoulders was Chinsŏ. Of course, Kŭnjo took part, too. The last time I saw Chinsŏ must have been more than three years ago. He'd put on a lot of weight in keeping with a typical forty-year-old manager of a construction company. He was forever complaining that he was so busy it was driving him crazy. It was so bad that his family said he was more like a lodger than a family member. He was tied up at building sites during the day, and stayed out late at night drinking to get rid of his stress. He plowed on without any concern for his physical health. The housing construction business was booming, and the three-story private housing units he built were selling well.

"I get my three meals a day just like anyone else, so why do I have to dash around like a damned lunatic just to make a bit more money? I've become a total Philistine. Yungu, that was a great time, wasn't it—when we charged up to the provincial office and we all got beaten up and hauled off to the police station? But now look at us—me a builder and you a publisher. Still, you're better off—at least you get to listen to intelligent people. We were the ones who lit the fuse for the April 19 Revolution, but I've got enough years under my belt to show me that the ones who prepare the way and the ones who take advantage of the times to get ahead are not necessarily the same people. So, what's left except to eat?"

I recalled Chinsŏ's disgruntled appearance as he railed on, glass of beer in hand. In terms of age I was also of the generation of the April 19 Revolution, and I had charged the police headquarters together with my fellow students. But the pure intentions of April 19 had been obliterated by successive military regimes. The souls of the 185 people who were shot down as they rushed forward with a naïve sense of justice to revive democracy in this land had been snuffed out in a moment. Our generation claims to have played a leading role in that "incomplete revolution," but people have kept emerging who've preferred to pander to the regime for their own advancement and have disgraced the name of the April 19 Revolution. That revolution started and finished with the righteous indignation of pure and honest youths without any central control providing tactics or strategy. As a consequence most of the participants felt compelled to return to their previous duties. I also tried to inherit the spirit of April 19, but without any real commitment. I got married and lived from day to day as an ordinary salaried journalist caught up in providing a comfortable life for his family. It was our politics of dependency as an undeveloped country that were to blame. Even so, I feel very ashamed that I was one of those who sold out the revolution, and to this day I've never claimed at any time or place to be one of the April 19 generation.

Kŭnjo ended by saying the death rate in South Korea for people in their forties was the highest in the world. He bemoaned Koreans' excessive ambition, their selfish worshiping of material goods, and their intense rashness and impatience.

"Think of it. Keeling over in your forties, in the prime of life. What's going to happen to his kids? They're at the age when they'll need a pile of money until they get married. Chinsŏ just dashed headlong through life believing in his own strength and then collapsed. In the old days it was enough just to have three meals a day—why do people today act the way they do even when everybody has enough? People who are living it up don't realize their own stomach is about to burst, they're so crazy grabbing money and land. And then on the other side of the fence are the damned students and the workers—they use violence and don't care whether they live or die. But do you think the fat cats are going to wave the white flag and share what they've got? I mean, we live in an age when politics and economics are tangled up together. That's a recipe for chaos, and meanwhile the economy is going to hell. If the workers get a raise by striking, the government panics and pulls up prices by the scruff of the neck. Why don't they realize that? Can't they just wait until we've reached an average annual salary of 10,000 bucks? . . ."

On and on went Kŭnjo. It was difficult for me to follow him. But then he returned to the subject of Chinsŏ's death, and the object of his ranting became the educational system. Why, his own daughter, a third-year high school student, was flying up to Seoul and back twice a week for individual lessons from a famous piano professor so she could get herself admitted to the music department at a university in Seoul. The fee for these lessons was "only" one million *wŏn* a month—it was like pouring water into a leaky bucket. Kŭnjo was one of the April 19 generation, and now he was immersed in the worldly upper class. I found his words utterly hypocritical. The only thing I could respect about him was that instead of using his TK background like the others to stake out a place for himself in that mound of greed known as Seoul, he'd remained in his ancestral home. But for all I knew, he may have been venting his frustration over precisely that fact. Finally I'd had enough of him.

"You know, don't you? About my brother? Hyŏn'gu's been admitted here."

"The one who's always getting himself into trouble?" Kŭnjo said with a sour expression. He said he'd seen a photograph of Hyŏn'gu in court in one of the local dailies. It sounded as though he was talking about the riot that had broken out when the people whose homes were being demolished in the redevelopment area of Pisan-dong had stormed the court during my brother's trial.

"I thought he was in prison. Is he ill?"

I explained Hyŏn'gu's medical history, then asked if Kŭnjo could find out how severe his condition was now all the tests seemed to have been completed, and what sort of treatment he could look forward to. Kŭnjo paused a moment then said he would try.

"Let's have lunch together. I'll meet you in the ward."

I understood from this that he'd tell me the result of his inquiries then.

Back in the ward, I saw five women seated in chairs or squatting in the corridor talking with Tongsu's mother. They all wore the same gloomy expression.

"Did you meet your friend?" Tongsu's mother asked me.

"Yes. He said he'd come here at lunchtime. He'll bring some news then."

"All right, I'll give you a call around that time. If you have to go out somewhere let Mother know."

So saying, Tongsu's mother went into the ward and then came out again to gently chide the women to get back to work. And with that she hurried off down the corridor together with them. One of the women wiped her eyes with the back of her rough hand, the way a man might, and said, "Mr. Pak had better get well soon and get himself released."

These women must have had children at the nursery school run by Tongsu's mother. All their faces were tanned and etched with deep wrinkles. Just like Sangju-*daek*, they wore baggy trousers and men's overalls caked with mud. One glance had told me they were day laborers at a construction site.

I took a seat in the corridor and had a smoke while mopping the sweat from my neck with my handkerchief. And then I saw my younger sister, Sug'yŏng, coming toward me, folding her parasol. She'd been studying at a leading university when she'd met Mr. Kim, who came from the countryside and was studying at a pharmacy college. They fell in love—I could never decide if it was his good looks or his generous character—and she married him soon after graduating. They now had three children and ran a pharmacy in an apartment complex in the suburbs. Each year Mother usually spent two or three months at our home in Seoul and the rest of the time with Sug'yŏng here in Taegu. Despite her age Mother would always be taking fixings for side dishes to Hyŏn'gu's home in the Pisan-dong shantytown—it was as much of a routine as a daily walk. It never took more than a couple of weeks at my house for Mother to start complaining that living in an apartment felt like being stuck in a chicken coop or a prison. And after that same couple of weeks Sug'yŏng would be sure to phone saying Mother must have stayed in Seoul long enough and telling me to send her back down. The pharmacy was only 300 yards from their home, and when Mr. Kim had to step out, Mother would mind the shop for him. Sug'yŏng also needed our elderly parent for household chores like feeding her sons when they came home from school. Then again, Mother had worked hard as a trader for thirty years in the local marketplace, where she was known as "the woman from up north." Even though she was not native to Taegu, after all this time she'd grown attached to the place. She still had friends in the Kyodong Market (formerly the Yankee Market) and her younger son's uncertain life-style tugged at her heartstrings. All of which meant that she was forever in a rush to leave Seoul.

Even though she would say things like, "I don't know what I'm thinking of, just waiting until I'm so helpless I have to stay with my eldest son," as I dropped her off at the express bus terminal on my way to work, her tiny frame looked buoyant as she walked off. But after Hyŏn'gu was imprisoned again, she never left Taegu. Visiting my younger brother in prison was Mother's priority.

"My husband looked up a doctor he knows here, but he couldn't get a straight answer, so it looks as though Hyŏn'gu's condition is serious." Sug'yŏng fastened the tie around her parasol as she spoke. In keeping with her bright character, there was no gloominess in her voice.

"We still have to see if they'll parole him. In this day and age once you're branded a political criminal, your life's worth no more than an animal's."

"But the thing with liver disease, there's no medical treatment once it's past the first stage of sclerosis. You can eat well and get plenty of rest . . . but even so the stomach and kidneys gradually stop functioning and then you can't digest anything, it gets difficult to pass water . . ."

There was not much difference between my own general knowledge of the subject and that of a pharmacist's wife who had picked up her knowledge selling all kinds of liver medicines. When I remained silent, Sug'yŏng said, "Mother's here, isn't she?" and turned to go into the ward.

"Wait—I want to thank you for last time."

I took a folded envelope out of my wallet.

"What's that for?"

"You know, for Hyŏn'gu's lawyer."

"What? You mean you want to pay that back? We're family, aren't we?"

Sug'yŏng looked serious as she pushed my hand away. At that moment I realized ours was truly a unique brother-sister relationship, and my heart filled with deep affection.

At the time Hyŏn'gu was released to the hospital, I was in the Soviet Union. And because I was only able to give my wife 900,000 wŏn a month for housekeeping, she had no savings from which she could withdraw a million wŏn in cash at short notice to post the bond. It appeared that while she was telephoning our publishing company's accountant, Miss Ch'oe, about how to raise the bond, Sug'yŏng had posted it already. Sug'yŏng had even gone so far as to phone her sister-in-law to tell her not to mention the money when I came back—she knew all the publishing companies were having a hard time. But it wasn't my sister's responsibility, and that's why I'd brought the check with me to Taegu.

Sug'yŏng kept refusing to take the envelope. She said she'd never made any distinction between her responsibilities to her own family and to her husband's family, and even though she was married this was the sort of financial responsibility she could undertake. After a struggle, I finally stuck the envelope into her hemp handbag and went into the ward.

Kŭnjo returned shortly after midday; he was no longer wearing his white coat. We prepared to go out, Kŭnjo saying it had been such a long time since we'd last met, he'd show me a good place to eat. Mother said she and Sug'yŏng would stay behind and have what Sug'yŏng had brought as well as Tongsu's mother's mung bean porridge, which would spoil if they didn't eat it quickly. Out I went after Kŭnjo. It was humid enough inside the building, but as soon as we stepped out into the sunlight, I felt as if sweat were being sucked out of every pore in my skin. The sun scorched my head. Even though the last of the dog days of summer was past, this was exactly the torrid weather that Taegu is famous for.

"You eat dog meat, don't you?" Kŭnjo asked me as he started his car. I said that was fine by me, and he turned down a road going out of town toward Kyŏngsan. The outskirts of Taegu were burgeoning with high-rise apartment complexes. But even if the midday heat was keeping drivers off the roads, the traffic moved much quicker than it did in Seoul, where the traffic is just as bad in the outskirts as in the city center. Kŭnjo proudly went into detail about all the ways dog meat is good for middle-aged people—that it's not just a tonic to be taken in the summer. He denounced the shallow elitist attitude of Westerners who, not eating dog meat themselves, look down on Koreans as barbarians. He insisted that every people's customary foods and tastes had to be respected as well as their basic right to enjoy themselves. According to Kŭnjo, the hospital had a "doggy club" and it was centered on the middle-aged staff. The club flourished and he himself was the general secretary.

The forested hills between Taegu and Kyŏngsan had plenty of large-scale restaurants specializing in dog and goat meat soup. The parking lot at our restaurant was packed with cars, and at tables inside and outside the restaurant sat gourmands of our age bracket, neckties loosened and sweating profusely, hard at work with their chopsticks. When we'd found an outside table in a small pavilion thatched with reeds, Kŭnjo summoned the restaurant owner, whom he seemed to know well, and ordered two pounds of neck meat for a stew.

"What did the internal medicine people have to say?" I asked while the meat and vegetables were cooking in the pan on the tabletop stove between us.

"Well, the cirrhosis is advanced, but they wouldn't say much more than that. I understand he's been charged with more than just a simple case of assault and that his case is under appeal. . . . I put some pressure on one of the younger guys, asked him if there's cirrhosis of the liver, then it's clear what the disease is, right? Which would make it impossible for him to go back to prison, because he'll need long-term treatment. And he told me that the consensus is they should operate—they'll need the family's permission."

"And?" I held my breath.

"It looks like cancer. The tumor is already about four centimeters. . . ."

So, Hyŏn'gu had liver cancer. I knew that modern medicine offered no certain cure for cancer of the liver and that it wasn't common for patients to last a year beyond their diagnosis. Patients who went back home usually came to the end of the road in three or four months. Otherwise they usually died in surgery or soon afterward from complications. Whenever I got a phone call saying that someone around my age had died, I assumed that if it wasn't a car accident then it was liver cancer. When I'd visited people's homes for a funeral, I'd several times heard accounts of the course liver disease runs from its beginnings as hepatitis until death. Listening to those clinical explanations had made me think of liver disease for Koreans in their late forties in terms of a brutal, knife-wielding criminal attacking you in the night, or else a small, crack suicide squad. Liver disease lies dormant with no pain or other symptoms, and suddenly you're told you have acute cirrhosis. To someone busy with his life and unprepared for his demise, it's a death sentence from out of the blue. The disease gathers its deadly poison in secret, fostering its own life force, knowing if it dies everything else dies too. And so it destroys not only the place it inhabits but all the living organs around it as well.

"What if they operate?"

Kŭnjo absent-mindedly wiped away his sweat with a damp cloth as he answered my question.

"Several things can happen. Of course, the earlier it's caught the higher the chances of success. To my knowledge, some people have hung on for three or four years after their operation, others have lived very normal lives for even longer. The liver weighs about three and a half pounds—it's the largest organ in the body. Its regenerative power is very strong, and even if just a third of it is functioning, you can still live a normal life.

"So will Hyŏn'gu have to have an operation?"

"If he doesn't go under the knife, there's no other treatment except diet and rest."

"Has it really got so bad that he needs an operation?"

I knew the questions were pointless but I asked them nevertheless, my tone faltering. I felt like someone clinging frantically to a branch, struggling not to fall off. I kept rubbing my sweating palms together.

"It looks as though the authorities couldn't come to a quick decision because your brother's case is under appeal. In fact if you can catch liver disease early, it's curable, but it's usually one step too late by the time people go into hospital. So, you can't just blame the prison authorities. It's not unusual for people to go into hospital for a check-up, complaining that they're exhausted from overwork, only to get diagnosed with cirrhosis of the liver. Three or four months later, one or two years at best, and it's all over. . . ."

I could no longer take in what Kŭnjo was saying. My energy was draining, I felt like a candle melting, and everything around me became distant. I no longer heard the chattering of the gourmands or saw them tucking into their hot meals, fighting the summer heat with heat, as if in the belief that eating enough tonic food was the easy way to a long life. I had always thought of death as something that bore no relation to me, and now I only saw the modest smile on Hyŏn'gu's gaunt, careworn, honest face as he lay in his sickbed. But I knew that his present physical state was not simply a matter of bad luck. I recalled a fragment of memory from our childhood.

During the winter of 1950–51 our family had trudged southward through blizzards from Tongduch'ŏn via Seoul and Ch'ŏnan to Osan without any fixed destination. Sug'yŏng and I were malnourished and wasting away, and Mother ate irregularly at best. Hyŏn'gu had been born without even the help of a midwife. There was no milk in Mother's breasts, which sagged like empty pouches. Hyŏn'gu was just a newborn, and even though he sucked until Mother's nipples were bruised and raw like mulberries, no milk would flow. My sister and I would wander the hard, icy fields gathering frozen, yellowed cabbage leaves to cook over a twig fire to stave off our hunger. Ever since we had been forced to pack up and flee south from the advancing communist Chinese forces, Mother had gone from house to house using Hyŏn'gu's wretched appearance to beg for food. She couldn't get milk but only gruel, and when she couldn't get millet gruel, she barely kept him alive by going to homes just before mealtimes and begging for water in which rice was being cooked. The life force is tough. Mother would have to walk at least five miles at a stretch, and if she didn't feel any warmth on her back, she would ask me to open the baby wrap and check on him. That tiny spark of life hung on by a single strand, and Hyŏn'gu survived all the way to Taegu, clinging to life by a fragile thread as if he were a growth on my mother's body. In Taegu we got through the winter in a refugee camp then built a house out of straw matting on a hillside in Sin'am-dong. Mother took to selling foreign cigarettes and American-made soap in the Yankee Market. I was enrolled at the refugee tent school together with my sister. After school I had to stand in line at the emergency food station run by the "big noses" to get a single bag of corn flour or dried milk. There were days when I waited in vain, but the single bag of food I did get after waiting three or four hours was essential nourishment for Hyŏn'gu. When he was three years old, my brother began to exhibit strange symptoms. At the time Mother had stopped peddling and instead sold her wares on a board laid out in the corner of the Yankee Market. When she went out to work she always took Hyŏn'gu. But she couldn't tie him up by the ankle all day, and so Hyŏn'gu would disappear when she was busy selling something or even if she just let him out of her sight.

In a flash Hyŏn'gu would toddle on his bandy legs to the garbage bin in the alleyway. There he found melon rinds, which he ate just as if they were a suitable food supplement for a starving baby. He'd once nearly died when a peach stone got stuck in his throat. So it was hardly surprising that he developed a swollen stomach. He looked almost like a tadpole the way his veins stuck out from his swollen belly. Only then did Mother take him to the clinic. She returned with no other treatment than a few capsules of Santonin and advice from the doctor to give him a liquid diet, reduce the amount of food he ate, and feed him regular meals. After Hyŏn'gu took the Santonin a mass of intestinal worms came out with his diarrhea. Mother, wiping his bottom, said they were like a black clump of threadworms. After that his stomach began to subside and his dark yellow face regained its normal complexion. I've read, though, that your health as an infant affects you until your eighties. So it's obvious to me that the starvation my brother endured as a young child must have affected his internal organs. Kŭnjo ordered a bottle of *soju* containing cucumber slices, saying that if we were going to be drinking during the day, it had better be strong and we should be washing down dog meat soup with it. Loosening his necktie, he picked out meat from the simmering pan, dipped it in seasoning, and began to wolf it down. He paused only to offer one last comment.

"With liver disease the first thing to do is to make sure you're getting enough high protein, and dog meat is a mass of unsaturated high protein. But the problem is, once you've got cirrhosis, the liver begins to harden and you can't digest protein any more." So saying, Kŭnjo picked out a chunk of neck meat with his chopsticks and proceeded to strip the tender flesh from the bone with his teeth and tongue as you might eat the meat of a crab.

Even though I'd missed breakfast, I had no appetite—there was a bitter taste in my mouth. I was confident there wasn't anything wrong with my own liver, but I felt guilty trying to protect it by eating high-protein food when Hyŏn'gu was suffering from a liver disease. Not wanting to drink on an empty stomach—and I never drink during the day—I forced myself to eat a few chunks of meat and sip some broth to go along with my three shots of *soju*.

Back at hospital, I counted, standing unprotected in the blazing sun, a group of eight youths, students or factory workers, I wasn't sure which, flanking the entrance to the annex building. One of them was a woman. One of the youths barked out slogans and the others shouted in response, vigorously punching the air with angrily clenched right hands.

"Save Pak Hyŏn'gu!"

"Save him! Save him!"

"Free Pak Hyŏn'gu!"

"Free him now! Free him now!"

"The authorities must take care of the poor and homeless!"

"Take care of the poor and homeless now!"

I looked with others who had gathered to watch the young people as they shouted and sweated. A strange feeling came over me as I watched Hyŏn'gu's youthful comrades. Was it courage I was seeing, or insolence? Had I looked courageous on April 19? I wondered about that.

As I made my way down the corridor toward Hyŏn'gu's ward, I was stopped by three riot police. The leader, equipped with a two-way radio, demanded to see my identity card. I obliged, telling him I was Pak Hyŏn'gu's elder brother. This was apparently deemed acceptable by whoever was at the other end of the radio, and I was allowed through. I found two more riot police guarding the door to the ward.

The propeller-like fan on the ceiling of the ward whirred. Hong, who was older and looked milder than the other guard, Ch'oe, whom I took for a non-commissioned officer, was looking wearily out the open window. Sitting in a chair and reading a newspaper, one leg crossed over the other, was a fat man with close-cropped hair, wearing a white shirt without a tie and navy blue trousers. The one man glanced at me in recognition, the other one scowled at me.

"Who are you?" asked the fat man. His tone was typical of a police investigator.

"I'm Hyŏn'gu's elder brother."

The man returned to his newspaper without a word.

Mother, Sug'yŏng, and a balding man in a frayed, short-sleeved summer jacket were gathered around Hyŏn'gu's bed. The man had just begun a prayer; his voice was calm.

" . . . O Lord, have you not said we will become your people and you will dwell with us, you will wipe away every tear from our eyes, death will be no more, and there will be neither sorrow nor crying, neither shall there be any more pain? Therefore, please wipe away the pain and tears from our brother. Just as you said, 'Behold I make all things new,' please sweep away arrogance, bury corruption, and grant rebirth to those who are good and yet weak. . . ."

Holding her Bible in both hands Mother added a heartfelt "Amen" in the middle of the prayer.

The balding man—only a few strands of hair adorned the crown of his head—was the Reverend Wŏn Hyŏngsŏp. He had founded a church for the poor by the time he officiated at Hyŏn'gu's wedding and had now opened a church in the Nogok-dong shantytown. The first time I'd met him was when my brother was at university, and he'd been sitting next to my brother in the dock at court after being arrested along with three students from the Christian Student Alliance for possession of seditious material. At the conclusion of the trial they received a two-year suspended sentence and were released. By then I was quite full of myself from hearing too many references to what an able journalist I was. I had the opportunity to talk with the Reverend Wŏn at a tea shop. Even now, although my wife and I never miss the Sunday service, I'd never think of calling myself an earnest believer. But back then I didn't even have the enthusiasm for church I have now. Anyway, I presumptuously asked whether he believed in Jesus' resurrection. I found such questions to be the trickiest and most frightening ones to answer. But the Reverend Wŏn gave his reply without any apparent difficulty.

"If I didn't, then how could I continue as a pastor all my life? Is it not the case that Jesus was nailed to the cross, died, was buried, and after three days returned to life? Many of his followers said they'd clearly seen the living Jesus, didn't they? Only the disciple Thomas said he couldn't believe Jesus had been resurrected unless he himself at least touched and saw the holes in Jesus' hands made by the nails. People nowadays, with their cold nature and emphasis on science, bear in their heart the same doubt. And so Jesus appeared in the flesh before Thomas and showed him his hands stained with blood from the wounds made by the nails. Granted I'm not living in the time of Thomas and so I can't see firsthand the bloodstained scars made by those nails. . ."

What the Reverend Wŏn said next, despite his leap of logic, struck me to the heart.

"Where I *do* apprehend Jesus' bloodstained scars made by those nails is in the groans of the poor and in their flowing tears and oozing sores. It is in those suffering people that Jesus has been resurrected on this earth. Just as Jesus died on the cross to redeem us and was resurrected and showed himself before Thomas, so the many poor people of today appear before us to demand of us what we can do for them. . . ."

After they'd finished their prayer the three visitors turned to me. The Reverend Wŏn and I exchanged greetings. As was his habit he gave me his hand without gripping mine. As always when I saw him, he was dressed like a worker or a market porter, in baggy trousers and cheap training shoes.

"Dr. Min came looking for you. I said we'd go find him after you came back. So what did your friend have to say?" Mother blinked back the tears pooling between her wrinkled eyelids.

"He didn't really know very much . . . I'll tell you later."

I looked at Hyŏn'gu. Even though his abdominal fluid had been drained, the swollen stomach beneath the coverlet had not shrunk in proportion to his emaciated body. Our eyes met and he gave me a smile. Despite the revolving fan, his face and neck glistened with sweat from the humidity of the ward. I wiped his forehead and neck with a damp cloth from the bedside table.

"Are you hurting anywhere?"

"Before you came I was always getting nosebleeds . . . but they've stopped, and now it's my back that's aching."

"Can I rub it for you?"

"Mother did already."

Breaking through the chirping of the cicadas, the shouting of the slogans grew louder. The fat man muttered, "Those idiots . . ." and rushed out, clearly worried.

"If only I could go send those kids away, but I can't leave the ward without permission," said Hyŏn'gu.

The Reverend Wŏn provided me with an explanation.

"There was a disturbance a little while ago. Two students and a worker knocked on the door asking to see Hyŏn'gu. The guard wouldn't let them in and locked the door. Then he made a phone call and all of a sudden the riot police showed up, and the students who'd been turned away went and got their group together . . ."

"I'm causing so much worry around here, I really ought to hurry up and get better. . . . Well, even though there's no hope I have to accept it—I've had that kind of thought, too. I've done my best in life, and I don't regret anything I've done. Even if I were to be born again in this country, on this land, if things were no different, I'd do the same thing all over again. That's just the way I feel."

My heart was moved—Hyŏn'gu's words sounded exactly like a last testament. They were also a kind of philosophical construction, a prison cell within his heart to which he'd been able to retreat ever since he was born. A life without regrets is beautiful, but in the case of Hyŏn'gu, it was not so much beautiful as heartbreaking.

"Now, don't talk like that," said Mother. "You're going to live twenty-nine years longer than your old mum. You were born to live a long life. Your brother and sister were too young so they won't remember. When you were baptized, the Reverend Yi at the First

Church said when your father, the Reverend Pak, had been taken to heaven, you were given as a new life. He said you would be like a descendant of Abraham, you would take up the task of your father and flourish from generation to generation. I still remember those words. A few years ago I went to visit the Reverend Yi when he was sick—he was in his eighties by then—and I told him what he had said. He laughed and said, 'You've got a good memory, Sister Mun.'"

I'd heard the story of Hyŏn'gu's baptism several times. Mother believed the Reverend Yi's words as absolutely as if she'd hypnotized herself with them. Even now when she told the story, her voice was filled with certainty. The belief that nobody could take her son away from her had solidified into an absolute faith, so that when he was in prison or on the run, and even in the "citizens' protest meetings," Mother was able to cope more confidently and resolutely than anyone. And in fact her son had always returned to her embrace.

"Mother, let's go see Dr. Min then."

As I spoke Hyŏn'gu tried to get up.

"Brother, I need to go to the toilet . . ."

I took hold of Hyŏn'gu's arm and helped him sit up, then held the IV bottle while I guided him to the toilet adjoining the ward. Using his free hand he fumbled with the opening in his hospital gown and found his drooping penis. But try as he might, nothing came out. It was always the same, he muttered. His legs were trembling and then as he gasped for breath his swollen stomach began to twitch. Finally a few drops of urine so cloudy it looked like rice water or pus trickled into the lavatory bowl. He must have been given a diuretic—but did this mean his kidneys were shot? My sole remaining hope—that he might still recover if he had an operation—had just evaporated. But even though I lacked Mother's faith, I didn't believe Hyŏn'gu's life would come to an end here. He'd overcome so much adversity just through the force of his mind and body. Nobody in this world was more worthy or valuable than he—I was convinced of this. After the

Seoul Olympics he'd retired from the labor movement to devote himself solely to the poor.

"The workers' situation is okay these days. At least they can form unions and carry out a concerted struggle. But the day laborers are genuinely poverty-stricken. They just get a daily wage and so they can't form a union. If you look at the composition of poor families, you'll usually see a sick or elderly member or two. Disabled children—physically handicapped, mentally handicapped—are concentrated in the shantytowns. I'm determined to live my whole life for them."

There was no doubt in my mind that God cherished this "practical movement of love for the poor," as Hyŏn'gu had once described it to me. In short, Hyŏn'gu had received a calling.

After helping Hyŏn'gu back to bed, I left him in the care of Sug'yŏng and the Reverend Wŏn and left with Mother to see Dr. Min.

As we headed down the long corridor we noticed a fuss between two elderly people and the riot police in the entrance hall. The two old people wanted to go inside and the police weren't letting them in. One of them, an old man with a long mustache and a straw hat, recognized Mother.

"Hello, Sister Mun."

Mother bowed and said, "Oh, little Ch'angil's grandfather."

I assumed from their appearance that like Hyŏn'gu's other visitors they lived in the Pisan-dong shantytown.

"They're saying we can't see Mr. Pak. Maybe they can get away with that with the youngsters, but how can they stop us old people from visiting a sick person? Is Mr. Pak's condition that serious?"

"If these people say no, what can I do? But the rumor that he's in critical condition is not true. Hyŏn'gu's condition is not serious," Mother said unequivocally.

"Mother, let's go."

I took Mother by the arm. Outside, the chanting of slogans had stopped and the students had sat down beneath the scorching sun, their clothing soaked in sweat. Apparently they'd changed to a silent

protest—they looked like Zen Buddhist monks engaged in medita-
tion. The fat investigator was admonishing them.

"There seem to be some students among you lot. If you think
you're so intellectual, shouldn't you be thinking about the other
patients? Is this some kind of marketplace? Also, Hyŏn'gu's condition is grave. No one's allowed to visit him except his direct family,
and do you think it'll help his mental state with you lot shouting slogans? Any more of that and I'll have you all arrested, every last one
of you. Have you got that?" And with that the fat man turned and
went back inside.

As we approached the main building I related to Mother what
Kŭnjo had told me. Knowing Mother's strong conviction that had
been hardened by faith, I felt it was best to share the facts with her
rather than give her a shock later. When I told her that in addition
to the cirrhosis a tumor had been discovered, Mother let out a groan.
"Oh my God!" And then her wrinkled mouth pursed shut and she
seemed to be thinking something over dispassionately. I fell silent as
well. Mother began to walk more quickly, but it looked to me as if the
tips of her rubber shoes were trembling.

Arriving at the reception desk of the internal medicine departments, I asked for Dr. Min Chonghak. The nurse told me he could
be found in Department 3. And there we waited for him in a private room inside his suite of consulting rooms. The air-conditioning
was on, and the small room was cool. After some twenty minutes Dr.
Min appeared. Whether to comfort the family or to lessen his own
burden, he gave us a detailed explanation of the incurable nature
of liver disease. Although he didn't mention Hyŏn'gu, the frequency
with which he used the word "fatal" left me with a feeling of menace.
Mother asked him directly if it was cancer. But Dr. Min replied in a
roundabout way that within the cirrhosis a harder portion, the size
of a red bean, had been discovered.

". . . the result of our first meeting is that the best method, in our
opinion, would be to operate and then provide radiation therapy.

You understand, of course, this has only a fifty percent success rate. But if the patient or the family objects, then our only option is insulin and dietary treatments—"

"If you use radiation," I interrupted, "doesn't that mean the tumor has spread?"

"In that case, I wouldn't suggest an operation but would advise that the patient be discharged."

"Have you reported the medical team's findings to the prosecutors?"

"Only the results of the tests and our opinion regarding treatment."

Dr. Min's expression was official, but his manner was relaxed and his voice gentle. I tried to read Mother's face. She was giving Dr. Min a piercing look. The draft from the air-conditioner set strands of white hair fluttering against her wrinkled forehead. Suddenly she jumped to her feet.

"I won't allow you to operate!" she shrieked. "Hyŏn'gu's body must not be touched by a knife. Far better to cure his liver by the laying on of hands than by using a knife. No matter what anyone says, God is on the side of my child!"

Small though she was, Mother seemed on the verge of toppling over, and so I lent her a hand.

"Dr. Min, first of all I'll try to see a lawyer. It's not so serious that you have to operate immediately, is it? If it *is* that serious, then the delay in getting permission for Hyŏn'gu to see a specialist will have cost him his life."

As I blurted this out I put my arm around Mother's waist and guided her out through the consulting room. I didn't hear a word behind my back—perhaps this was the first stage of the shock treatment for the patient's family.

On our way back to Hyŏn'gu's ward Mother asked what I thought about taking her youngest child to an open-air prayer retreat. There was a spiritualist minister whose laying on of hands had cured even terminally ill cancer patients. A church elder who knew all about liver disease was planning to come tonight with a bottle of earthworm broth and had assured Mother that if Hyŏn'gu took it, with God's help he could be cured. Mother had acquired a fairly good knowledge about liver disease, and her voice was surprisingly clear, and even her pace was energetic. It was also clear from her lack of tears that Mother was making an effort not to think despairingly about my brother—a judgment born out by what she said next.

"You've just got back from abroad, and you must be busy, too. Do you have to hang around here? Go on back and get on with your work. I'll let you know if anything else urgent crops up. It's only four hours from Seoul to Taegu, isn't it? Tongsu's mother and I took care of Hyŏn'gu when he was in prison before. We saved him. And now that he's been let out of prison into hospital, shouldn't it be possible to take him home or to a retreat? I'll meet that lawyer Chu. That young man is a church elder so he listens to me."

Here was Mother worrying about me in addition to everything else. I said I would meet the lawyer but that the lawyer wouldn't be able to weigh the pros and cons of surgery. Tongsu's mother was closer to Hyŏn'gu than anybody, and I didn't know her stance on the matter, but I was against him having an operation. A liver operation was the last resort, the last strand of hope. But who was I to say? And so I decided to consult one of my classmates who was a specialist in internal medicine after I returned to Seoul on the night train.

Next I visited Chu Yŏngjun, the human rights lawyer, whose office was near the courthouse. Chu had handled many cases involving violations of the Emergency Measures. He was about the same age as Hyŏn'gu. I told him the results of Hyŏn'gu's medical tests, then asked whether Hyŏn'gu might be moved to Seoul National University Hospital, where there were specialists in liver disease. Why not arrange for another battery of tests there? We could then decide about the operation.

"In my opinion it doesn't matter to them whether they operate," said the lawyer. "And whenever doctors say 'If the family objects,' I have to wonder if their real intention is just to play for time. I'll apply to the court for a transfer of location for the purpose of seeing a specialist. It will have to be for Seoul National University Hospital and not his Pisan-dong residence. The court may grant permission for the hospital, but they won't grant it for his home. Because the shantytown in Pisan-dong and the nearby industrial complex are the base of Hyŏn'gu's activity, and the more that Hyŏn'gu's problem gets known on the outside, the more headaches for the authorities." Chu promised to hand in the application for the transfer the following day.

By the time I returned to the university hospital, evening had arrived. I realized I hadn't noticed the setting of the summer sun. The students who'd been staging the sit-down demonstration had disappeared. A new shift of riot police were guarding the entrance hall and the ward; they seemed ready for any eventuality.

Ch'oe, the young guard with the crew cut, was back on duty in the ward, and the fat police investigator was gone. Sug'yŏng and the Reverend Wŏn had also left, and my sister-in-law had arrived with my nephew Tongsu. She was standing behind the bed massaging my brother's lower back by pummeling it with her fists. Hyŏn'gu had perched his son on the edge of the bed and was having an intimate father-and-son conversation with him. Tongsu's mother listened to the conversation with a smile on her face.

"I'm going to be a doctor. 'Cause then I can cure Daddy," said four-year-old Tongsu.

"Sure you have to cure Daddy, but there are lots of sick people in our neighborhood, aren't there? You'll have to cure those people too, won't you?"

"Yes, yes. I'm definitely going to be a doctor. Daddy, if you're sick and you can't walk let's ride a taxi home. Not a bus, a taxi. I never went in a taxi. Daddy, I'll show you my painting—it's on the wall at school."

As Tongsu pestered his father in his lisping voice, Mother glared at him over her spectacles as she thumbed through her Bible. "That little rascal . . ." Even though the specter of death was absent from the ward, I couldn't help wondering what would happen if Hyŏn'gu were to close his eyes and leave behind his young wife and his little youngster. Even though I was nearly fifty, I felt overwhelmed with sadness and felt a sharp pain in the bridge of my nose. Finally I produced from my travel bag the presents I'd brought from Russia—knitted woolen shawls for Mother, Sug'yŏng, and my sister-in-law and a couple of toy cars made of tin for Tongsu. One was an ambulance and the other a fire engine. I placed the two cars in Tongsu's hands.

"Wow, great! I can show my friends tomorrow. Thank you, Uncle." Tongsu displayed the toy cars above his head as he chattered on proudly, his face blossoming with happiness.

I went out into the corridor for a cigarette. Through the window I could see the shadows in the courtyard lengthening. There was an orange glow to the patches of sky visible among the trees. A breath of wind had set the leaves trembling. Patients in wheelchairs had come out to the courtyard to relax in the temporary cool of the evening now that the heat of the day had dissipated. I heard low voices and went up to the windowsill and looked down. Right beneath the window were four old people sitting together chatting. Among them were the two who'd greeted Mother when we'd gone to see Dr. Min.

". . . It was when they were demolishing the A zone. Well, that was the first time I ever saw Mr. Pak get angry like that—normally he's gentle as a lamb. The grandmother in the Ŏms' house was sick in bed and Mr. Pak kept trying to block the entrance. He asked for just one hour's breathing room. But would those ignorant demolition workers listen? They were just doing their 'public duty,' so they didn't have to show any human feelings. They just shoved Mr. Pak out of the way and began to take down the board walls with hammers and crowbars. Then there was a shriek and Sangju-*daek* comes rushing out the side door with her child in her arms, shouting at them to wait—her mother was inside. But the workers pretended not to hear. And then a section of board came flying off the wall and hit the child smack in the forehead. You should have seen the blood. When Mr. Pak saw all that, he got really angry. I was next to him and his eyes were burning like fire. I knew something was going to happen, and sure enough he ran up to one of the workers, snatched his crowbar and began to swing it around. He was crying and shouting like a madman: 'Aren't you human, too?' And then he started hitting the demolition workers."

"I would have had to do something, too. That kind doesn't seem to have any blood or tears."

"Reverend Wŏn was there, too. After Mr. Pak was arrested, he said something about what had happened. It sounded kind of strange, you know, but he compared it to when Jesus in the Bible drives out the people who are buying and selling in the temple and overturns the chairs and tables of those who are selling doves. He said he felt as if he was looking at that scene."

"Mr. Pak is so precious, and yet the times are killing him. He spent nearly twenty years in the labor movement, and then working for the poor, and then in prison. Do you suppose he ever had time to eat three meals a day? My son told me Mr. Pak fasted many times in his prison cell. And now his liver has dried up."

"People who don't eat and have a hard time should at least have a healthy liver. He's really unlucky for such a young person."

"If anything happens to Mr. Pak do you think people are just going to stay quiet? A lot of people are waiting to see what happens. You know, the workers at Sŏng'an Dyeing and Weaving and the women at Hanguk Electric? It looks like they're taking the lead and starting a collection for his hospital fees . . ."

I stubbed out my cigarette and went back inside. Calling Tong-su's mother out into the corridor, I told her what Dr. Min had said about Hyŏn'gu having an operation, and we talked it over. She too knew already that Hyŏn'gu had cancer as well as cirrhosis, and she too was opposed to surgery as a first option. As he was still under the jurisdiction of the court and couldn't be moved without the court's permission, it seemed best to monitor his condition for a few days and see how his treatment was progressing.

"I've been asking around," she said calmly. "Three days from now is Sunday and some sort of decision should come by then. I've heard there's a new treatment—when the tumor's still small, it's wrapped in a thin film, something like cellophane, to stop it from spreading. When you're back in Seoul please see what you can find out. It would be good to reserve a bed at Seoul National University Hospital. I'll go to court with the lawyer tomorrow."

She bit down on her cracked lower lip, her expression serious. I took strength from her—she was already preparing herself for the worst. It was fortunate that even at this critical juncture she did not waver and handled everything sensibly.

"Tongsu's mother. We're over here. If we can't visit Mr. Pak, perhaps you could come over here for a moment? There's something we want to say to you." One of the old people chatting outside must have recognized her voice, and had stuck his head through the open window to address her.

"Are you good people still here? All right, I'll come out," she replied.

Later that day I left East Taegu Station on the slow train to Seoul that departed near midnight. I planned to return to Taegu four days later, after scheduling the work at the publishing company so it could be carried on in my absence.

My second day back in Seoul, I was constantly on the go at the publishing company and following up for Hyŏn'gu. I phoned Hyŏn'gu's ward and Sug'yŏng's pharmacy to ask how things were going. They told me Hyŏn'gu was about the same except that he wasn't able to urinate and the pain in his back had gotten worse. By the time I got home it was midnight and I went straight to bed, not bothering to wash up first. For the first time in a couple of weeks I was able to sleep deeply.

Around half past one the following day, just as I got back to the office from Seoul National University Hospital, I had a call from Sug'yŏng.

"What'll we do? It's Hyŏn'gu, he's in a coma . . . you've got to come quickly. From dawn he was complaining that he couldn't take the pain . . . he woke up and then he lost consciousness . . ."

The connection was clear enough that I could hear Sug'yŏng weeping, but somehow it sounded like a faraway echo. All of a sudden I felt my energy drain away. Finally it was happening, and now what? I was aware of dropping the receiver and then I went blank. The next thing I knew, our accountant, Miss Ch'oe, was asking gingerly if I'd had some bad news. I closed my eyes a moment and heaved a sigh.

"Can you find the Chut'aek Bank passbook and withdraw whatever's in the account . . . five hundred thousand in cash and the rest as a check."

Next I called home. I told my wife about Hyŏn'gu and said I'd leave for Taegu straightaway. My wife, her tone urgent, said she would call her mother in Ch'ŏngju and have her come up to Seoul to take care of the children, and then would join me in Taegu.

"Don't take the car. You absolutely mustn't. If you drive in an agitated state . . . you know, don't you?"

I never would have thought of that—women certainly are shrewd and precise. After promising her up and down that I'd do as she said, I ended the call.

Seoul Station was closer than the Kangnam express bus terminal, so I took the train. After the stop at Yŏngdŭngp'o Station, we gradually left Seoul behind and fields and mountains began to appear outside the window. Luxuriant trees absorbed the hot sunshine and gave off an intense greenness. If only those who were dying could be revived by moisture and sunlight. Once again I imagined the deep yellow cast of Hyŏn'gu's face, his haggard form, his body filming with cold sweat as he oscillated between life and death. Summer is hard enough as it is for any invalid to endure, and this sauna-like heat was causing Hyŏn'gu to break down. When a refrigerator is disconnected or the voltage drops and the inside of the fridge gets lukewarm, then the contents sealed tightly inside are sure to go bad quickly. If I were to compare Hyŏn'gu's body to a refrigerator, then it was as if the cord were constantly being plugged and unplugged. Under such conditions wouldn't his liver break down, not to mention his kidneys, stomach, intestines, and lungs? It was horrible to consider. Better to call up a different image of Hyŏn'gu. When our family had pushed south as refugees that winter, we were moving in the same direction the train was now traveling. Mother had carried a tiny spark of life strapped to her back, a spark that had kept burning all this time. What was the difference between survival then and death thirty-nine years later? Was it simply that there was now a child to remain in the future? If not, was it that now he was grown up, God wanted to see his beautiful handiwork and was calling to him, saying, "Now that you have done your share, come to my side . . ."? God's providence was beyond my ken, but in any event, cold-hearted reality was taking no notice of it. I went to the restaurant car and had myself two bottles of beer for lunch.

I arrived at East Taegu Station shortly after six to the sight of the sun sinking behind the buildings of the city. I hurried to the taxi stand and caught a taxi to the hospital. I arrived to find the front gate closed off and two riot police buses, grills over the windows, parked next to it. Several riot police were guarding an emergency side entrance, which had been left ajar. The people lined up there were being admitted after showing their citizen's identity cards and explaining the purpose of their visit. I took my place in line intuitively realizing the precautions had something to do with Hyŏn'gu. When my turn came, I gave the name of the hospital building and Hyŏn'gu's ward.

"Your relationship to the patient?" the riot policeman asked, examining my citizen's identity card.

"His elder brother. I got an urgent phone call, and I've just arrived from Seoul this very moment."

"Let him in," came a voice from the vicinity of the custodian's booth. It was the fat police investigator I'd seen in Hyŏn'gu's room two days earlier.

I walked almost at a run. As I turned the corner of the main building, sweat streaming down my face, I heard from near the annex building containing Hyŏn'gu's ward a chorus of singing as well as hands clapping in time with the music.

"See where the green pine grows

With no one to tend nor care

Winds may blow and snowstorms howl

But it is green to the ends of the earth . . ."

It was quite a sight. There in the spacious courtyard of the annex were row upon row of fully equipped riot police surrounding some fifty students, workers, and shantytown women, who were themselves sitting in rows as they clapped and sang. Next to a jeep with grill-covered windows stood a pair of burly middle-aged men with two-way radios, who appeared to be in charge of the police. Tongsu's mother was gesticulating and berating them energetically, but to no avail as the men silently concentrated on the demonstrators. I glimpsed a banner held up by two women in the back rows of the demonstrators. One of the women was Sangju-*daek*.

"Light of the poor, Pak Hyŏn'gu forever!"

Realizing I had gaped long enough at this scene, I glanced for a moment at the Reverend Wŏn, who was among the singing demonstrators, then entered the building, identified myself to the riot policeman at the entrance and the guard at the ward, and finally I was there. I could feel all eyes turning toward me. Without greeting anyone, I went up to the bed.

"Hyŏn'gu!"

Deep in a quagmire of sleep, he didn't respond. His face was a sickly green, no longer the color of a living person. Now and again he frowned, and his breath came in heavy sighs, as though he was being tormented by a nightmare. Beneath the coverlet his bulging stomach was much more noticeable, looking like that of a pregnant mother about to give birth—a symptom of the uremia that had spread throughout his body. I clasped my brother's hand. It was damp, emaciated, chilly. Sweat or tears, I'm not sure which, fell from my face onto the coverlet. I could barely choke back the sobs surging within me.

"There doesn't seem to be a shred of hope," said Mother, who was keeping a bedside vigil. "They're saying the end will come tonight. There's no one who can save this child now. . . . I don't believe in that doctor, but I have to believe what he said. . . . It's just like it was with your young father. This child must be really important for God to want to take him for His own purposes. His wretched old mum is left behind. . . . We must do as He asks, but . . . is there anywhere on earth a story as pitiful as this? . . ." She was wiping Hyŏn'gu's face with a damp cloth as she muttered these words as copious as her overflowing tears, muttered words that to my ears were a wail pouring out in tears and blood.

Now even Mother, taking care of the comatose Hyŏn'gu, was no longer insisting that her youngest child lived inside her. Mother had turned down the coverlet nearly to his waist, and his hospital gown had been undone, laying his chest bare. His gaunt ribs bore a dew-like film of perspiration. His chest was the yellowish brown color of earth. With a towel Mother slowly wiped away its layer of sweat.

"You never saw him when you were born, and now you're going to see the daddy you missed so much. Is your Daddy in heaven still looking as young as he was when he died at thirty-three . . . ?"

Despite the ceiling fan whirring round and round, not a strand of Hyŏn'gu's long, sweat-soaked hair stirred. Cold sweat oozed from every pore of my brother's body, as though it were emptying itself of all moisture. His breathing would die away and seem about to stop, then explode with the sound of someone blowing his nose and become rapid again. When that happened, I had the impression that my brother would open his eyes just the slightest bit and give his usual modest smile as though he were slowly about to rise. But soon his breathing faded again. A single tear trickled from the corner of his eye.

"How long has he been in a coma?" I asked Mother.

"More than half the day. He hasn't come round in all that time. They wouldn't release my son, so he couldn't get the laying on of hands at the prayer retreat. . . . I ran to them and I fought and I pleaded with them to let my son go. I was going to carry my child on my back in my bare, bleeding feet to the Kŭmho Mountain prayer retreat but . . . for the first time I'm not able to save this child. . . . Oh, Lord God, behold this child. How difficult it must be for him, leaving with all the cares and sighs of the poor people in his heart. Look how he's gasping for breath. He's crying, isn't he . . ."

I backed away from Hyŏn'gu's bed and looked about to see Sug'yŏng sitting half turned away with Tongsu on her knee, wiping her eyes with a handkerchief, her shoulders heaving as she sobbed. Tongsu, still holding his toy cars, was glancing at me with frightened, bloodshot eyes. The older guard, Hong, and a middle-aged man in a lightweight jacket who seemed to be a police investigator were keeping an eye on me.

The chanting of the slogans was louder now.

"Release the prisoner of conscience Pak Hyŏn'gu!"

"Release him now, release him now!"

"Give us back the prisoner of conscience Pak Hyŏn'gu!"

"Give him back to us, give him back, give him back!"

As I stood there like someone in a trance, Hong looked out the window and pointed.

"Look at those idiots—they're climbing over the wall!"

I looked out the open window and sure enough, several students or workers were clambering over the ivy-covered wall. Out rushed the police investigator.

The air outside was full of the chirping of cicadas and the shouting of slogans. I felt stifled by the oppressive heat and the heavy silence in the ward. I just couldn't bring myself to look toward the bed, where Mother was repeating something over and over as she looked down at Hyŏn'gu. I went out to the corridor, and as I smoked, I looked out the window through blurred, watery eyes.

"If you don't disperse by seven thirty, you'll all be arrested. Everyone must leave within twenty minutes!" One of the middle-aged police officers standing beside the jeep was speaking through a megaphone. The demonstrators whistled and jeered at him, then resumed their chorus. This time the clapping of hands was reinforced by the booming of a drum.

Behind the cordon of riot police, I spotted Tongsu's mother hurrying toward me, accompanied by three young people. The young people remained at the entrance to the annex while Tongsu's mother entered. Outside the shadows were deepening, and inside the corridor was very dark. Tongsu's mother came to a stop in front of me.

"They won't let him out until he's dead—not that I expected any different. Everyone wants to take Hyŏn'gu home before he dies and hold the funeral at the community center, but they'll never allow it. The police are expecting a riot, so there's no way they'll listen to our insignificant wishes. For all I know they'll keep his body and cremate him just to get rid of him."

All of which told me that Tongsu's mother too held out no hope for Hyŏn'gu.

"Why in God's name would they do that? I'll talk to Sug'yŏng's husband about the burial place." Saddened to be talking about funeral arrangements, I realized that I had now accepted Hyŏn'gu's death as an established fact.

Tongsu's mother seemed lost in thought, and then her eyes suddenly brightened. Looking around her determinedly, she spoke to me in a conspiratorial tone.

"No matter what happens, we're going to take Tongsu's father home before he passes away. We decided this afternoon."

While I stared at her blankly, unable to process what she was saying, Tongsu's mother walked briskly into the ward.

In the meantime, the number of demonstrators had swelled to perhaps sixty, and now they burst out with new slogans.

"Pak Hyŏn'gu's about to die, free him!"

"Free him now! Free him now!"

"Give us permission to hold the funeral in our community!"

"Give us permission! Give us permission!"

The one calling out the slogans was one of the young people who had been with Tongsu's mother just now. His chanting had become desperate, and I wondered if he'd come to some sort of tacit understanding with Tongsu's mother. The next moment it struck me—that's what they'd been talking about a moment before. Responding to the urgency of the young man's slogans, the demonstrators stood up as one and punched the air with clenched fists as they shouted. They looked at a loss, and I could hear some of them asking if Hyŏn'gu was really dying, or if his condition was really that bad.

"The authorities must take responsibility for the death of Pak Hyŏn'gu!"

"Take responsibility! Take responsibility!"

The shouting of the slogans became more urgent. The young people had gathered at the forefront of the demonstrators. Before I knew it they were putting their arms over each other's shoulders. Soon all the demonstrators were linked in this way and they began to advance in a huge wave, as though they meant to break through the riot police blocking the way. The riot police were like a concrete wall and did not yield behind their phalanx of shields.

"Disperse, or you will be arrested!"

Just as the harsh voice crackled through the megaphone, a Molotov cocktail flew from the back of the demonstrators toward the jeep and exploded with a bang. From the rear came great shouts—

"*Wa, wa! Oshya, oshya!*"—and again the demonstrators advanced, arms around each other's shoulders, fiercely determined to breach the wall of riot police.

"No violence! Violence can't solve anything!"

I couldn't see him but I recognized the voice—it was the Reverend Wŏn.

Bang! Bang! More Molotov cocktails exploded. The Reverend Wŏn shouted, "This isn't a street! This is a hospital!" and then his voice was swallowed up by the yelling of the crowd. Finally the police had had enough, and hospital or not, tear gas canisters began to burst with a dull, popping sound.

"Arrest them all!" shouted the police chief through the megaphone.

The riot police rushed the demonstrators and began to arrest them right and left. The next moment the broad courtyard had become a pandemonium of shrieking and yelling. The riot police guarding the ward came running down the corridor, boots clattering, and rushed outside.

I could smell the tear gas. Tears came to my eyes and I burst out sneezing. I hurried back into the ward just as a young man with a stick climbed inside through the back window. He was followed by several others, all wearing masks. Bunching together, they menaced Hong with their sticks. White-faced and open-mouthed, Hong put up his hands in surrender.

"Mrs. Pak, let's go!" a youth in overalls shouted at Tongsu's mother. "We need to get out of here! There's a minibus waiting at the back gate."

"What are you doing? W–where are we going?" Mother stammered. She was in shock as she protected Hyŏn'gu with outstretched arms, as if trying to gather him up.

"Mother, we want Tongsu's father to be able to die in our room in Pisan-dong. Tongsu's father is not a criminal, he can't die locked up in this place under guard!" Tongsu's mother spoke quickly as she wheeled the bed toward the corridor. Her eyes glistened with tears as she looked down at Hyŏn'gu struggling for breath.

"Yes, yes. You're right," said Mother, suddenly focusing in response to her daughter-in-law's words. "Tongsu, we'll go first, you and me!"

So saying, Mother snatched Tongsu from Sug'yŏng and in one swift movement put him on her back.

"Grandma, is Daddy really going home?" Tongsu asked in a clear voice.

"That's right, he's going home. Now you've become Daddy. And you're going to do everything Hyŏn'gu couldn't do. You are your Grandma's youngest son now!" Mother shouted as though possessed.

Just as Mother had hurried southward with Hyŏn'gu on her back during that winter long ago, now carrying Tongsu on her bent, narrow back, she took the lead and flung open the door of the ward.

"Brother, is it going to be all right?" Sug'yŏng asked me, bewildered.

"Nothing we can do now. It's out of our hands. Let's go." In a daze I prodded Sug'yŏng along.

"We can't go out through the entrance. Go the back way—hurry!" said Sug'yŏng. She seemed to have made up her mind, and out she went following Mother.

The corridor was full of the acrid smell of tear gas. In the gathering dusk I saw thick smoke in the courtyard as the chaos of the riot continued.

The young people wheeled the bed along from the sides and from behind. As we emerged from the corridor into the dim light of dusk, Hyŏn'gu's form became indistinct. I felt anxious. And then a sudden resolve ran through me like a jolt of electricity. Each of us had now begun to make a prison cell in our hearts to which Hyŏn'gu could retreat and live and breathe. I finally realized it wasn't right that Hyŏn'gu should pass away in detention. If Hyŏn'gu died, his arrest for assault and interference with a government official would never be resolved. Still, even if it was only symbolic, I now knew that I too had the responsibility to take Hyŏn'gu, while he yet breathed, to a place of freedom, even if we never managed to reach the rented room in Pisan-dong.

With Tongsu's mother I took hold of the handles at the foot of the bed and we helped roll it headlong down the tear gas–filled corridor. Leading the way just as much as I was, Mother with Tongsu on her back and Sug'yŏng with her arm around Mother's waist hurried toward the back door. And just when we got there the door was flung open by a waiting group of young people. Our path had been blocked, but now we had an exit to freedom. Just as we three children had hurried southward with Mother that winter, we now pushed through the tear gas as if through the smoke of artillery, hurrying the bed along. It was at that moment that I felt in my heart the same overpowering excitement as when we'd rushed shoulder to shoulder toward the police battalion on that April day so long ago.

THE PAGER

Kim Yŏngha
Translated by Dafna Zur

Kim Yŏngha was born in 1967. To date he has published
three story collections and five novels, in addition to film
criticism and travel writing. In the summer of 2008 he
and his wife sold their apartment in Seoul and began living abroad part-time, in places ranging from Vancouver
to Hong Kong to New York City. By then Kim had left his
teaching position at Seoul University of the Arts and was
writing full time. ▓ Kim's father was in the military and
the family moved frequently during his childhood. At
the age of ten, Kim almost died from carbon monoxide
poisoning (resulting from incomplete combustion of the
coal briquettes formerly used to heat Korean living quarters), the exposure depriving him of memories of his life
till then. Kim has spoken of how this experience shaped

his development into a writer, the creation of his stories becoming a surrogate for reclaiming the lost narrative of his early years. Not surprisingly he is one of the most imaginative and most visual writers of his generation. ■ Kim's earlier works, such as his debut novel, *I Have the Right to Destroy Myself* (Na nŭn na rŭl p'agoehal kwŏlli ka itta, 1996), and the story "Lizard" (Tomabaem, 1997), are rife with sex and death. Although Kim has joked that in this phase of his career he was unmarried and full of raging hormones, he was in fact tackling two subjects that had rarely received sustained attention by writers in the authoritarian, neo-Confucian culture that characterized South Korea at least until the democratization process of June 1987. He has since published an intertextual novel inspired by the story of a *kisaeng* and an evil magistrate, *What's the Matter with Arang?* (Arang ŭn wae? 2001); a diaspora novel involving the first Korean immigrants in Mexico, *Black Flowers* (Kŏmŭn kkot, 2003); a novel whose protagonist is a North Korean national living undercover in the South, *Your Republic Is Calling You* (Pit ŭi cheguk, 2006); and a coming-of-age novel describing the online culture of present-day South Korea, *Quiz Show* (K'wijŭ shyo, 2007). Readers of these varied works have compared Kim with Murakami Haruki, but a more apt comparison might be with Mishima Yukio, who like Kim dealt initially with sex and death but evolved into a writer with a broader vision of his culture and society, both past and present. ■ "The Pager" (Hoch'ul) first appeared in the Summer 1996 issue of *Munhak tongne* and is the title story of Kim's first volume of short fiction, published the following year.

Visionaries dream about reality. Believe me, reality is what visionaries dream about.

—Chang Chŏngil,

The Woman Crazy for Sylvia Plath

1. Pager

Should I?

I picked up the phone, started to dial, put it down again. Hmm, maybe now's not the best time. She may be sleeping, in which case she'll be a little short of pleased to hear from me.

Bottom line is—I behaved totally out of character yesterday. Maybe that's why my heart starts to race when I recall the scene. I hadn't tried a stunt like that in all the twenty-eight years of my life. I'm the vacillating, wishy-washy type, who ends up doing a whole lot of nothing.

Then I thought of Suji. Three months ago, she tells me she's going overseas to study. "You mean, your parents agreed to send you?" I said, surprised. She stared back at me with a very perplexed expression. "Obviously I'm not going alone." I was still clueless. "What are you talking about?" I said, annoyed, pressing her for an answer. "You still don't get it?" she said sharply, picking up her pocketbook. "I'm breaking up with you, I'm marrying someone else, and I'm going abroad to study. Now do you get it?" I nodded. As she got up, I grabbed at her pocketbook and blurted, "Good luck in your studies." She gave me the most pitiful smile. And that was it. My parting words sounded ridiculous even to me.

I remained in the coffee shop after she had gone. Our last moments had left me completely red-faced, so that the full realization that I'd made a mess of the relationship escaped me. I thought about it long and hard. Where did I go wrong? And what made her so pompous and confident? How could she do it? How could she walk out on our two-year relationship, marry someone else, and go off to study? At that point, I was a bit angry.

On reflection, I knew I'd gotten it wrong. Breakups aren't one-sided. They don't happen because of one or the other's mistake. Relationships end because they're meant to end—isn't that what love is all about? Still, I agonized about where I had gone wrong. If I'd made mistakes, they'd include my habit of religiously watching two videos a day, buying her only cheap earrings, and never attempting to write a resume or CV. Anyway, she was gone. At this moment she's probably parked her Japanese car in front of a supermarket in Boston and she's inside with her husband buying an armful of frozen meals, just being happy. Of course, Suji's husband is presumably ecstatically happy, too. Suji's the kind of girl who knows how to hide her feelings.

Good luck in your studies. I started playing with the idea of showing up at her wedding to take back what I had said. I fantasized endlessly about walking up to the bride in her waiting room, surrounded by all her friends, and whispering something devastating. Fantasies— they were all the revenge I was capable of, my only entertainment. My best line: "I was in the neighborhood, so I stopped by." Picturing myself hanging over her, whispering in her ear with a nonchalant smile put me in the best of moods. She'd be tense, expecting the worst, and then she'd giggle nervously in relief.

My final fantasy was about the moment at the end of the ceremony when the photographer asks the friends of the bride and groom to step forward. I'd squeeze in on the groom's side. Later, when they look at their wedding photos together, they might even get a strange thrill from seeing me standing there.

But I never did go. I stayed home and rented the comedy *Four Weddings and a Funeral.* I took part in the movie's four weddings and one funeral. I remember enjoying the film, but I can't recall the storyline now. That's the way it always is with me.

Should I try to page her again?

I fingered the phone again. As I did so, she came alive in my mind.

It was about 3 P.M. yesterday, at the Ch'ungmuro subway station. I was walking along the yellow line, the one in the announcement: "The train is arriving; for your safety, please step behind the yellow line." Maybe I was safe, maybe not. I like that kind of tightrope walk. My favorite tightrope is the one that divides reality from fantasy. Sometimes I think that reality is fantasy; sometimes I go through life believing that my fantasies are real. But this blur never struck me as problematic. It's like watching a film: I explore my fantasy world within a fixed framework of time.

It was on that subway tightrope walk that I met her. She wasn't standing on the brink like me; she was leaning back against the much safer wall. Strands of straight brown hair fell over her shoulders; a long, voluminous knitted sweater came down to her behind, complementing her oval face; and her jeans, frayed at the bottoms, dragged along the floor, giving her a sexy aura of decadence. But it was the girl's pose that held me spellbound. She was leaning against the wall, one leg stretched out straight, one slightly bent, and her hands were in her jeans pockets. But this doesn't really describe her. The key was, she knew how to adopt the pose that would make her look most beautiful. I'll bet she has a full-length mirror in her room. Because I'm sure that only people who watch themselves endlessly in the mirror can pose so impeccably. I imagine her looking at herself naked in the mirror. Stripped bare, she slowly walks up to the mirror. And she strikes that pose, listening to her Walkman, swaying ever so gently. The music? Schubert's "Death and the Maiden" would be best. Nudity and death—I liked the combination. The two have one thing in common—exposure. Nothing to hide. Nudity exposes that original human form normally hidden by our clothes; death exposes the secrets of the dead. Death snatches away

the sexual complications, absurdities, and extravagances from the
defenseless hands of the dead.

The girl also had big eyes, and her gaze stayed fixed. Only people who are used to being the focus of public stares can do that. Like
anchors on the nine o'clock news, or TV stars. Normal people look
all around in subway stations. Those who don't look around know
that if they do, they're most likely to clash eyes with someone else.

Yesterday—the day we met—started off on the right foot. A Taegu
university magazine commissioned fifty pages of manuscript. They
wanted an analysis of recent commercial ads, specifically those
that borrow words and concepts that used to be used exclusively
by social movements. For example, they asked me to decipher the
social significance of ads like this one, for jeans: "The motion of tire-
less revolution." Blue jeans and revolutionary motion. Commercial imagination is such a melting pot. Throw in Lenin's collapsed
bronze bust; add rhetoric born of radical ideas. That's why this kind
of imagination can't really be called imagination at all. This kind of
imagination probably dreams up chemical defoliants and industrial
mergers. Anyhow, they'd pay 200,000 *wŏn* for those fifty pages. That
would be enough to cover books and cigarettes for the next while.

How long do you plan on living like this? Suji used to ask. To be
honest, I wasn't all that content with having to survive on the ran-
dom articles I was paid to write for school papers and magazines. But
answering that type of question with the "I promise to get my act
together" line was even worse. Moreover, there was no reason she'd
believe me. You say things like that to justify yourself in politics. She
was going to leave me, and this was her way to secure the foundation for a final farewell.

Fortunately, I feel the girl I met yesterday suits my tempera-
ment infinitely better than Suji. Suji always blamed other people for
the misfortunes in her life; this girl didn't. The kind of girl that can

pose like that, the kind of girl that watches her naked reflection in a full-length mirror couldn't maliciously blame others for her own problems. And when you think about it, my pathetic attempt at a farewell—*Good luck in your studies*—was not entirely my fault either. Inevitably, I became flustered and hesitant in front of a woman who played her role to such "political" perfection. She was always whining about how I'd ruined her life. She kept saying that had she met a decent man, she'd have continued her studies.

Imagine how refreshing this new girl is!

The moment the train appeared, the girl leaning against the wall stepped behind me. I heard a faint jingle. I stole a glance in her direction. The sound must have been coming from the two rings hanging from each ear that were swinging even as I looked away. Did she know that the accessories dangling from her ears emitted a sound that stimulated some man's auditory function?

A love affair with a stranger. What an exciting thought! And a totally new experience for me. I've always dated women I knew long and well, women I met at work or some gathering. I'd find an appropriate weekend, watch a second-rate porn film, drink draft beer in the back alleys of Kwanch'ŏl-dong, and spend the night with whoever. Soon, formal speech turned mutually familiar, and next thing I know she's demanding I say I love her. Affairs devoid of any imagination. It was scary, sometimes. Nothing was up to me—I just had to fit together the right puzzle pieces.

But the girl from yesterday—she's different. In that brief moment of time between the jingling of her earrings and the opening of the train door, I was able to construct a photo album with hundreds of still shots. That's how different she was. I imagined her in a minor role in a soft porn film; then as an understudy appearing only in the sex scenes; then as the fiancée who lost her husband-to-be when the Samp'ung Department Store collapsed in 1995; and finally as the heroine of a tragic love story, whose beloved runs off with another girl to study abroad. Of these, the body double role was my favorite: a girl who does the full nude scenes that big movie stars avoid. She dreams of stardom, but necessity forces her to do this kind of work from time to time. She's got the perfect body and a face to match, but she hasn't had her lucky break, and so she makes a living as a body double. She loved a man, but one day he discovered her on the screen and dumped her.

The doors slid open. A man in a suit with a sports tabloid in his hand got off first. Next, a man with his hair drawn back in a ponytail, and a woman holding a black drawing board. They were followed by two or three hefty middle-aged women who pushed me clumsily yet determinedly out of their way. Thinking of the girl with the jingly earrings staring at the back of my head, I waited until everyone had gotten off. Inside, I leaned against the exit door and she stood opposite me. We were in a perfect position—all we had to do was look up and we'd be facing each other. But of course, she didn't look around or lose focus.

"The train is about to depart—please watch the closing doors," came the announcement, and the train left Ch'ungmuro for Tongdaemun Station. Only three stops left to Hyehwa, my stop. Will she get off at the same station? And if she doesn't?

When I get anxious, I start fiddling with my belt. It's a bad habit I acquired growing up. I got all my brother's hand-me-downs, and I was always scared my pants would fall down. It's about time I stopped since I'm at the point in life where I buy my own clothes. But whenever I get antsy or uneasy I still keep pulling up my pants. Thanks to that habit, though, I remembered my pager. I read a story once about a girl who only gave her pager number to her boyfriend, so that every time it went off, her heart would skip a beat. The Pavlov effect, I think it's called. The story made me laugh. Even if she dated other men, her reflex reaction wouldn't easily disappear. People may disappear, but conditioned reflexes stay on.

I pulled out the beeper and started fingering it. A generic model, selling for 30,000 wŏn, it was the most basic of pagers—a stumpy thing with a black frame, unimpressive design, of course incapable of giving the time, showing nothing but the phone number of the caller. And now that I was stuck at home all day struggling with my writing, it was a pure nuisance, swallowing a monthly service fee of 10,000 wŏn.

Then it came to me—why not just give it to her? That's it! I started to fidget. What if I just hand it to her and quickly get off the train! She'll be completely confused. Still, I don't think she'll throw it away. She just wouldn't feel right about it. And since she doesn't know the number, she won't be able to use it for herself. The pager will be waiting for my calls only. That's when I became aware of my erection. I was aroused. Never in my life had I attained such control—someone's destiny lay in receiving my call.

She's about to face her destiny. To acknowledge the fact that she can't just toss the pager away, that she has no choice but to wait for the call that will set it off.

"Next stop is Tongdaemun Station. Tongdaemun Station. The doors will open on your left." One station to go. The palm holding the pager started to get clammy. What should I say when I give it to her? I'll be in touch. No, that's weird. I'll page you. That won't do, either. At times like this I either go mute or else everything I say comes out garbled. What will I say? The sweat I felt in the palm of my hand I now felt running down my back, and my groin felt moist. I shut my eyes tight.

"Next stop is Hyehwa Station. Hyehwa Station. The doors will open on your right." I took a step toward her. And for some reason noticed a National Security Bureau poster on the wall of the car: "Drugs, Smuggling, Industrial Spies—International Criminals Threaten Our Society . . . " She looked up wide-eyed, as if she'd noticed my existence only then. The expression on her face froze me in my tracks—it was the kind of refined expression that only those with heightened self-awareness are able to pull off. The door slid open. Desperate, I blurted out the one thing that came to mind. Maybe it was the dizziness. I think I was swaying slightly when I came off the train.

Strangely, those moments felt like a dream. Isn't it true, though, that the most decisive moments in life are always so intense that they are, in fact, elusive. First kiss, first sexual experience, first confession—you can talk about them, but that's all. It's like when a typhoon comes—you only know its power after it has passed through. Anyhow, I have just a vague memory of what I said:

"It's set to vibrate. Please, carry it on you at all times."

I remembered that much before exhaustion overcame me. I'll page her tomorrow. With a blanket over me, I fell asleep on the sofa.

2. Pagee

She was about to get her period. Her head was starting to pound, and moving around just made her grumpy. Tomorrow or the day after, she thought to herself. PMS was awful—this time of month she invariably felt like having her womb extracted.

She kicked off the cashmere blanket, stood up, opened the door, and walked toward the kitchen. The kitchen of her eleven-*p'yŏng* apartment was always too dark because the windows were so small. She took out the cornflakes, poured the milk, and started to eat. It's supposed to be a low-fat meal, great for her figure. Should I try the grape diet? But grapes are so pricey. Can you survive on grapes? She liked the sound of it. Living and dying on grapes.

Beep. Beep. Beep. The pager in her room went off. She pushed aside her bowl of cornflakes and went to get it. Looks like they're filming today after all. She picked up the cordless phone and returned to the kitchen.

"Hello? It's me, Songhwa. . . . Yes. . . . Two o'clock this afternoon? How long will it take? . . . About two hours? Yes. That's fine. I'll see you then."

She placed the phone and pager on the table and went back to her breakfast. Of all days, why does the bowl of cornflakes never seem to end? She spooned the food into her mouth, utterly aggravated. The director says two hours, but that's just his estimate—she knew very well it all depended on what time the lead actress would decide to show up. She'd been working as a body double for two years now, and not once had she seen the lead show up on time. Especially on days like today, when they were shooting the sex scenes. If you think about it, it's pretty amusing. It actually wasn't hard to understand why they were always showing up late for these scenes.

Her mind wandering, she suddenly stood up. She walked back into her room as if she'd forgotten something and took a second pager out of her pocketbook. She checked to see if any calls had come in, and seeing that none had, she went back to the table. She stared at the pager for a moment. Black frame, cheap, nothing special. With all those lightweight, pretty models out these days, "fashion" pagers and "card" pagers, why on earth would someone walk around with this thing? And yet looking at it put her off less than she expected. *It's set to vibrate* . . . The expression on his face as he spoke to her, placed it in her hands, and hurried off was still fresh in her mind. And like he said, the pager was set to vibrate. But why wasn't he calling? Why wasn't he paging her?

She had felt his presence even before they got on the train. He was balancing himself along the yellow line, walking in her direction. He walked as if on a tightrope, his arms angled like a penguin, and when he stopped, she realized that he had his eye on her. So she did what she always does—she lowered her gaze and quietly felt his movements. She always believed that you should learn to enjoy being looked at by strangers. No matter what people say, she thought, I'm still an actress. He seemed to stare at her for a while, and then as the train arrived, he went to the front of the line and waited. And she went right up behind him. But something seemed to have surprised him, and he looked back at her. He was sensitive to her movements. And it wasn't such a bad feeling.

She got up from the table, planted the bowl of leftover cereal in the sink, and went back into her room. She took off the t-shirt she'd slept in and stood in front of the mirror. She was now completely naked. She admired her hips and back in the full-length mirror beside her dressing table. It'd been four days since she'd worn panties, so that the line along her hips had now almost disappeared along with the bra line across her back and underarms. She had to stop wearing underclothes four days before a shoot because of those lines. She stared at her body absent-mindedly. She'd been at this for four years now. The first job her modeling agency got her was a lingerie commercial, and that seemed to have shaped her destiny. It was always like that. Grades, aptitude tests, details of home and school life—they never seemed to affect her future one way or the other. The mood of her modeling teacher, the color of the sky that day, the humidity, the chance moment a certain man spotted her on the screen—these were the things that had decided the direction of her life. They were it. And that "certain man" . . . she'd loved him once. Or rather, through him she'd allowed herself to dream of a different world.

They had met in a jazz bar in It'aewŏn, and he had said he worked for a semi-conductor company. His company logo was stitched onto his smart gray suit. She introduced herself as a student majoring in theater and film. When he started discussing Eisenstein's montage techniques in *The Battleship* Potemkin, she was thrown off. She hesitated, and he quickly covered up for her embarrassment, politely saying "So, you're an actress, then?"

"I was never a good student," she said with a weak smile.

"I thought you looked familiar," he offered.

Three months later, on a summer vacation together in Pusan, he proposed. "Marry me," he said, slipping his hand inside her clothes. She believed him—back then, anyway. A month later, he told her he'd spotted a girl in a video who had the very same freckle on her bottom. "What a coincidence!" she said, denying any connection. But then he waved a girlie magazine in her face with a triumphant smile. Inside, wearing nothing but a girdle, her face turned, was a girl who was unmistakably Songhwa. He seized her arm as she turned to leave. "Give it to me one last time?" he said. She came back in and stripped. She stood under the fluorescent light, looked into his eyes as she peeled off her panties, and took him in her arms. For the longest time he stayed soft. As she left the house, she heard the iron door slam shut behind her.

She probably always knew how it would end. But thinking about it just made her more miserable, so she shook the thoughts away. So what if I knew? And what if I didn't? It's all in the past anyway, and there's no way he's coming back. She started getting ready for work.

She placed a thin band-aid on her nipples to keep them from protruding and shaved her armpits. She loved the feeling of shaving cream on her skin. She slid a slip over her bare skin and put on a dress. It's not see-through now, right? She checked herself one more time in the mirror and left. The cold draft that snuck up between her thighs reminded her that it was autumn.

She was on her way out of the building when she realized she'd forgotten something. Back in she went to pick up the stumpy, generic pager and stuff it in her pocketbook. She knew she was being ridiculous, but so what.

He's probably going to page me today, she told herself with considerable conviction. He would have been too shy to call as soon as yesterday and I'm sure he's got his own busy schedule. That would explain why he didn't follow her but just shoved the pager in her hands and took off. It's probably better not to lie this time, not to tell him the bit about majoring in film and theater. He seemed like a man who wouldn't leave her if she told him she was a body double in sex scenes. If he's the kind of guy to say what he did passing her his pager, and if he's the kind of guy to embrace that kind of indecisiveness and originality, then presumably he wouldn't leave her. But what if he really does page me today? Should I meet him like this, no panties on? Or should I suggest we meet tomorrow?

The pager seemed to exude a female animal fragrance. As long as she had it on her, he'd be able to call her anywhere. Carrying it meant that she had already accepted him. She wasn't particularly proud of her reasoning, but she still couldn't throw the pager away. She was somehow convinced that if she were to discard the pager, she'd be cut off from all relationships for the rest of her life. The pager was another scrutinizing gaze. Somewhere in this world, there were eyes focused on her. And she was used to this kind of scrutiny.

Once she had been in a small pub that featured skewered snacks. She spotted herself on the wall, right above her head, wearing a bathing suit and lying on a rock. It was a wall calendar, advertising a brand of clear rice brew that people drink chilled. That day, she felt like the girl in the photo was someone else, and she turned her head away and drank quietly. But after a drink or two she began to steal glances at the calendar she'd been ignoring. She ended up with tears in her eyes. Now, why should I be crying like this, over nothing? It's not even pornographic. I've got a bathing suit on and everything. And dammit, it's my job, what I get paid for! I'm not crying because I'm sad, she decided, but because I look so cold in that photo. And in fact the day of that shot was really cold—it must have been in October. Pretend it's summer, the team leader was saying. That was easy enough. She could pretend Kyŏngp'odae was really Phuket, and that she was advertising some beauty product rather than gracing a calendar. But the goose bumps covering her all over, they couldn't be fooled.

Arriving at the studio, she steadied her nerves. It was ten to two; she started fiddling with her makeup but then stopped. What's the point? Her face won't even be seen clearly on screen. Two-thirty, and the lead still hadn't shown up. Typical! Cho, the director, was calling the actress's cell phone but he didn't seem to be getting any-where. Cell phones, Songhwa thought to herself, staring at one. If a pager is a cheap prostitute behind a showcase window in Seoul's Miari red-light district, then a cell phone is a high-class call girl. She passed such a show window in a cab once, and the driver told her the girls were sitting there waiting for someone to ask for them. But there were also high-class call girls and famous *kisaeng* entertainers like Hwang Chini, who had the privilege of choosing their partners, or, for example, paging whoever it was they wanted. Yes, the pager was definitely a low-class prostitute, she repeated to herself in self-scorn. At the same time, she made sure it was turned on. Nothing yet. Could he have forgotten? Hell, any of his friends will do as well. Could someone please just get this pager vibrating? She grasped the pager in her right hand and uttered a feeble half-prayer.

I'm cold. She rubbed her arms. It was early fall and the studio was chilly. It would warm up in a minute, once the lights were turned on, but for now it was cold. The staff huddled in groups of twos and threes, all waiting for the actress's arrival. Forty minutes later, she walked in wearing dark, pert sunglasses. Traffic? the director inter-jected on her behalf, before she had a chance to offer an excuse.

Songhwa stared vacantly at the actress, who'd set herself up in a corner of the set and was doing her makeup. Of course, she must do her makeup while we film the sex scene. As soon as she's done, the filming starts. The actress and the lead actor pretend they're drink-ing cognac at the table by the bed. The cognac bottle is filled with flat Coke. She delicately sips it. A moment later, she staggers, and when he tries to catch her, she shakes him off and slaps him across the face. "Cut" calls the director. "That hurt, didn't it?" the actress titters, rub-bing the actor's face.

"Hey, body double!" Songhwa is rarely called by her name. She gets up obediently and walks toward the bed. The director gives her a few instructions. You saw her slap him? He's really angry. He slaps her back, throws her on the bed and rapes her. Got it?

She follows the actress to her dressing room, to change into what the actress was wearing. She steals a glimpse at the actress's body—way below her expectations. "Great body," the actress tells her, a tinge of envy in her voice.

Songhwa got slapped four times. The actor never asked if it hurt. He threw her on the bed five times, and tore her clothes off four times. She had to stand naked for about three hours, enduring the actor's sweaty odor. "Try not to bruise me," she protested gently, but it was as if he hadn't heard; he didn't bother answering.

The filming complete, Songhwa was about to leave when the director came over and handed her an envelope containing her fee. Outside, she bought two bottles of Gatorade and gulped them down. Gets absorbed quicker than water, they say . . . But while the glucose was being absorbed in her body, the pager had still not vibrated.

On her way home she stopped at the corner store and bought four bottles of Hite beer and a bag of peanuts. On days like this she had to have a drink. Drinking alone? Well, what can you do? She walked in, pulled off her dress and dug out a pair of panties and a bra. That's better. Without underwear on, she felt restless, ungrounded. She sat down at the table and cracked open a beer.

What's he like? she wonders as she fondles the pager. She makes him into a cabaret-hopping pimp, then a poor student, then a rebellious second-generation corporate son, then a writer. Of these, she liked the writer best. *It's set to vibrate.* Only a writer would be capable of saying something like that. He probably got dumped by his girlfriend because he doesn't have a steady job and does nothing but write all day. His ex probably ended up marrying somebody else and going abroad to study, and he was battling loneliness when he saw her in the subway. He's probably thinking about her right now and writing a short story about it. That's why he's so scared of meeting her. Because if he does, and the fantasy is shattered, he'll never be able to finish the story.

She decided to wait. Until he finishes the story. And when the pager does vibrate, it will signal that the story is completed. She'll buy him a drink with the money she made getting pretend-raped. Under a calendar advertising a clear, chilled rice brew.

3. No Page

When I opened my eyes, it was well past one. As soon as I was up, I deliberated again: should I page her, or not? Let's wash up first. I dragged myself out of bed and went into the bathroom. In the mirror a scruffy-looking man looked back at me.

"Imagination is another level of reality," I mumbled at the mirror. Suddenly, I was dying to see her. The girl I'd seen leaning against the wall inside Ch'ungmuro Station. The girl posing with absolute, perfect charm.

I began to feel hungry. I rummaged through the fridge and found a slice of cold pizza and some orange juice. The fridge was full of all kinds of food. Several times Suji had given it a good cleaning, going after the job with religious zeal, like a priest at Holy Communion. But for some reason, I'd never really warmed up to that sparkling fridge. It was so clean and neat that eating anything from it actually felt like Holy Communion. She was like a descendant of light, and as befits a descendant of light she had no interest in the power of imagination. When you think about it, she did the right thing by getting out of this dark den and going to study overseas with a guy who has it together. Were we to break up all over again, I'd probably send her off with the same line: *Good luck in your studies.*

I chucked the pizza box in the garbage and sat at the desk. I was behind on the article for the university in Taegu, and after that was done, I had to write a story by the end of the year to enter in a literary competition. Suji was right—I couldn't live like this forever.

Okay, let's get going. But first, some unfinished business to take care of. I have to page the girl. I have to call her, now that she's carrying my pager, my plaything. I took a deep breath and picked up the phone. Slowly I dialed the ten-digit number, and my voice greeted me on the other end. "Hi, you've reached Yi Yŏnshik. To leave a numeric page press *one*. To leave a voice message, press *two*. I'll get back to you as soon as possible." I pressed 1 and carefully entered the seven digits of my phone number. Then I hung up.

Would she have kept the pager on vibrate? What would she be doing at this moment? Could she possibly be thinking about me?

I didn't have to fantasize long.

Beep. Beep. Beep. Somewhere a frantic signal was going off. I was surprised and completely confused. Turning my room upside down, I finally discovered the source of the commotion. It was in the inner pocket of my jacket—my black, stumpy, generic pager, my number flashing desolately on the display. I'd had it all along.

So nothing had changed. As usual, I'd chickened out at the last minute. What would have happened had I really given her the pager? Whatever—real life is tedious, and fantasy is exciting. *It's set to vibrate?* What a joke! My laughter seeped into the corners of the tiny apartment.

As I turn on the computer, I decide to let go of the fantasy of paging the girl. I mean, it's just my own number that's going to end up on display. I ended up paging myself. That's what my fantasies amount to: an ex-lover's shadow, empty booze bottles piling up night after night, twenty fairy girls that can be created in the course of a single night.

I decide that this is a story waiting to be written. A short story that would start "She was about to get her period."

While making this decision I notice my calendar. Today is October first, but the calendar is still showing September. I get up and tear off September and scrutinize the half-naked girl lying on the rock. She looks so familiar . . . where have I seen her?

WAXEN WINGS

Ha Sŏngnan

Translated by Janet Hong

Ha Sŏngnan was born in 1967. Since her debut in 1996 she has firmly established herself as one of Korea's most important contemporary writers. She has been honored with numerous awards, including the thirtieth Tongin Literature Prize for "Blooms of Mold" (Komp'angi kkot, 1998) and most recently the fifty-fourth Contemporary Literature Award for "Alpha Time" (Alp'a ŭi sigan, 2008). ▨ In "Waxen Wings," one of her earlier stories, we see the beginnings of her interest in the themes of ambiguous alienation and anonymity. We also discover the traits we enjoy in her more recent work—clean and compact sentences, meticulous but perceptive description, and plotlines that move between reality and fantasy. ▨ "Waxen Wings" features a nameless character who is obsessed with being airborne, or escaping the confines of gravity. We are offered intimate glimpses of this character as we move through various episodes of her life. The distinctive feature of this story is the second-person narrative. Although it is the least common narrative mode in literary fiction (and difficult to pull off), here it is well suited to the nature of the piece. A tragic story risks becoming sentimental if told in the first person, but may become too detached if told in the third person. In "Waxen Wings," the second-person narrative affords the reader the best of both worlds: enough distance from sentimentality and enough intimacy for empathy. That the story is told mostly in the present tense also lends it a sense of immediacy, enabling us to closely follow the repeated frustration of the girl's desire to take flight, culminating in a memorable climax. ■ Like a microscope, Ha's eye inspects the smallest object or incident in such detail that even the most familiar becomes strange and menacing. However, her view is never cold or clinical. This is precisely her gift—the ability to elicit sympathy and tenderness through a constant accumulation of details. In "Waxen Wings" and other fictional works, Ha Sŏngnan examines the truth about ordinary people and the loneliness of their existence, affording us a fresh glimpse of our society while making profound statements about the human condition. ■ "Waxen Wings" (Ch'onnong nalgae) first appeared in the spring 1999 issue of *21 segi munhak* (21st-century literature).

—Janet Hong

Your watch stopped at 3:14. The second hand fell off when the glass cover shattered. Within minutes you were unconscious. During what seemed like a nap that continued a little longer than usual, the seasons slowly changed in the front lawn, right below your hospital room window.

When you could walk on your own you pushed the IV stand out onto the lawn and sat in the sun. Sometimes you glanced at your watch as if waiting for someone. It was always 3:14. From the lawn you had a clear view down to the main entrance. The gate was always crowded with ambulances and visitors bearing gifts. But the girl wearing a large backpack and carrying a shoe bag caught your eye; she stared about while picking her way through the bustle. She walked not on the sidewalk but up the middle of the entrance road, and ambulances with their patients and taxis with their passengers passed through her as they sped away. Each time, the girl went fuzzy like an image on a television set with poor reception. From where you sat, you waited for that little girl. Leaping through a hole in time, a ten-year-old you came mirage-like to visit the you who was now twenty-seven.

You, ten years old, are cutting across the school field. You're alone once again, unable to tag along with the others. They had burst outside, crashing into you in their rush while you were still in your indoor shoes. They're probably hanging around the snack stand, the comic-book shop, or the stationery store in front of the school right about now. You are shorter by a foot than the other girls your age. When you're standing next to them your small size becomes even more obvious. You look maybe six or seven at the most. The kids in your class call you Birdie. Your backpack straps dig into your shoulders and the shoe bag drags on the dirt, leaving a lazy, winding trail. The abandoned field looks all the more vast today. You've never cut across it before. You prefer walking along its fringes, always in the shadow of the school building. Already you feel that walking across like this is too much; never again will you cut across another field, hotel lobby, or lounge. You had taken this shortcut in your rashness to catch up with the others, but your steps lag. You finally make it to the school gate, but lack the courage to step out and talk to them. You walk toward the playground where rainbow-colored tires are half embedded in the ground. The swing is swaying gently, as if someone has just been on it. You sit on the wooden seat without taking off your backpack. As you trail your toes in the dirt, the swing starts to move back and forth and soon you're in full motion. You toss your backpack and shoe bag onto the sand and kick your feet in the air. Once you fall into the rhythm of the swing, you become one with the motion and are carried out and back, like seaweed rolling on the waves. The arc of the swing gets wider and the seat goes up as high as the metal crossbeam from where the chains hang, and your body becomes parallel to the ground. You're covered with sweat and your mouth is pasty.

One day, after pumping yourself up as high as the beam, you let go of the chains. Freed from the swing, your body soars—only for the briefest moment, but you feel as though you're flying. If not for the law of gravity you would have risen into the air, past the leaves of the sycamores flanking the field, and disappeared beyond the five-story school building. But like Newton's apple, your small, light body is pulled to earth, and you land deftly on the sand.

Soon enough you learn that your hang time—the time you're able to remain airborne—is a little longer than the other children's. Five swings hang from the crossbeam and sometimes five children are on the swings at once. The other kids try to copy you and jump in midair. But no sooner have they jumped than they tumble onto the sand. By now, you can even pick a spot to alight on while you're pumping your legs. Where you've landed there are prints, as neat and clearly etched as a bird's.

While others grow tired of the swings and move on to the adventure playground and the seesaw, you stay on the swings. While

swinging, you think of different ways to make a bigger jump, different ways to hover longer in the air, but in the end, you curl up in midair and do a somersault. In a flash, all the kids abandon their games
and gather around you.

Hey, that's easy! I can do that too. A jealous classmate tries to copy
you and jumps from the swings. But she thuds head first into the
sand, and in the next moment she's howling through her sand-filled
mouth. She's bleeding from the nose and her face is scratched up.
Your homeroom teacher comes running.

This is very dangerous! Who started this?

All at once, every gaze is directed at you. But now the eyes are
cold. After this incident, you never see anyone jump from the swings,
at least not on the school playground. You don't dare go near the
swings again.

Teacher, I want to fly, but the ground keeps pulling me down.

You sit facing your teacher in the empty classroom after everyone
has gone home. For the first time the teacher looks at you very closely.

What a small child. She recalls the woolen dress she recently
bought; it had accidentally shrunk in the wash. Every feature is
smaller on this child, just like the shrunken dress. Suddenly, an
uneasy thought flashes across her mind. This child who wants to
fly, what if she decides to take flight from the roof of the school? The
teacher shakes her head as if to dislodge this disturbing thought, but
in her mind you keep falling from the school roof. The teacher looks
into your small eyes and speaks, emphasizing each word.

*I want you to listen very carefully. Only birds can fly. It's impossible
for people to fly. You're just able to stay in the air a little longer than the
other kids, that's all. Can you please tell your mother to come see me?*

But your mother comes home from work at seven o'clock every
night, and if she misses even a single day, she'll lose three days' pay.
For lack of anything better, your teacher makes you write "People
cannot fly" over and over again on the chalkboard. Because you're so
small, your writing reaches only halfway up the board. The teacher
stands behind you, watching. *So that's why they call you Birdie.*

When you enter middle school you push aside thoughts of flying; you are too old to play on the swings, and you're no longer naïve enough to confess your desire to fly. You learn more about this gravity that keeps pulling you down to the ground. Back then it was the fashion among students to write famous quotes in their notebook, but instead of writing something like "Even if I knew that tomorrow the world would go to pieces, I would still plant my apple tree," you write, "The force of gravity between two objects is directly proportional to the product of their masses and inversely proportional to the square of the distance between them." You believe that if people could escape the confines of gravity, they could fly like birds. But you find that even the task of simplifying the law of gravity is difficult. Although you're in middle school now, you're still smaller than the other girls. The average height of a middle school girl then was five-feet-two, but you're a mere four-feet-nine.

One day, you're about to go back to your homeroom after gym class, but the teacher tells you to stay behind. Thick exercise mats cushion the concrete floor, and you're shivering from the cold—the gym feels like the inside of a fridge. A voice rings out from the dark.

So you're the girl the gym teacher mentioned? Come over here.

You hesitate because of the mats.

It's okay, just walk across with your shoes on, but it'll be the last time.

You walk toward the voice but because of the padded mats, you keep stumbling. A young woman with short hair is sitting on a vault. In her hand is a long stick that touches the ground. Although it's March and still cold outside, her legs exposed below her short skirt are bare. On her small dangling feet are kid-size indoor shoes.

Shall we have a look?

She hops down from the vault. Up close she's much smaller than you had guessed.

From now on as soon as you're dismissed from school, you run straight to the gym. There, no one calls you Birdie. Everyone is small like you. You finally feel at peace. You put the vault the older students will use into position and clean the gym after practice. On sunny days you drag all the mats outside to air them out. Because the school sits on top of a hill, you can even see them laid out in front of the gym from the bus stop at the bottom of the hill. The light reflecting off them makes the gym look like a snow-capped peak. Practice starts with front and back rolls, then the splits. When you sit with your legs spread out, straining to do the splits, the coach instructs the older students to sit on your shoulders. If you cry out, the coach jabs you in the stomach with her stick. The tender flesh around your groin turns black and blue. You wear the same leotard as all the other gymnasts, but you are so scrawny that the leotard keeps riding up to reveal the cheeks of your small bottom. You get home later and later. Now, it's your mother who waits up for you. She buys you a wristwatch, but your wrist is so small that you have to punch a new hole in the strap. Summer comes and you practice your vaults. You don't take off the watch, even though the sweat that collects under the leather band makes your skin swell, leaving a pale strip around your wrist. While you perform your endless tumbles, autumn changes to winter and winter changes to spring.

Your first period still hasn't come. You've noticed that every month, the girl sitting next to you in school sneaks a hand into her bag, whisks out a mysterious object and hides it in the folds of her clothes, then slips away to the bathroom. You also don't show the usual signs of sexual maturity. No habits that are common to middle school girls like pulling down a bra that keeps riding up. No photos of golden-haired boys, singers, and movie stars in your bag. On your way to the gym after school, you see the other girls flock to the TV station to watch a broadcast on the big monitor outside. They've never even heard of the people you're interested in, like Nadia Comăneci and Nellie Kim. Because of practices and meets, there are many days when your desk is empty. For this reason, you earn the envy of others.

In eighth grade, you start watching a girl named Yunhŭi—a tenth grader and already the Seoul representative at the national games, where she won gold in the balance beam. Sometimes you leave school and linger around the nearby high school field. When Yunhŭi does a demonstration on the beam, you study her every move, transfixed. Just from the way she mounts the beam, you can tell she's special. Instead of placing the springboard at the end of the beam like the other gymnasts, she positions it alongside the beam. She does her approach run, jumps, and then lands doing the splits, on a surface that's only four inches wide. Even though you're still learning the basics, you sometimes go up on the beam when no one is around. Every time you take a step, you have to flap your arms like a bird to keep your balance. Like Yunhŭi, you let your hair grow out and pull it back into a knot at the crown of your head. You need a dozen bobby pins to anchor the willful strands. With your hair pulled back so severely, your eyebrows and the corners of your eyes are yanked up, making you look perpetually angry.

Your event is the uneven bars. When you soar between the 8-foot and 5-foot bars, it's easy to see how small you are and how long you hang in the air. But when you try to keep yourself straight during the handstand, your arms keep shaking. Full turn after cast handstand, swing to low bar, then transfer to high bar. But then your hands slip and you fall to the mat. Every time this happens, the coach's long stick jabs your stomach. As further punishment, you have to do an hour-long handstand in the middle of the gym. If you fall over or break your form, you have to start all over again. Blood pumps down into your face, and your arms that are holding up your body start to wobble uncontrollably. Bare legs—some pale, others reddish or sallow—pass by, and an occasional sarcastic remark is tossed your way. A pair of pale slender legs stop in front of your face. The calves and thighs visible above the legwarmers are covered with dark purple bruises. You raise your blood-gorged face. It's Yunhŭi. Because it's Yunhŭi, your face turns even redder.

With handstands, try to forget that it's you you're holding up and pretend that you're holding up the ground. It works for me. And that landing earlier was really impressive.

You don't get to see Yunhŭi at the gym anymore. She was selected for the Asian Games and so she's moved to the athletes' village. Every night, you write her a letter. You lose interest in going to the gym. For being late, you have to do leapfrogs and handstands or hang from the bar. You see a photo of Yunhŭi in the sports section, in a feature on athletes to watch in the Asian Games. You're confident, of course, but so is your coach, that Yunhŭi will receive a medal. But when the news arrives, it's not about medals. Yunhŭi has had an accident. She took a bad fall in practice, damaged her spinal cord, and is paralyzed from the neck down.

Yunhŭi doesn't come back to school. Now, you no longer struggle to keep your body straight when doing a handstand on the bar. After a full turn on the high bar, you can even perform two and a half flips before you land. You recall how you used to ride the swings as a ten-year-old. Once again, the desire to fly takes hold and you begin the familiar battle against gravity. In ninth grade, you become the star athlete of your school. Your peculiar way of walking—body straight, chin and heels raised high—becomes ingrained in you.

Once you visit Yunhŭi instead of going to the gym. After her accident, she remained in hospital care. She is having lunch when you arrive. She clamps her mouth shut when a middle-aged woman, who appears to be her mother, tries to feed her. After attempting to pry Yunhŭi's mouth open with the spoon, the woman smacks her daughter on the head. Yunhŭi falls across the bed and her face is buried in the pillow, but she cannot get up. The mother starts to weep; she pulls her daughter up and places a pillow behind her back. The girl who is leaning pathetically against the bedframe is not the Yunhŭi you knew. She is plump and white. Even her wrists that peep out from the cuffs of her hospital gown are covered with fat folds; they look like silkworms. Her hair that used to be pulled back in a neat knot is cut so short it leaves her ears in plain sight. You go home without entering the ward. That day, you cut your hair short. Because you skipped practice and cut your hair, your coach yells at you while jabbing your stomach with her rod. You have to clean the gym, a lowly job reserved only for seventh graders, and you stay behind, practicing well into the night to make up for missing practice. You keep falling off the uneven bars and you run toward the springboard only to stop and repeat the approach run. Once on the vault, before you can take a step, you tumble to the mat. All of a sudden, you get sharp pains in your stomach as if your coach is jabbing you again with her stick. It's your first menstruation.

In high school the routine is the same. You still go to the gym, you still train under the coach with the bare legs. When there's a tournament coming up, you don't go to class. Swing, support, release; while you repeat these steps, the bruises on your body multiply. Countless times a day you squeeze the rosin bag with your callused hands. Even though you chalk just your hands, you're covered all over with powder; there are white handprints on your leotard, legs, and arms as if someone has slapped you. Menthol sports rubs are now your brand of perfume. Your face is angular and as you've grown more accustomed to the bars and support stance, your torso has taken on the shape of an inverted triangle.

You unfasten your watch. When you put the pin through the next hole in the strap, an ominous feeling comes over you. You're at the Seoul tryouts for the National Games to perform your uneven bars routine. And there, your premonition becomes a reality. You could have done the routine with your eyes closed, from the countless hours of practice. Swing from low bar to high bar, grip, then cast to handstand, hold, release and catch bar three times in a row, somersault and catch bar again—the routine was as familiar to you as breathing. But instead of catching the bar again, you clutch at air and fall helplessly to the mat. To finish your performance, you take hold of the bar again. In the hope of making up for your deductions, you become too ambitious, and attempt a triple somersault instead of a two-and-a-half for your dismount. You've been practicing the triple *salto* on your own, but making it barely two times out of ten. You release the bar and flip three times in the air. Instead of landing on both feet, you plant your rear-end on the mat. You receive a 7.8 out of a perfect 10. A student from another school becomes the Seoul representative.

At school, you sit at the very front of the classroom. You copy down the math problems from the chalkboard, but because of your frequent absences you can't understand any of the questions. Just then, the student behind you pokes you in the back with a pencil. *Hey, you mind lowering your head a little? I can't see the board because of you.* In half a year you've grown nearly five inches.

You're now the tallest on your team. For your dismount, even before you can do two flips, you land bottom first. Your rear-end, somehow having filled out, hits the mat with a dull thud, like a ripe persimmon bursting as it plops to the ground. The other gymnasts laugh. Once again people start to call you Birdie, but this time, it's for a different reason. Every day you stay late to practice on your own, but even hanging from a bar becomes difficult because of the weight you've gained. The girl from your childhood, the one who fell face first into the sand from the swings, comes to mind. You keep falling off and each time, you chalk up, spit into your hands, then leap up to the bars again. You even run out of saliva to spit into your hands. The gymnastics equipment is spread around you. You find yourself thinking more and more about falling off an apparatus than climbing onto it.

The coach calls out to you as you're about to remove your shoes. *It's okay, don't bother, I just need to see you for a minute.*

You realize that at some point you've started to tower over her. You recall the day you first met her. Since then, she has gotten married and become the mother of two, but she hasn't changed a bit; as always, she is barelegged and dressed in a short skirt. She taps the springboard with her rod. *What in the world are you eating? Did somebody come up with a magic growth pill?* Her voice echoes in the gym. *Who would have guessed you'd shoot up like a bean sprout overnight?* She's the one who is angry. You stand in front of her with your head hanging down, as if you've actually eaten something you shouldn't have. *I've seen cases where people had to quit because of an injury to their Achilles tendon or spinal cord, but never something like this. . . . Maybe it's better this way, since a gymnast's career is so short.*

As you shove open the gym door, the coach calls out to you. *Study hard, all right?* Walking down the hill, you consider your options. Your palms smelled of rosin and spit no matter how often you scrubbed them with soap, and you felt more comfortable with the uneven bars, vault, and balance beam than with math, English, and Korean. You and your coach had believed that you were done growing. Never, in your wildest dreams, had you imagined that you would one day be tall.

You return to your eleventh grade classroom. It's almost midnight when you get home after the review sessions. You take out your old textbook from tenth grade, but it's scarcely any easier. You occasionally go to the gym to practice. When you make a mistake, the coach no longer comes running. You don't even get in trouble. Sometimes you walk up to the gym door, but end up loitering about the building, unable to go inside. The orange glow coming through the window seems inviting. You stand outside and listen to the sounds of practice: the thump of bodies hitting the mats, the gymnasts' spirited cries, and the coach's fierce voice. Then you head home.

Dressed in a tracksuit with your gym bag in hand, you stand in front of Ch'anggyŏng Palace. To this day, you still don't understand why you went there. You probably remembered the zoo you went to as a child, but it's been moved to a new location. While you wait for the palace doors to open, you eat a corndog and some fish cake soup to take the edge off your hunger.

At the break of dawn you are the lone visitor. A few times, you walk slowly past Ch'anggyŏng, then across the bridge toward Ch'angdŏk Palace and back. You're joined by a crowd of Japanese tourists; they chat nearby, their language like the whine of mosquitoes. You sit on a bench in front of an old hut, an area that most people don't seek. A flock of pigeons swoop down and peck at the ground. You buy a bag of popcorn at the concession. Every handful you throw causes a swarm to chase after the popcorn. Amongst this flock is one that's missing a left toe and one with a sty in its eye. There's also one that stands motionless in the same spot, blinking very slowly, while the other pigeons surge greedily. You watch this pigeon. The P.A. system announces that it's closing time. You grab your bag and are about to get up when the pigeon collapses. For the first time in your life, you witness the moment life escapes from a living thing. All the visitors have left. You continue to stand there even after the concession clerks have gone home. The sun starts to set, and everything gets dark quickly. All the pigeons have flown off except for the one by your feet. Rigor mortis has set in. You open your bag to find something to dig with, but find only your leotard, a roll-on muscle relaxant, a notebook, and some pens. You start to dig with your pen. The ground is harder than you thought and your pen breaks. You use your fingers instead and dig a small hole. Blood forms under your dirt-filled fingernails. You shroud the pigeon in your leotard, lay it to rest in the hole, cover it up with dirt, and pat it down with your foot. Two security guards walk toward you. Before they see you, you scramble up onto the old hut behind the bench. The guards' flashlights move away. You sit on the tiled roof and gaze out into the woods, toward the lake and the bridge, but all you see are different shades of darkness. You peer at shadows to guess where the zoo used to be. From the top of the roof, you watch the sun come up. You climb down from the roof and walk toward the main entrance, but it's closed. For you, climbing over the Ch'anggyŏng Palace wall is a piece of cake.

You miss a day of school, but nobody notices, since it's more common for you to be absent. You no longer go to the gym. Around this time you hear that Yunhŭi has entered a seminary. By the time you're off the gymnastics team for good, you've grown even more. You're now five-feet-five.

Your old watch stops more often now.

Excuse me, Miss, do you have the time?

You're on your way back from the bank, where you rushed to make a deposit before closing time. You help with the accounts at an apartment manager's office. Six years older and a graduate of a trade high school, the bookkeeper you work for always wastes time and completes her work only when the bank is about to close, making you run to the bank every day. The way back takes twice as long.

Miss, what's the time, please?

The scooter that's blocking your path—you realize you've seen it before. You look at your old watch. *It's two thirty.*

Confused, the man looks up at your face. *That's strange. It was around two thirty when I was having lunch. Are you sure it's two thirty?*

There's a kind of belligerent quality to his eyes. The second hand on your watch isn't moving. You hold your wrist up to your ear, but don't hear anything. When did it stop? You realize you haven't looked at your watch for a long time.

It's okay, thanks anyway. Hey, do you take the number 62 bus?

You are confused by his question.

Same time every day, I see you at the bus stop. Do you know what a water strider is? The insect with long skinny legs that stands on water? You reminded me of a water strider, the way you stood at the bus stop. There's a watch repair shop on the main street. And beside it there's a store with a big sign that says Movie Town. I work there. It's right across the street from the bus stop. Well, I guess I'll see you around.

With that, he starts to putter off on the scooter. But then he yells, *It's actually five to five right now. And my name is Kang Hyŏkchun!*

While the watch repairman puts a new battery in your watch, you look out the window. Across the four-lane street is your bus stop.

Wow, it's been a while since I've seen this. I used to wear the same brand myself when I was young. They don't make this kind anymore. They've come up with these ones instead.

The man slides open the glass display and takes out a couple of watches from a bed of cotton. He lays them down on the glass.

Here, take a look. All these watches are from the same manufacturer. The design and quality are just as good as imports. I'm not asking you to buy them, all I'm saying is take a look. Isn't it normal these days to own a few watches? This one with the leather strap is nice as a more casual option and this one right here with the gold bracelet is an excellent choice if it's a dressy look you're after.

You hold one of the watches up to your ear in order to hear the ticking of the second hand. But the shop is full of the ticking of clocks large and small. On the wall facing the window are all sorts of clocks, from wall clocks to alarm clocks with cartoon character designs. The hour and minute hands all point to the same time. You pick one out and use it to set your watch.

Next you stop by a neighborhood bookstore and buy a full-color insect picture book. Within its pages is a photo of a water strider darting over the water with its long slender legs. Its legs are taut like guitar strings. If it gets hit by a raindrop or if the current should suddenly turn rough, it looks as if it would get swallowed up. But as vulnerable as it appears, it also has a kind of charm. Why must a water strider stand on water? There is more than enough land in the world for its legs to stand safely on. It uses surface tension to stand on water and the long hairs on its legs to skate across. You picture the strider gliding across water.

The front window of Movie Town is plastered with posters advertising video release dates for the latest movies. While you wait for your bus you keep glancing at the store. The man's job is to deliver, then pick up the videos that people order on the phone. There are times when his scooter would be parked out front on the tree-lined sidewalk. At age twenty-three, you watch him as you once watched Yunhŭi. The #62 comes and goes without you on it.

Hey, you just missed your bus! What are you doing?

You didn't notice the scooter drawing up behind you.

Did you hear me? Your bus just left. That's already the second one you've missed.

Instead of getting on the third #62, you're sitting across from him at a café called Jardin. You didn't realize it when he was sitting on the scooter, but the man is much shorter than you. A girl in a green apron sets down two cups of coffee.

Wow, you're taller than I thought. Five-foot-six?

You grew a little more after you graduated from high school. You've never actually measured yourself, but when you talk to the men you work with, you're at eye level with all of them. You're no longer a small high school girl who picks out clothes from the junior section.

Do you like short guys? He smiles awkwardly while adding sugar to his coffee.

You saw many male gymnasts at various tournaments. They too were short compared with the other male students. You were used to seeing short men.

He tells you that he was a child star who had the main role in a children's show. *Believe it or not, there are still people who recognize me. It's really embarrassing when they ask for an autograph.*

The man goes on to list a few actors he worked with who have risen to stardom. The names are familiar. He didn't grow after the age of fifteen. He is still waiting for the opportunity to make his big screen debut, and in the meantime, working at the video store wasn't a bad idea—he might as well hone his acting skills and watch movies for free. He has memorized every famous movie line and could even talk with a cigarette dangling from his mouth like Humphrey Bogart.

The person who's supposed to grow stops growing and the person who isn't supposed to grow ends up this tall? That's life for you. 'Life isn't always what one likes, is it?' Have you seen Roman Holiday*? It's a line from that movie.*

So like all couples, the two of you sometimes go for a beer or catch a midnight flick. He tries to recite the right movie line at the right time and place, but he makes you laugh instead by toasting you with the famous line from *Casablanca*—"Here's looking at you, kid"—when you clink beer glasses together. He also makes you laugh when he says, "Nor art, nor nature ever created a lovelier thing than you" as he is leaving after walking you home. When he kisses you for the first time, it's "Don't kiss me. If you kiss me, I won't be able to leave."

He's not at the place where the two of you decided to meet. You wait for his scooter in front of the video store. But when it arrives, it's a stranger who's riding it.

Didn't Hyŏkchun come in today?

The man says he doesn't recognize the name and tells you to go ask inside. The owner, who is checking in some videos, recognizes you.

That guy, he won't be coming in anymore. What do you expect with guys who work at a place like this? They migrate like birds, flying around from place to place. He asked me to give you this.

He hands you an envelope. There's a single sentence written in the center of an A4 page: "I'd rather lose you than destroy you" and below, in tiny print, "Maria in *Maria's Lovers*."

What's it say? He didn't tell you some nonsense about how he used to be an actor, did he? Told you his name was Hyŏkchun? I bet you that's fake, too. Probably has over ten names he goes by. Hyŏkchun—yeah, right!

You decide not to believe the owner. You cross the street and stand at the bus stop. The #62 goes by. You don't even know his name. Everything he did and said to you for the last six months—he could have taken it from some movie. Although he borrowed a line to say goodbye, you think that the words "I'd rather lose you than destroy you" are true. A movie you once saw crosses your mind. In it Audrey Hepburn says to Cary Grant, "Oh, I love you, Adam, Alex, Peter, Brian . . . whatever your name is." As you walk down the street you mumble to yourself: *Oh, I love you, Hyŏkchun, Kyŏngshik, Ŭnho, Ch'angmin, Minsu . . . whatever your name is.*

Your hand shovel doesn't work very well—the ground is too hard. And you can't quite remember the exact location either. Since the hole you dug wasn't deep, you should be able to feel it if you poke the ground with the shovel. The pigeon should have rotted away without a trace, but your leotard, made of a cheap nylon weave, won't decompose even after you die. Perhaps a heavy downpour swept away the top layer of earth, leaving the leotard in plain view, and the custodian tossed it out. All day until the sun sets, you poke and prod at spots that look right, but nothing turns up. You end up digging dozens of holes in front of the old hut you climbed that night. In the end, you start to think that perhaps you had it all wrong and you buried it somewhere entirely different, maybe Ch'angdŏk Palace and not Ch'anggyŏng Palace. That day you walked back and forth between the two palaces at least five times. You're not even sure which wall you jumped—the one near the Tonhwa Gate or the one near the Honghwa Gate. To your inexperienced eye, all the traditional buildings look the same.

Twenty-six years old, you soar through the sky. You, who stayed airborne for only a moment when you jumped from the swings, can now stay in the air for as long as you want. You belong to the hang gliding club called Icarus Wings. From high up, the houses and trees below look like they're stuck together. Once you have completed your test flights on ground and the bunny hills, you are able to hang glide from higher places. Once a month you attend the club meetings. The president of the club warned beginners not to be too ambitious. In hang gliding, there is something called the "glide ratio to target," the ratio of the distance glided to the distance fallen. Although you haven't quite mastered it, you are able to stay aloft longer than the other beginners. In order to turn, you twist yourself to the left and to the right. You navigate the glider by moving the bar, which changes the direction of the sail. When you land, your gymnastic training is obvious. While others waddle unsteadily with their rear-ends sticking out like ducks and then are dragged by the glider, you pull off a flawless landing.

You go up a mountain with expert pilots. Your hang glider, transported to the end of the road by car, must be carried to the summit. Under your waterproof parka, your clothes are soaked with sweat. At the top, you assemble the glider, attach the sail, and put on your helmet. You are fully aware of what to do in case of an emergency. Those who are more experienced go first. They sail slowly down the mountain in wide, gentle arcs. Since the current can change at any time, depending on the temperature and topography, you pay close attention to the person who goes before you. Below the cliff is a dense growth of pines and an occasional crag jutting out from the deep green. You must sail over this area and land in a flat field. You take a running start and jump. You find yourself buoyed upward. It's as exhilarating as sticking your head out the window of a racing car. The sweat you worked up from the climb dries. Far below you can see the path you took, snaking its way to the peak. As you begin to pass the pine grove you see the landing area. Your companions who have already landed are waving at you. But the moment you try to square yourself to land, your sail begins to rattle violently. Suddenly, the wind hitting your face changes direction. You lean the control bar to the left, but a gust of wind from below sends your glider shooting up. In the blink of an eye, you're far from the field. You move the bar this way and that but the sail doesn't obey. Another gust of wind hits you, this time from your right. Your glider starts to nosedive. You struggle to stay in the air a little longer, but it's no use—you're sucked into the pines. A wide crag looms up, you let go of the bar, and cover your face with your hands.

There is a flower basket on top of the bedside locker. *We wish you a full and speedy recovery.* It looks like you've had a visit from the club; the words "Icarus Wings Hang Gliding Club" are written on the pink ribbon that trails from the basket. The roses are withering into a blackish red. Your mother tells you what one of the members said— if not for the sail, your injury could have been much worse—but you know it's your long hang time that spared you.

People are meant to have both feet planted on solid ground. Every time you wake, your mother says these words over and over again. You get moved from the ICU to a general ward. Because of the chitchat of visitors and the coin-operated TV, the room is always noisy. After the scars heal and a period in rehabilitation, you're discharged.

The president of the hang gliding club calls occasionally to see how you're doing. You assure him that you'll never make a mistake like that again. After your crash, two other women dropped out of the club. The next scheduled flight is in Chŏlla Province. You recall the sensation of being up in the air. You see an aerial view of the narrow trail you followed to the top. *It might be a little difficult this time, but next time you go, please let me know.* You hang up with a chuckle. But you never hear back from him.

On nights you couldn't fall asleep, you went out onto the glassed-in balcony and looked out the window. But too often you failed to catch the outside view, and there were more and more days where you found yourself gazing at your reflection. You told yourself that the sleepless nights would stop once you started exercising again. Illuminated by the security light, the playground sand shone like a glacier field. The shadows cast by the swings grew and shrank as they undulated on the sand. It was then that you saw her—the girl on the swing. You recognized this girl. It was you, ten years old, still on the swings. You threw on a sweater and opened the door. It had been a long time since you last took in some fresh air. Walking to the swing set was as difficult as cutting across the school field as a child. But the girl was gone. You sat on the swing and gripped the metal chains. You backed up two paces and lifted your feet. The swing began to move slowly. The playground safety-rule board loomed up, then grew distant. You felt dizzy. The chains started to squeak. It took much longer than before to propel yourself up. The moment your swing went as high as the beam, you let go of the chains without thinking and jumped. Your body hung in midair. You curled up in a ball, clutching your legs and drawing your chin into your chest. But there wasn't enough time for even one somersault. Like a gunny-sack, you flopped onto the sand. As you hit the ground, you heard your right leg crack and out it popped from under your skirt, glancing off the seesaw and dropping to the sand. *My leg!* As you tried to stand to fetch your prosthetic limb, you noticed your watch. Even in the dim security light, you could read the two hands—3:14.

When you had woken up in the ICU, you had looked at the curled-up petals on the wilting rose wreath and the white bed sheet. Unlike the bulge in the sheet where your left leg was, the area covering what should have been your right leg had been flat and smooth.

You managed to rise on one leg and moved toward the seesaw. Your shadow was stretched out long on the sand. You looked at the shadow cast by the stump and the empty space below it. In that shadow, half of you could now forever hang in midair.

CORPSES

P'yŏn Hyeyŏng
Translated by Cindy Chen

Women's fiction in South Korea has flourished since the
mid-1990s arrival of a new generation of writers, most
of them born in the 1960s and 1970s. One of the primary reasons for their collective success is the increasing
diversity of their voices, and one of the most distinctive of
these fictional voices is that of **P'yŏn Hyeyŏng** (b. 1972).
To readers accustomed to stories set in the calm interior
landscape of memory, to women's stories of what it has
meant to be a woman in Korea, P'yŏn's debut story collection, *Mallow Gardens* (Aoi Kadŭn, 2005), is likely to
come as a shock. The stories in it are visceral and violent
and rife with strong images—not necessarily a pleasant
reading experience, but at the same time an experience
that will leave few readers complacent. The title story is a

prescient tale of a grotesque family attempting to survive
an apocalyptic plague. It seems inspired in equal parts
by actual events (a SARS outbreak in 2003), American
pulp fiction (Richard Matheson's *I Am Legend*), and such
visionary films as Peter Weir's *The Last Wave* (which
shares with P'yŏn's story frog-infested rainfall). It is an
unsettling story in which the characters' ages are inde-
terminate, the narrator's biological mother is referred to
as "the woman," and reproductive capacity is the main
signifier of one's existence. A fortress mentality is in play
until the end of the story, which in its image of the protagonist taking flight strangely echoes the ending of Yi Sang's
"Wings," one of the most subversive of modern Korean
short stories. ■ P'yŏn is herself a profoundly subversive
writer. Whereas the Korean literary establishment has
long privileged fiction that addresses issues deemed relevant historically, politically, or culturally, her stories are
image-driven, and the images are strong stuff indeed—
body parts, body fluids, decay, fecundity, lushness. In a
society whose contemporary history has been marked
by the rationality and logic of authoritarian government
and economic development, P'yŏn offers us a surreal,
irrational world of chaos and confusion. In a tradition-
ally patriarchal culture she tells her stories from the point
of view of men who are subordinated to women and at
the mercy of animals. In the literary tradition of modern
Korea confinement is arguably the most important motif,
but P'yŏn invests her stories with the opposite of confinement—space, which is equally disorienting be it psychological, as in "Corpses," or physical, as in the title story of
her second story collection, *To the Kennels* (Sayukchang
tchogŭro, 2006). ■ The stories in *To the Kennels* are
only slightly tamer. The title story is ironic in that a cho-

rus of dogs, presumably bred for slaughter, beguile and disorient the protagonist. And the most recent story in that collection, "The First Anniversary" (Ch'ŏtpŏntchae kinyŏm'il, 2006), short-listed for the 2007 Yi Sang Literature Prize, is a very unusual love story. Both of these stories, like "Corpses," feature male protagonists caught in a chaotic, surreal world over which they have little control. Translator Cindy Chen's interview with P'yŏn (see "Suggestions for Further Reading") reveals an author trained in both creative writing and in literature (a rarity among Korean writers), one who has read widely in international literature, and a writer who is unusually visual and imaginative. If any among the current generation of women fiction writers in South Korea may be said to have carried out Virginia Woolf's dictum that killing off the gentle, egoless, self-sacrificing "angel in the house" is part of a woman writer's job, then those writers would be Ch'ŏn Unyŏng and P'yŏn Hyeyŏng. ▨ "Corpses" (Shich'e tŭl) first appeared in 2004 in *Hanguk munhak* (Korean literature).

The call from the police station came about a month after his wife had gone missing. A body part had been recovered from the same ravine where she was presumed to have drowned—and it belonged to a woman. He said he would be there first thing in the morning, and hung up. It was a five-hour drive, not counting a stop at the service area where he would fuel up on a bowl of *udon* noodles. He could leave immediately, but still wouldn't arrive at the city until 2 A.M. at the earliest.

The recovered body part, he was told, was a severed right leg. And with that leg he was to seal his wife's fate. The leg of an average adult was supposedly half her height. His wife was five feet three inches tall. He held his hands two and a half feet apart. "About this long," he mumbled.

His mind inched over his wife's body—from her feet to her knee-caps, from her kneecaps to her privates, from her privates to her nipples, and from her nipples to her head—and visualized a rough sketch of a female body. Whether that body belonged to his wife or to the prostitute he had picked up, he could not tell.

He struggled to remember how his wife's right leg had looked. She used to complain that her legs were fat. Was she being serious? And did she mean that her legs were only slightly fat? Was she comparing her legs with her long and unusually skinny arms, or with the legs of other women her age? He couldn't recall if his wife's legs had much hair on them. Had he ever actually felt his wife's legs? In response, his hand reached out to caress the right leg of the woman his mind had sketched. Was her leg flawlessly sleek, or muscled and lumpy? Was the ankle concealed inside her trailing skirt thin enough for him to wrap his hand around, or was it as thick as her calf? He was drawing a blank. He lay down, and began to erase the woman before his eyes. Apparently she didn't want to be erased, because she removed her right leg and plopped it down on his head.

The leg was boring into his brain when it came to him—wasn't there a tiny little fibroma on his wife's leg? It was no larger than a grain of rice, and soft, but as far as his wife was concerned, it was practically a fist-sized eyesore. She sometimes said she felt she was nothing but a pair of legs; she blamed the fibroma for that. Some-body had told her it would fall off if she could strangulate it with a strand of hair. She couldn't find a hair long enough to wind around the base of the growth and so she noosed it instead with a length of thin black thread, causing it to shrivel up and blacken. And yet it never did fall off. That blackened growth could be the key to the mys-tery of his missing wife.

She was presumed to have drowned. A fisherman claimed to have seen his wife—or more accurately a woman—falling into the water, screaming and flailing. This witness could recall no details—manner of dress, length of hair, facial features. The only thing he remembered was a woman falling into the water, hands clawing at the air. The duty detective hypothesized that the woman in question was the missing wife.

The man re-imagined the woman's leg from his head back into the air and zoomed in for a close-up of the growth. Hmmm. Now which of his wife's legs was that growth on, anyway? He couldn't blindly assign the artifact to the wrong leg, lest she mistakenly be pronounced dead when in fact she was alive, or else be shelved away as a missing person when she should have been labeled dead. The woman's leg punctuated this thought by thumping down on his head again. He felt like a detective watching a criminal slip through his fingers. It was a shitty feeling. He was flustered, too. It was unacceptable that his wife's fate should be in limbo. She should not be presumed to have drowned. Innocent until proven guilty; alive until proven dead by the existence of remains. And he was flustered because he was faring no better than his wife. In his ineptness, he felt more dead than alive. How was it possible that he remembered nothing of his wife's body, a constant in his life for more than ten years? He stomped out to his car and set off for the city. *I'm going to look at that leg—and I will know if it's hers when I see it.*

Along the way he was met with a downpour. *Strange, they never mentioned it in the forecast.* On with the wipers. They labored back and forth, but before they could do their job, the left blade stopped dead. Rain streamed down the windshield alongside the motionless blade. The right blade continued to lurch along by itself—*thunk, thunk.* And then he nearly lost his grip on the wheel. *What the—was that the right-side wiper blade or a woman's right leg?* Off with the wipers. But not for long—the rain was coming down too hard. His wife's rain-blurred right leg once again cleared the windshield.

In the waiting area at the police station he hunkered down for a cat-nap while he waited for the duty detective. He heard a sound from the direction of the hallway—footsteps. His eyes jerked open. A shadow was approaching, its footsteps heavy and squelchy, and with it a rampant raw-fish stench, the very same stink that emanated from his fishmongering wife. He stared at the shadow . . . it *was* his wife. She was laboring toward him on one leg, the right one; it resembled a sodden stump of wood. He tried to get up but his wife stuck the mis-shapen stump right in his face, menacing him, warning him to stay put. He tried to dodge it anyways. That was when he woke up—the duty detective was shaking him by the shoulder. The detective didn't ask him why he was there early. Just as well. He didn't want to be blurting out in confusion that there was a growth on his wife's leg but he couldn't remember which leg. And what would the detective think if he started blabbing about how his one-peg-legged wife was kicking him in his dreams?

The right leg was with the unnamed bodies in the morgue. With some indifference, the detective slid out a refrigerated steel body tray, and there it was, one cold and hardened right leg, all by itself. Mixed with the confused jumble of odors from the formalin, the chemi-cal solvent, and the detergent was the sterile metallic smell of the body tray. He gagged—overwhelmed not so much by this onslaught of odors as by the putridness of the flesh, which no longer looked human. Shreds of it hung like unraveled seams where the leg was severed. Poking out from the end was the femur, the bone almost flu-orescent in its blackened casing of rotten flesh, looking as durable as molded plastic. The patella looked lifelike and sturdy. And the tibia glistened white. The flesh and the skin belonged to a decomposing corpse, no two ways about it, yet the bones seemed to belong to a living person. The toes were crushed beyond recognition, a shapeless mass, making him wonder if the person had been born toeless.

The leg could have belonged to anyone. The Jane Doe to whom this dead, black-as-coal leg was once attached—could she have foreseen being consigned to the deep waters of a ravine? The leg, before it decomposed, could have belonged to a college girl on the run, a department store saleswoman who had massaged her cramped calf in between customers, or the high-jumper who had planted her foot on the ground before torquing herself over the bar. Could this leg and its partner have danced until they could dance no more? Could it have been the leg of a new bride who had knelt to offer up bows to her elders? Yes, it could have belonged to any of them. And not necessarily his wife.

He stared mutely at the leg. It was a single solitary body part and yet its unrelenting decay bespoke his own mortality. The leg was bereft of all organic matter—water, proteins, nucleic acids. It was dead, plain and simple. It placed in stark relief the fact that the human body was merely an agglomerate of proteins, susceptible to breakdown. He had half a mind to comb his body for rot. *Note to self: Take preservatives—one handful—before kicking the bucket.*

His eyes fished the lump of flesh for a fibroma. Spots of blackish purple discolorations were particularly pronounced around the knee, making it difficult to tell a tear in the skin from a fibroma. His eyes met the detective's and he shook his head.

"It's not my wife." Then he stammered, "My wife had all five of her right toes."

The detective shrugged. "So does this leg."

His eyes followed the detective's finger to where pearl-white bones sprouted forth like baby teeth from the torn flesh of the mashed toes. The detective told him that the tears in the flesh were from fish bites. The man rejected the detective's implication, arguing that his wife's leg never had this much fat on it.

"Not fat—bloat," the detective corrected him.

That did it. Out spewed the *udon* he had slurped down at the rest stop. Bits of shaved kelp that had garnished the broth now garnished his vomit, blackening it so that it blended perfectly with the rotten lump of flesh on the body tray. He felt as though he was crunching down on his wife's toes. Again his stomach churned. The detective quietly slid the body tray back into the refrigerator.

The leg had been discovered by a fisherman in the lower reaches of the ravine. No items of clothing or other body parts—just the leg. The detective asked the man if his wife had ever had surgery on her leg.

"No, never," he was quick to respond. Only then did it occur to him that he could not have known about any procedures that might have been done on his wife's leg when she was a girl or before she had met him. He corrected himself accordingly and told the detective that actually he did not know. The detective did not buy the idea that a body slammed by the current into a boulder or a body gnawed by fish could have shed a leg as a result—something was not adding up. The markings on the leg looked like they had been made by a saw. Or maybe they were the vestiges of a simple surgery or a dislocation of the femur, the detective added when he noticed the man's puzzled expression.

"An unnatural death invites all sorts of speculation," the detective said, to which the man nodded dumbly.

His wife had gone missing during their first ever fishing trip. She was standing atop a lichen-matted rock. He had repeatedly urged her to find another spot, and she had repeatedly refused, insisting that the water was shallow and smooth where she was standing. She had no idea that a recent torrential downpour had raised the water level more than twofold. Nor could he have predicted the depth of the water or the speed of the current. His wife was sucked away the instant she hit the water. The fisherman who claimed to have seen her thrashing about in the water was fishing downstream from them. He did not dive into the swollen river to rescue her. Which was not to say that the man would have acted any differently had *he* been the one to see her being swept away. The rapids had looked knife-sharp, like they could drive through his heart if he so much as touched them.

The police questioned him. They suspected that he had pushed his wife in. He maintained his innocence, but he could tell that nobody believed him. No one could attest to his alibi that he was by himself, exploring the upper reaches of the ravine, at the time. But there was no hard evidence of his guilt, either. And so the duty detective had declared the wife missing. Without a body this was his only option under the law—even though he believed that the woman had drowned. The body could have sunk to the bottom or been wedged among rocks in the ravine. It could also have ridden the waters to a city far beyond her husband's reach. The ravine, with its raging daggered water, had kept the secret of the wife's whereabouts to itself.

The man and his wife might have enjoyed the fishing trip if it had been motivated by something other than the fact that their savings, which he had been shelling out faithfully in installments for a lease on a new business establishment, had pretty much vaporized. And he was only one of several dozen victims, the lot of whom had banded together to come up with a countermeasure; it was about all they could do. He and his wife might have had better results if they had just gone after their own lost money. Perhaps then his wife would still be alive.

His wife was the one who had suggested that they take their penniless selves off to the ravine for a respite. The ravine was located beside a city far from where they lived, a long and complicated way to go for a breather. It had taken about five hours just to reach the park. And then through a toll gate and a long winding drive upstream alongside a river. *This must be it!* his wife had gushed. *The water that flows through this ravine,* she said, *is more secretive than the ravine itself, it's cold like dagger steel. And the water is so transparent it*

*looks almost shallow, but with the water in a ravine, the more transparent
it is the more unfathomable its depth.*

Up alongside the ravine they drove. The pavement had long
since ended. The occasional parked cars seemed to belong to the
fishermen who were dispersed along the winding stretch. There was
no end in sight to the meanderings; they could have driven until
sundown without reaching the headwaters. So they settled for a
relatively secluded spot. It was his wife's first time fishing, but she
was not put off by the bait worms. She was, after all, forever elbow-
deep in stinking fish. He watched as she dug through the bucketful
of squirming worms for the meatiest and the fattest one, and felt a
rush of resentment. He wanted to blame their dire situation on his
wife, she who feared and loathed nothing. For all he knew, some of
the meals she prepared included rotten fish that she didn't want to
waste. She probably even served their customers fish eyeballs. He
dropped his fishing pole and glanced at his wife. She was hooking a
plump worm onto a bobber. He knew she wasn't to blame for the fail-
ure of their restaurant. And he was the one who had thrown their
money away on the new-business scam. Yet he couldn't ignore the
growing temptation to beat his wife with his fishing pole. And hell,
it wouldn't be hard to push her into the water. But he resisted the
impulse and instead returned to the car, fists clenched, leaving his
wife to bait the fish hook with the worm. When he last looked back,
she was casting the bobber into the water.

He was determined to reach the head of the ravine and calm
himself down along the way. The path stretched on and on, one bend
turning into another. He couldn't tell if he was driving upstream
or going around in circles. Finally he was tired enough to want to
rejoin his wife. He turned the car around, but when he found their
spot after what felt like a long and disoriented drive, he saw only
the bucketful of worms slithering about on the ground. His wife was
nowhere in sight.

The rain was still coming down hard on his way home from the police station. On with the half-defunct windshield wipers. His mind churned over the image of the putrid right leg. It was a skinny leg, but his wife was most assuredly a rotund woman with breasts that sagged practically to her hips. That leg was too skinny to be his wife's. *It couldn't be hers*, he grumbled. He had repeated the exact same thing to the duty detective. In all likelihood, his wife's right leg was still being slowly rendered by the merciless water of the ravine, decomposing into sediment on the riverbed. It would turn into food for a fish, and then into a tasty dish for the lucky man who caught the fish. Her left leg, her torso, her arms, and her head would suffer the same fate. He realized he was drooling, and rolled down the window and spat into the rain. The rain streaks were as fat as the worms that his wife had turned into bait.

The building was a dump. Long abandoned but not yet demolished, it seemed to be crumbling on its own. When first unveiled, it was supposedly the toast of the neighborhood—the grandest structure ever constructed there, worthy of receiving homage from people in neighboring localities. It was the first building in the region to have an elevator. And the elevator became so popular with young pranksters that security had to be posted in front of it instead of at the building's entrance. A good forty years ago, this was. And in that time the building had shed all of its grandeur. But it didn't take the building forty gradual years to fall into decay. It happened suddenly, the way that water in a ravine rises after an unforeseen downpour. The way that water can sweep you away and swallow you up. The way that water can fill your lungs the instant you're sucked under.

The building's misfortune began soon after two developers announced plans to put up a retail-condo building on each of the two vacant lots flanking it. Construction workers started to assemble on the lots. Tall gray walls were erected, sandwiching the building in the middle. Hand-painted on those walls were groves of trees so exquisite and detailed that birds crashed into them by mistake. In contrast with the fake groves of trees, the building and its hard cement walls had all the majesty of a trash can. Worse, the walls limited access to the building at a time when visitors to it were already dwindling. Tenants started to take leave of the building. With his back against the wall, the building's owner finally sold it to the two developers. The owner could have profited from the transaction had he sold earlier. But with construction of the retail-condo buildings already well under way, he could only dump the building for a fraction of its market value.

Demolition was to begin in earnest next week, at which point their restaurant, along with the rest of the building, would be stripped down to a skeleton of bare steel surrounded by a heap of broken glass and cement blocks. He and his wife served seafood—fish with steamed rice—on the ground floor. The restaurant was their only child and they had toiled for the last decade or so to nurture it. They took care of the restaurant in its early years and the restaurant took care of them in its later years. It gave them laughter. It offered them a place to sit when they had migraines. It kept peace between them when they were angry with each other. And, he found out only years later, it provided his wife with her much-treasured fish eyeballs. His wife would rip out the eyeballs before stewing or grilling the fish for customers. It was not an issue for the customers, who could not have cared less whether the fish in their meal could still gaze at them. His wife took immense pleasure in inventing recipes for the eyeballs. And because she ate no meat, the eyeballs were her only source of protein.

He hoisted the restaurant's storefront shutters and went inside. The stench of rotten fish, which had made itself known to him outside, even with the shutters down, stung his nostrils. The restaurant had been closed down ever since his wife had gone missing, the fish still in the freezer from the day they had left on that fateful fishing trip. He pinched his nose and opened the freezer door. When the building's power supply was cut off, the stocks of fish were left to fester and stink up the freezer. Halibut, sole, pike or mackerel—there was no way of telling one fish from another in that rotten jumbled mess. He donned a pair of rubber gloves and scooped out the fish. Black fluid leaked from their putrid innards. He dropped them onto the floor and the black effluent spattered his pants, reminding him of the livid spots on the severed leg.

Next he retrieved a plastic bag of fish eyeballs—no doubt his wife's collection. The eyeballs had been left to rot along with the bodies that had once housed them. Awash in a black juice, the eyeballs looked teary. He turned on the tap—nothing. The water must have been cut off too. That left the stale barley tea in the refrigerator, and he used it to rinse the eyeballs. Most of them had disintegrated by now. Among those that remained, he popped the shapeliest one into his mouth. A disgusting rancidness filled his oral cavity and with each breath, out came the fishy stink from the recesses of his body— or was it the stench of his own body, dying from the inside out? He took his time sucking on the eyeball. Finally he burst into tears—it dawned on him then that his wife had to be dead.

Several days later there was another call.

"Sorry for being such a bother but I'll need you to come down to the station again. It's nothing urgent, you can come in at your own convenience, but I think the earlier, the better." The duty detective was hemming and hawing; he sounded embarrassed.

The man listened patiently and said he would leave at once. Just as he was about to hang up, something occurred to him. "What did you find this time?" The pause at other end made him regret the question.

"You'll find out soon enough." But then the detective changed his mind, and soon enough became right now. "We found a left hand. We weren't able to take any fingerprints, so we've hit a bit of a snag."

After hanging up the man stared at his own left hand. Underneath webs of blood vessels and nerves, underneath layers of membraned muscle, the hand was attached to his thick wrist. And, the furthest extension of that wrist, five digits with gnarled knuckles. His fingers were stout and a healthy shade of pink from their rich and steady supply of blood. Vessels bulged underneath his skin as if to prove that his hand was, indeed, a living thing. Yes, that was his hand. He closed his eyes and tried to memorize what his eyes had just captured. He could picture his gnarled knuckles. And his wrist, so thick he could not wrap his other hand around it . . . But that was it. Further details seemed to have been lost.

If he was having trouble recalling his wife's face—he remembered only her cold and severe lips—why should he be expected to remember what her left hand had looked like? Then it hit him. *Of course, her ring!* He hadn't bought it until several years after they'd been married. The ring was unprepossessing, one humble diamond on a thin band. It was the kind of nondescript ring you could find practically anywhere. The numerous scratches on the protruding diamond were visible to the naked eye. The ring may have fallen into the water along with his wife, but luckily, he could visualize it pretty well. Now if only that hand still had all of its fingers, and one of those fingers still had the ring on it.

This time he wouldn't stop for food along the way. He had no wish to throw up black shaved kelp at the sight of a ragged severed arm. But before he could leave, there was another call, this one from the owner of the building with the restaurant. He had to empty out the restaurant by tomorrow; whatever was left would go down along with the rest of the building. He told the owner that he would stop by the restaurant and sort out the things he'd like to keep. Not that he actually wished to keep anything. Everything in the restaurant could be tossed for all he cared. Except for his wife's kitchen knife—*that* he wanted to bring home. His wife used the same knife for everything—from trimming and chopping, to gutting and scaling a fish. It was a carbon-steel sashimi knife with a long thin blade. She liked it even though it wasn't the best knife for preparing fish for stewing or grilling. Other cooks would probably prefer a cleaver with a thick rectangular blade for that sort of work. His wife enjoyed the dexterity involved in scaling and skinning a fish. But she often ended up slicing into her own wrist. The knife blade was long and the blade tip sharp. When she slit a fish's stomach in one sidelong stroke, the tip of the knife would oftentimes graze her wrist. His wife had likened it to being pricked by a dull needle tip. Even so, it seemed to him as though his wife was trying to slash an artery in her wrist, and this did not sit well with him.

Cuts from a sharp object on the wrist of the recovered left hand could probably tell him if the hand was his wife's. *An identifying mark!* He was ecstatic. *If she ever comes back,* he vowed, *I will analyze her body under a microscope.* He would memorize every detail. How many of her molars had fillings? How long were her nose hairs— were they dense and untrimmed enough to poke out of her nostrils? Was her nose crooked to the left or crooked to the right? How did her earlobes crease? Was the cartilage of her ears hard or soft? Was her hair stiff or silky? Where were the moles on her body? He wished he knew if the pubic hairs concealing her most private parts were darker and longer than other women's. He wished he could remember the look of her vaginal lips. And the size of the uterus nestled inside her pelvis—having never borne a child, was his wife's uterus really no larger than a fist and shriveled like the lips of a toothless old woman? If he had the answers, he could easily recognize his wife— even if her body was dismembered, even if the only things he had to work with were scattered remains discovered in a ravine's waters.

The duty detective began with an embarrassed apology: he was sorry for the bother. The man said nothing, not even voicing his hope that the left hand would turn out to be his wife's.

The left hand reminded him of the right leg—bloated, putrid. The skin, flaps of it missing, sagged like a piece of paper. The finger tips had been gnawed off. Dozens of threaded bundles of blood vessels were splayed out from the severed wrist. His wife's hand had pinched a plump bait worm and hooked it onto the bobber; it had scaled and gutted a fish, then rinsed it under water and sprinkled a dash of salt on top before putting it on the grill—was the hand in front of him now the same one that had done all of that? He could not be sure. What about the typist whose hands could input six hundred characters a minute? Or the violinist whose hands could play a concerto? Could the left hand not have belonged to either of them? He asked the detective if a ring had been recovered.

"Nope, nothing like that." Looking stumped, the duty detective continued, "It does look as though the individual could have worn a ring—I mean, if you look closely, you can see that the skin at the base of the finger is especially white. What we can't tell is whether the coloration is due to bloating or a ring."

Once again he had to confess to the detective: he couldn't tell whether the left hand was his wife's. The detective nodded, as if to say, *I thought as much.*

Without a head, the identity of Jane Doe would continue to elude them.

Goosebumps stood up at his every pore as he tried to visualize his wife's decapitated head—her nose chewed off, the roots of her teeth cracked, her cheeks patchy with mold where the flesh had peeled off, water weeds bursting out of her eye sockets. . . .

"If only there had been a ring," he offered.

The detective apologized again. "That ravine has a reputation as a mass grave. We've had a lot of drownings. People slip off the rocks—they're kind of mossy, you know. And people go in for a swim and get swept away by the current. And some people, they just stuck their feet in and then suddenly got pulled in after. And we've had homicides, too. What starts out as a happy excursion ends up with someone pushing in a friend, a family member, you name it—a crime of passion. And let's not forget the suicides. Especially the ones who leave no trace—missing persons for eternity. And it's nearly impossible to search a river that's as long and deep as that one. The local people, most of them, don't mess with the ravine unless they like to fish. And the legends that have grown up about the place—the main one being that evil spirits hide in the ravine and snatch people. We've had no shortage of sightings of these spirits—several of them made it into the news. You've never seen them in the news?"

The man slowly shook his head. The detective took off his rubber gloves and continued. "Supposedly fishermen from all over the country flock there—even though the ravine is deep in the mountains and the roads aren't paved—*because* it's a mass grave. Thanks to the drowning victims, the meat on the fish is absolutely delicious." The detective finished by asking why the man and his wife had bothered to travel so far for a day trip.

The man knew he'd be coming back. He'd be asked to identify another body part—a skull, breasts, or perhaps buttocks. While the detective was talking he was thinking about his wife's hand. Her hand that had stroked his cheeks, cooked for him, fondled his penis. Her hand that had scooped out fish eyeballs, pulled out bloody fish innards, a hand glistening with sticky fish scales. Her hand that had smelled of marinade, that had rolled the restaurant's metal shutters up and down a thousand times, that had wiped away tears from her face after a hard day at the restaurant, the hand that had waved a clenched fist in his face when he came home after losing all their money. Her hand that had pinched a bait worm and then clawed frantically at the air before disappearing beneath the ravine's waters.

That hand was gone. The hand shown him at the police station was just a body part, too decayed even for worms to feed on.

The restaurant was pitch-black inside—no more power. From the freezer the man pulled out the bag of fish eyeballs from last time. They were even more putrid—he chucked the bag into the trash. The smell of death hung dense in the restaurant, causing him to gag again and again as he cleaned out the refrigerator and the freezer.

The sight of every rotting item conjured up an image of his wife's body decomposing at the bottom of the ravine, her body that had sunk below the surface as it rode the current, her body dismembered by collisions with jagged outcrops, the body parts carried away by the raging waters and shredded by ferocious fish. Hearing was supposedly the last of a dying person's five senses to fail. His wife would have heard the rushing of the waters mingled with her own screams as she was dragged along by the current, the thrashing of schools of razor-toothed carnivorous fish, the cracking of her bones as her body slammed against a boulder, the flitting wings of avid droves of carrion flies that had scented her death. She would have heard the splash of fishing lines dropping onto the water and the boisterous cackle of the fishermen above who were oblivious to her desperation. Had she reached for those fishing lines?

Just then he heard noises in the kitchen. And saw a black flickering shadow. The shadow was cleaning a rotten fish.

"Hello? Is that you?" His voice was a croak. He tried to remember when he had last uttered a word.

His wife's left hand was cleaning the fish—the same dead, black left hand whose flesh had been shredded by the fish in the ravine. Her body listed, as if she was standing on one leg. No, she was leaning on one leg—the putrefied right leg he had seen at the police station. His wife didn't turn around. She was engrossed in what she was doing. She was holding down the fish with her left hand and plucking the eyeballs with her right thumb and index finger. Blood vessels still attached to the eyeballs stretched out from the sockets. Her fingertips were stained with the fish's black blood. The fish was unwashed and probably infested with vibrios and parasites. He watched, unable to turn away, as his wife gulped the fish whole. When finally she glanced at him she was about to put the eyeballs in her mouth. And then she disappeared.

The restaurant seemed even darker now. He picked out his wife's knife, sharp and glinting, from an array of rusty kitchenware. The handle was warm as though someone had been holding it only moments earlier. A rotten eyeball sat on the cutting board. He picked it up and popped it into his mouth. A caustic fishy odor spread deep into the recesses of his body. He cleaned the bloodstained blade on his clothes. He would take the knife home and leave everything else behind.

Soon there would be nothing left of the building. The man cringed in pain every time the wrecking ball slammed into the walls; he felt as though his bones were cracking with each blow. He and his wife had spent all their energy nurturing the restaurant, their only child. It had put food on their table, offered them chairs on which to sit, provided them with money, supplied them with fish eyeballs. But soon it would be a scrap pile. And underneath that pile he would bury his wife and their restaurant. He recalled the burial ceremony of a South African tribe, something he had seen on TV. When a member of the tribe died, those left behind would tear down the roof of his hut, cover his body with the dirt and rocks, and leave him there. No special formalities. Likewise, his wife and their restaurant would rest where the building used to stand, their graves marked by a mound of cement blocks. The building's sign had been stripped off. The glass doors had shattered without a sound. Just then his cell phone rang. It was the duty detective. Not quite ten days had passed since the last call.

"Sorry for the inconvenience but I need you to come down to the station again." The detective sounded calm.

Another body part. He didn't feel up to it. Sure, it might have belonged to his wife—but so what? By now it was just another part of a dead body that no longer bore any relevance to his wife. And so he told the detective that unless they found his wife's head, he would much rather avoid another trip. After all, there was no predicting when a right arm, a left leg, a limbless torso—or even another right leg—might be found. There could be a myriad of body parts in the ravine's secretive, bottomless waters just waiting for a fisherman to fish them out. He couldn't be expected to drive down to the station to try to identify every last one of them, could he now?

"Well, as a matter of fact that's exactly what we've recovered— a skull, and we think it belongs to your wife. We had a craniofacial analysis done, compared it with all the people who have gone missing recently, and the closest resemblance is with your wife."

The man's heart began to pound. His wife's head, finally. The last step in closing the case—his wife would no longer be "missing" but "deceased." He would never have to identify another body part. He let the information sink in before asking how his wife looked. The detective hesitated.

"Floaters don't present a very pretty sight. Most of them are face down, with their extremities hanging down into the water. Blood gets pooled in their scalp, their face, their neck. And decomposition tends to go faster with the bodies of drowning victims—they get all bloated with gas, it's awful unsightly. And I'm afraid it's the same here, even though we don't usually find only the head."

In a roundabout way, the detective was saying that his wife's head was a disgusting mess. The man told the detective that he would leave at once and hung up.

The man had stared at his own hand as the eyewitness recounted how he had seen a woman falling into the water. Fourteen phalanges in the fingers, five metacarpals in the palm, and eight carpals in the wrist—this was his hand, held together by bones more fragile than those elsewhere in his body. This hand would feel the same pain at the touch of anything hot, cold, and burning, and instantly withdraw in a reflex dictated by thousands of nerves. Could this hand have killed his wife? Could it have felt the same pangs he felt as he watched the bait worm squirming helplessly between her fingers? Could it have then unknowingly pushed her into the water?

He returned home, hands hanging limply at his sides. He picked up his wife's knife. At her funeral, her head alone would have to suffice. Had she drowned with her eyes wide open? Water weeds would be trailing out of her eye sockets like streams of black tears. Frothy, foaming masses of worm-spawned eggs would line her purple, decomposed lips. Her head would be so bloated he was not sure it would fit into the coffin. Her body would be a burial dress stuffed with balls of cotton. He would bury his wife's knife with her. The knife's sharpened blade would never decompose. It would be his wife's spine, her thigh bone, the sole of her foot. That knife alone would accompany his wife to eternity.

He took a detour to the ravine before heading to the police station. The evening sun was half hovering above the horizon. Just when he thought he was nearing the end, a turn would bring him face to face with another stretch of road. The farther upstream he drove, the more difficult it was to spot fishermen. *Where did we park last time?* But he could only remember driving continuously upstream. He rounded a bend and was wondering if he should drive farther upstream when he saw a large group of fishermen near the ravine's edge. All as one they cast their bobbers into the water and reeled in their catch. They even wore the same expression, like they had all struck gold. This spot must have offered the most fish. By now he had been driving for more than two hours, but the dirt road continued to snake upstream. How much farther were the headwaters? And how much farther before he arrived at the spot where his wife had disappeared? He had no idea. So he stopped the car and approached the fishermen.

The transparent water lapped against the bank as though trying to lick his ankles. He remembered his wife warning him that water so clear looked deceptively shallow. *So this is what swept her away? This is what took off her head, tore off her legs and her hand?* Shut in by the trees' shadows, the ravine's frigid water must be numbingly cold. Had the water temperature been higher, his wife might have been able to hold out a little longer. But as it was, she couldn't have lasted more than thirty minutes.

He came near the fishing party. The men were silent. No boasting of hooking a fish of record size, no cursing of bad luck in catching nothing but minnows. They were occupied with jigging their fishing poles. Every one of them seemed skillful, every one kept pulling something out of the water. He got close enough to see the ends of their fishing lines, and a shriek escaped him. One fisherman was lifting an arm, dripping blackish blood, out of the water. The next man was pulling in a buttock with the white pelvic and tail bones sticking out, blood leaking where the flesh had been eaten away. Another man, beside himself with joy, fished out a bloodshot eyeball the size of a ping-pong ball. Everywhere he looked, body parts were being reeled in—a head with a protruding tongue, a dead black toe, tangled weaves of weed-like hair. Even an undulating length of slithery blue intestine. Over there a man held up a winged upper body, its torso marked with blue patterns and its face fixed with a red-and-white beak. Several men together were hauling out a grossly bloated torso. Covered with fish scales, the torso was glistening under the evening light. These body parts had all taken the fishermen's bait, the big, meaty worms. One man grabbed a handful of worms from his pocket and flung them into the water—no time to bother with hooking them through the bobber. The worms had knotted themselves into a squirming ball that did not come apart even upon hitting the water. In the now stagnant water dismembered limbs and body parts swarmed around the ball of worms. Transfixed, the man lost his footing. His feet slipped out from beneath him and as he plunged toward the water his hand caught the outstretched root of an old tree. *Thud*—a slimy lump of something landed on his head. The lump untangled itself and slithered all over him. He needed both hands to scrape the creatures off, and he let go of the tree root. Into the water he went, plummeting toward the bottom.

The sun had set and the the water felt icy enough to flash-freeze his intestines. The still water, loath to flow, constricted drawstring-like around him. Desperate to stay afloat, he grabbed at the haphazard network of fishing lines cast around him. Like the roots of black water weeds tossed by the current, his legs kicked frantically beneath the surface. Darkness had obscured the fishermen. He screamed at them to toss him a fishing line. Schools of fish were closing in on him. They had already bitten off his toes. A fish hook caught on the crown of his head. A strip of his scalp peeled off as the hooked bobber was reeled in. Worms floating on the surface were quick to dig into the raw wound. Slowly he was reeled out of the water and then he was tossed into a huge fishing net with all the other body parts. More skin was rubbed away by the coarse weave of the net, his body now mottled with patches of raw flesh.

His abraded form lay supine on the dew-dabbed ground, which smelled damp and earthy. He listened to the nighttime sounds of the ravine. Every rustle of the wind through the trees sent leaves fluttering softly onto the fishing net. Worms streaked with white light crawled toward the net, coiling and uncoiling themselves. Water splashed like the crack of a whip as fishing lines were cast. The water remained stagnant save for the whirling drone of the eddies. That drone sounded like his wife's whimpers. Worms had covered every inch of his body and the fishing net that confined him. A queue of them were creeping up the dead trunk of a tree, looking like a white line being carved into the bark. Soon they were at the top. From there they fell weightlessly through the air and onto his body like raindrops. And there, in the thick of the night, in this ravine, he was laid to rest.

THE GLASS SHIELD

Kim Chunghyŏk
Translated by Kevin O'Rourke

Kim Chunghyŏk was born in Kimch'ŏn, North Kyŏngsang Province, 1971, and studied Korean Literature at
Keimyung University in Taegu. He debuted as a writer
in 2000 with "Penguin News" (Pengwin nyusŭ), which
became the title of his first story collection, in 2006. He
is the recipient of the 2008 Kim Yujŏng Literature Prize.
His most recent books are *The Library of Musical Instruments* (Akki tŭl ŭi tosŏgwan, 2008), a story collection,
and *Zombies* (Chombi tŭl, 2010), a novel. ▰ "The Glass
Shield" (Yuri pangp'ae) was first published in 2006
in *Ch'angjak kwa pip'yŏng* and was reprinted in *The
Library of Musical Instruments*.

We sat in the subway unraveling tangled balls of yarn. The work was simple. All we had to do was catch one end of the yarn and carefully loosen the kinks; look for the tangled bit, pass the yarn through, and the kink untangled easily. We each had a ball of yarn in our hands. We concentrated all sensation in our fingertips, working in rhythm with the rattling subway car.

There were very few people on the subway, so our yarn operation went ahead smoothly. One or two stole suspicious glances at us, but there really was no need for suspicion. You couldn't blow up the subway with yarn; nor could you set a fire or kill someone with yarn. Yarn was just yarn. If the crowd did the *wave* in support of our efforts to unravel the kinks, that would be great, but there was no reason to stop us doing what we were doing. We stretched the unraveled yarn along the subway seats. As the yarn grew in length, the distance between us increased. Blue and red yarn heaped up on the green seats.

"This is too easy," M said. "Why didn't it work earlier?"

M's ball of blue yarn was reduced to half its original size.

"That's us," I answered weakly as I unraveled the red yarn. "Screwing things up is what we do best."

Two hours ago M and I had taken our thirtieth job interview. At the end of it the panel gave us the standard "That's all right, you can go now."

"Screwing everything up," M repeated. "Why didn't you put that in our CVs? Under special skills maybe? They might take pity on us and give us the jobs."

"Did you list slagging your friends under hobbies?"

As we talked we kept our eyes trained on the balls of yarn. It was a miserable morning and our situation was grim. We shut up and concentrated on unraveling the yarn.

"Is this the circle line?"

"I think so."

"Maybe that's why I'm a bit dizzy."

"It's not the circle line that has you dizzy, it's looking at the ball of yarn for too long. We need a rest."

I looked out the window and saw that we were above ground again. It was almost as if the subway had waited for us to take our eyes off the yarn before clanking its way above ground. Bright lights and small buildings and myriad signboards opened like a collage in front of us. Not so much a landscape as a series of paintings stuck together. We looked out the window as we waited for the train to go below ground again. Tightly stretched electric lines showed the way. The subway stayed over ground. We were in the last car, so if we stuck our noses to the glass and contorted our bodies, we could see the curve the front of the train was running. This made the circle line idea come to life. Two stations later, the front of the train dipped and disappeared underground. The scene topside went with it. The window became a mirror, reflecting the two of us instead of the scene above. We began to unravel the yarn again.

I flushed when I thought of the laughter of the interview panel two hours ago. M and I always took company recruitment exams together. We wanted to work in the same company. That was part of it. But the heart of the matter was that M and I couldn't take an exam on our own. We were inseparable, two sides of a coin, front and back of a single person. Without M, I was a page of paper so thin I couldn't stand on my own. And I believe I meant the same to M. We took thirty company entrance exams together. A hundred games, a hundred losses. Our win ratio was zero, but we never once entertained the thought of taking an exam each on our own.

We also took the interviews together. We even went into the interview room together. We were once asked if we were homosexual. Some companies said they only wanted one new recruit. Still we were obdurate. We insisted we had to do the interview together so that we could show our true worth, and we drove the personnel managers crazy in the process. Some companies refused our demands; but more often than not the personnel man just said "As you wish."

We tried out new approaches, in the belief that we could rewrite the history of interviewing, but we found the interview panels rather cool to us. We tried to impress them with our repertory of tandem jokes, but very often they threw us out before our time was up. We couldn't understand why. Once when we were being thrown out, we asked the personnel manager why we were being failed. He looked at each of us in turn. "Try a gagman exam," he said and pushed us out.

"Well, at least it's fun," M said with a laugh.

We did a gag routine in an interview for an Internet management company— we didn't even raise a laugh from the panel. In an interview for an animation production company, we tried a clumsy magic show. M set off the sprinkler system in the ceiling when he was trying to light a handkerchief he had prepared as a prop. We did a parody of peddlers selling their goods in the subway in an interview for management personnel in a company that publishes English-language textbooks. The peddler piece got the best response. We used outrageous English back and forth between us to advertise one of their books. One man on the interview panel laughed so hard he fell off his chair. When the personnel manager was explaining why we failed, he said, "You know, our book is not the kind of bogus text that's sold on the subway." We had forgotten the first rule of interview preparation. You've got to research the company. We prepared diligently, but all we knew about the company was that it sold English textbooks. We never gave a thought to the quality of the texts the company was selling.

Our preparation for yesterday's interview was thorough by our standards. Over supper, we read and reread the company materials we had downloaded. It was a computer game company and they were looking for recruits in concept planning and testing. In addition to having the basics of programming, applicants needed to be bursting with ideas, to have outstanding imagination, confidence in all game situations, and the grit to finish any game they started. We didn't have any of these qualifications, but we sent in our applications anyway in the belief that we could always play games.

"Don't you think we have some imagination?" M asked.

"Of course we do," I said, "and lots of ideas too."

We didn't know if our imaginations were the kind the company was looking for, but we felt that this company best suited our sensibilities.

"But how will we show our imaginations? Should we try the magic show again?"

"No, not that again. Do you want to set the company on fire? We'll hit their weak spot. We'll prepare an interview totally unrelated to imagination. That'll put them thinking. We'll get better scores that way. Our approach will be the direct opposite of all the other applicants."

"How do you mean?"

"What do applicants lack most?"

"We just studied that. Patience and loyalty."

"Right. We'll show them patience. There's nothing more important for computer game testers."

"So how do we do it? You mean we should do a trial of strength—stand on hot stones for ten minutes, or something like that?"

That was the genesis of our yarn-unraveling routine, which we duly performed in front of the interview board. No practice was necessary. You don't need practice to unravel a tangled ball of yarn; you need patience and determination. We prepared a few introductory remarks and went to bed early.

Next day.

"Gentlemen, instead of introducing ourselves, we'd like to make a little presentation. We believe that testing computer games is like unraveling a tangled ball of yarn. We'll show you how to unravel the kinks by patiently loosening the yarn step by step."

I thought we had a terrific concept. And the reaction from the interviewing panel was good. As we pulled the blue and red yarn from the paper bag, I thought I detected a stir of interest from the panel. But we had a problem. We had tangled the yarn too much in the waiting room. Beads of sweat dotted our foreheads by the end of the first minute. Three minutes later the situation was no better. After five minutes our bodies were drenched in sweat. The sweat on our hands made the yarn even more knotted. All we managed to unravel in five minutes was about a foot of yarn. M began to pull instead of unravel. I sighed. Finally, M muttered "Ah shit" in an undertone. That finished it.

"Okay, that's enough. Very good idea. But you both seem lacking in tolerance. Practice unraveling the yarn and apply again."

The panel laughed. I felt like throwing the balls of yarn at them, but they had done nothing wrong. Outside the interview room, one of the applicants waiting his turn saw our pickled appearance and said, "What sort of questions did they ask to produce a sweat like that?" I wanted to hit him, too, but it wasn't his fault. We were the problem.

"If you hadn't sighed back there . . ."

"So it's my fault?"

"No, no, if you hadn't sighed, I'd have sighed first."

"If you'd sighed first, I'd have said 'Ah shit.'"

A hundred games, a hundred losses. That was us. We got on a subway with good air-conditioning. We had sweated so much, and it was so hot! When I had cooled down a bit, I thought I'd like to complete the unraveling.

It took thirty minutes to unravel the yarn completely. The volume of blue and red yarn on the subway seat seemed enormous. The sight of so much red and blue against the background of the green seat overwhelmed the onlookers. It was like an artist's painting, like the landscape of my heart. It was beautiful, I thought.

"It's pretty long."

"Fifty yards maybe. What do you think? Longer maybe. A hundred yards? More?"

"We'll measure it. Each car is twenty yards long. If we keep going back and forward with the yarn we'll get the length."

"How do you know the car is twenty yards?"

"It's written over there, stupid!"

I pointed at the notice over the door. The length and width of the car and the car's number were written there. When I rode the subway on my own and had nothing particular to think about, I used to read that notice. Sometimes I remembered the car number. It would be nice to get on the same car on the same train. People going to work at the same time every day probably get on the same train every day, but none of them could tell you the number of the car.

There were only four other passengers in the car. No one would think it strange if we went back and forward with the yarn. M took the end of the blue yarn and got up. He took a firm grip on the yarn, moving slowly like a man walking an invisible dog. The yarn on the seat uncoiled like a snake and followed him. M got to the end of the car and twisted the yarn. But he had nothing to fix it to, so it just followed him when he began to walk back. We wouldn't get an accurate measurement this way.

"The yarn keeps following me. Will you stand at the other end and hold it?"

"Who'll hold it at this end then? Do you want me to hire someone part-time? Come on, just keep walking to the end of the train."

"Fine. Why didn't you say so at the beginning, bollix?"

M began walking again with the yarn. He was afraid the yarn would get caught in the doors between cars, but there was no problem. M kept walking, matching his movement to the rhythm of the car. I let the yarn out a little at a time so it wouldn't tangle. It was like flying a kite. M was already out of sight, but I could feel him on the yarn. The blue yarn kept following him. After five minutes, I was at the end of the blue yarn. I wrapped the end of the yarn around my finger so as not to lose my grip on it. Would M know I was at the end of the ball? Suddenly the yarn tightened. More force would break it. I could feel M at the other end. Then the yarn fell to the floor.

A few minutes later the connecting door opened and M's smiling face was revealed.

"This is really fun. Everyone stared at me. Go and see for yourself. The expression on the faces is priceless."

"Did you get the measurement? How far did you go?"

"At first I counted the cars, but with everyone looking at me I forgot the count. The length doesn't matter anyway. If you don't want to go, I'll go again?"

Before I had time to reply M had the yarn in his hand again. I couldn't figure out where all the fun was, but if it was enough to get M this excited, then I couldn't afford to miss it. I took the end of the yarn from him. Disappointment was written across his face, but for my sake he was willing to let the yarn go. Just as I took the red yarn in my hand the connecting door opened and the porter came in.

"Is this your yarn?" he asked. He had the ball of blue yarn in his hand. What had taken us thirty minutes to unravel, the porter in one sweep had returned to its original tangled state. I had the red yarn in my hand, and red yarn was coiled on the seat. There was no way out of it.

"Yes, it's mine. Is there a problem?"

"There's been a report of a suspicious man in a suit setting a bomb."

"A bomb?"

I didn't realize my voice had risen. Someone thought the blue yarn was a bomb fuse. Clearly someone somewhere was using colorful bomb fuses.

"What's the yarn doing on the ground? Have you set a bomb?"

"Ah please, sir, you're not accusing me of setting a bomb. Would I set a bomb?"

"And why isn't it going off?" M interjected. "Isn't it about time it exploded?"

The porter looked at each of us in turn. Two men dressed in suits with a ball of red and a ball of blue yarn was not a common sight. M kept giggling.

"I'm afraid you'll have to come with me."

The porter grabbed the red yarn on the seat, went through all the newspapers on the luggage rack, and examined every corner of the seat. The porter knew there couldn't be a bomb. Anyone could see we didn't have bomb faces. I don't mean that a bomber is a separate entity, it's just that someone who's going to blow up the world would have a different light in his eyes. Our eyes said firecracker rather than bomb. The passengers moved to the next car when they heard the bomb talk.

"I'm sorry," I said quietly to the porter. "The truth is we're in the art business. . . ." The porter turned his head and looked at me. It was as if he were hearing the word "art" for the first time in his life. And I felt as if I were saying the art word for the first time in my life.

"What do you mean, *art?*" The porter and M looked at me at the same time.

"Don't you know what art is?" I asked.

"Is setting a bomb art?" he said.

"There's no bomb," I said. "My friend over there has an acute sense of fun. It's obvious if you look at the yarn. It's not a fuse or anything like that, it's just an ordinary bit of yarn. We're just ordinary people stuck in the daily grind, creating a special experience; you could call it a performance, or an event. We're into art."

"You're telling me that laying yarn on the floor is art?"

"You could call it an event that links the splintered heart of mankind to the yarn image. What better space than the subway to represent modern life?"

M kept giggling, but the porter listened attentively to what I was saying. He hesitated, unsure what he ought to say. His attitude had softened considerably, perhaps because of the impact of the art word or perhaps because I was so respectful in my bearing.

"I understand what you're saying," the porter said, "but you can't do that on the subway."

"Can't do what?" I asked.

"Art things," he said.

"Ah art!" I said. "Okay, I understand."

"This is a public space. You'll appreciate that you can never tell what's going to happen next in a public space."

"Ah yes, I'm sorry. We'll find somewhere else."

"I'll have to confiscate the yarn. Will you show me your identity cards? I need to record some details."

The porter checked our ID cards and moved to another car. We got off at the next station. We had never seen the station before, and we had no idea what part of the city it was in, but that didn't matter. We were afraid the porter would come back and say he'd changed his mind and we'd have to go with him.

"Art my ass!" M cried. "You didn't get to do any art. I was the only one got to do the art. What a pity!" M was giggling again.

And truth to tell, I did have a sense of missed opportunity. This may be seen as a casual remark, but I was genuinely curious about the reaction of passengers when they saw me taking the yarn through the cars. For folks stuck in humdrum daily routines, it could be a special experience.

"One man told me he thought my pants were unraveling. Maybe I should have bared my ass? There was a guy taking photographs too. It was fantastic fun. Such a special experience for me . . ."

We rode the bus until we were nearly home. We got off the bus and went into a beer hall. Our suits stank, we had sweated so much. As we drank beer, a yarnlike liquid infused itself throughout our bodies. Eyes closed and feeling the beer, I figured I could calculate the length of my body.

We discussed our next interview. We had one tomorrow with a

company making kitchen appliances. The more I talked with M and the more interviews we did, the more it seemed that we were evaluating the companies rather than the companies evaluating us. We had developed a basic principle: we would not take a job in a company that didn't accept our unique interviewing style. We were the losers, of course, but the loss seemed inevitable. We had started this way and we had to see it through.

"Why don't we cook something for the interview?" M suggested, his face already red from the beer. He must have swallowed some red yarn.

"Feed the interview panel some shitty dish and then say, 'Now we see the necessity of kitchen scales!' Is that what you mean?"

"What a brain! What insight!"

"We'll fail anyway. Maybe we should throw in some diarrhea pills?"

"And if they say thank you for helping us lose weight and give us the jobs, what then?"

"It will mean a life selling kitchen scales."

"I wouldn't like that."

"So why did you apply for the job?"

"I thought we could use the scales for a fun interview."

"That's what I thought. The bottom line is we'll never get a job. We're twenty-seven already."

"Twenty-seven? Is that all we are? We'll get something eventually."

"What'll we get? Is there anything we do well?"

M grew sullen. We drank in silence. Every beer we drank, we put the price of it on the left hand side of the table. The money on the right kept moving to the left. We hoped to get drunk before the money was all gone, but we couldn't get drunk as long as we kept watching the money. We were still clear-headed.

"Four beers left."

"Why can't we get drunk?"

"Let's put the next one down the hatch."

We took the beers in our hands and gulped them down. We belched, we were dizzy, we were drunk. When the money was spent, we went home.

When I woke the next day, I had a ring of pain wrapped like Saturn's rings around the general area of my head. The ring turned in a circle pressing down relentlessly on my head. M seemed in a similar state. We shared a bowl of *tchamppong* Chinese noodles but just ate the soup part. Looking at what was left, I recalled yesterday's interview. The noodles like the yarn offended the eye. We put the bowl outside the door, lay down again and looked at the ceiling. We had nothing to say. We had to prepare for tomorrow's interview, but we were not in the mood.

The cell phone rang about three in the afternoon. It was a friend of ours who got a job a couple of months ago in an Internet newspaper company. He was drinking with us when he got the news, and he was so happy he smacked a big kiss on my cheek. M sweet-talked him into drinking with us until four in the morning. Our newly employed friend, of course, paid the bill. He lost his cell phone and wallet that day, and he was left with a cut on his chin that he couldn't account for.

"You fellows were so jealous of me getting the job you hit me, right?" he grumbled, but we weren't the kind of guys that were jealous of such things. The company that had taken him on was pretty prominent, but it was also well known for long hours and poor wages. Next day he had us meet him at a department store and bought us a tie each. Good luck in your interview, he was saying. He treated himself to a new suit, the latest model of cell phone, and a leather wallet.

As we left the department store, he said, "Now I'm going to begin the exotic second half of my life."

"He figures he'll score a lot of goals in the second half since he used so much energy in the first half. Twenty–nil maybe?" M said. The sarcastic tone may have been because our friend's "exotic second half'" remark had stung. Anyway we had no contact with him for a while. Age twenty-seven and the second half, I figure, are concepts that don't belong together. As far as we're concerned, we still haven't finished the first quarter.

"Is M there by any chance?" My cell phone friend lowered his voice as if he wanted to say something to me privately.

"He's lying here beside me. We've taken pills, we're doing a double suicide. . . . We've no jobs, no money and our heads are splitting from beer."

I was so hoarse, I suppose I could have been taken seriously. I hawked up the mucus in my throat and swallowed it again.

"Don't be going on like that. . . . So you're together. Ask M if he was on the subway yesterday."

"Here, I'll put him on. Ask him yourself. I think he's still alive."

"Come on, you know I rub him the wrong way. Just ask him, was he on the subway?"

M was asleep. That or he knew we were talking about him and was pretending to be asleep.

"He was on the subway. We both were."

"You were on it together. Did you go around the cars carrying blue yarn?"

"How do you know about that?"

"Ah, I'm right. It was M, wasn't it? It's hard to make him out in the suit."

"How do you know about the suit?"

"He's on the Internet. Take down this address."

I typed in the address he gave me. It was a private blog called "Street Scene." Sure enough, M's photograph was there. Dressed in a suit, eyes cast down, M was walking toward the camera. You could see the blue yarn faintly behind him. Actually it looked more like a line superimposed on the photograph than a piece of yarn. There were five photos in all. The last one, a rear view, gave a clearer view of the yarn.

The photos had been uploaded five hours ago, and already there were two hundred comments. The comments reflected a wide variety of opinion. Someone who had lost a sweetheart in an accident thought the unraveling yarn was a symbol of an unforgettable love. Someone else thought the yarn symbolized a trip around the country. A third party thought the blue line had been superimposed on the photo. I woke M. He laughed when he saw the photos. The more he read of the comments, the more he laughed. When he finished the last comment, he fell on the floor laughing.

"Yah," he exclaimed. "What incredible imaginations! How do they do it? Imagine thinking it was a picture of someone pulling a lily-livered lover's rotten tooth!"

M rolled across the floor. I didn't think the comments were funny enough to warrant rolling on the floor, but M obviously did. Such a variety of comment was unbelievable. And to think that I could have been the hero!

"My paper is going crazy trying to make contact. M obviously considers himself some kind of street artist. What the hell was he doing with the blue yarn?"

Our friend sounded annoyed. Perhaps he had heard M's laughter on the phone and thought it a bit ridiculous. He had never liked M's tricks and jokes. "I can't understand why you stick to him like glue," he often said. And for every such remark I liked him that much less. It was the word *understand* that irked. You can never understand human relations, I thought. When he made such comments, I wanted to say something back, but I was afraid I'd lose a friend. I liked his earnestness and I liked those big eyes full of curiosity.

I wanted to tell him the long, complex story of the interview room, but I was afraid M would be demeaned in the telling. And I'd be demeaned too.

"Actually we were doing art."

"Art? What do you mean, art? What art are you two into?"

"Subway performance art. Joining the splintered heart of modern man with yarn. That sort of thing."

"How long have you been at that sort of thing? You two and art don't mix."

M was sitting at the computer, writing something. Another joke. I was curious what he might write under the pictures.

"We've been at it for a long time. You just didn't know about it. Recently we did a performance on the bus."

"What did you do on the bus?"

I imagined a bus. What could you do on a bus? Let's see . . . a driver, seats, a bell to get off, straps to hold on to . . .

"We heaped blue yarn on an ad on the back of the seat."

"Why did you do that?"

"It was an experiment to see what people could do with yarn."

"And what did they do with it?"

I wondered what you could do with a piece of blue yarn while sitting in a bus. I couldn't think of anything. I covered the speaker on the phone with my hand and asked M, who was inputting something in the computer.

"You could strangle the person in front," he said.

"People have very poor imaginations," I said. "Most of them just knit."

"I'm surprised to hear you two are at that kind of thing. I'll call you again later."

After the call, I saw what M had written in the computer. "Maybe it was an attempt to tie up the subway with blue yarn?"

"That's a bit weak," I said.

"Weak, you say. Okay, I'll think about it some more. Not much imagination, I'm afraid."

We lay down again and thought about what you could do with the blue yarn, but we got sleepy. It was seven o'clock when we woke and it was dark outside. Time, we felt, was being stolen from us. Everything was too fast. Maybe we thought the first quarter wasn't over yet, but what if our friend was right and the second half had begun. Maybe we were asleep in the locker room while everyone else was running around in the stadium.

M got up abruptly and spilled the coins from the piggybank onto the desk. He separated them by denomination, very carefully, like a dealer in a casino. He counted the coins in stacks of ten. The operation didn't take very long because we regularly took money from the piggybank.

"How much is left?" I asked, looking at the ceiling. More to know how bad our situation was than to know how much was actually left.

"Maybe enough to buy a box of *ramyŏn*."

"Let's buy the *ramyŏn* before the money runs out."

M divided the coins between his two side pockets and went out. I lay there quietly, imagining life without M. I couldn't visualize it very well, but I figured the time had come for each of us to make his own life. The room I was lying in was like a sinking ship. We were living in that sinking ship with our arms tightly wound around each other. Life had become a sort of three-legged race. Running with one leg tied, trying to match the breathing of the other, was bound to be slower than running with two free legs. It was fun, but inevitably it was slow. I figured we were too far behind now. We would have to loosen the ties that bound our legs before it was too late. I wondered what M's reaction would be. Maybe he was just waiting for me to loosen the ties first. The phone rang while I was wondering how I'd say my bit to M.

"I told the editor about you two. He wants me to interview you. Have you time tomorrow?"

"We have a job interview tomorrow."

"Won't you be free in the afternoon? We'll meet at five."

"But what sort of interview have you in mind? We don't do interviews."

"The editor has already written the captions. 'Blue Yarn Imagination,' 'Street Artists.' It'll be okay? Come on, do it."

"I'll ask M."

"What's there to ask? You two are like an old married couple. Come to the office at five. We'll take some photos in the subway nearby. Wear your suits. You'll have suits on for the job interview anyway."

I put down the phone and stared at the ceiling again. Blue Yarn Imagination, Street Artists. Art. Art be damned! It was all a pain in the neck. I didn't want to do anything. I didn't want to do the interview, and I didn't want to go to the office. I wanted someone to grab me by the scruff of the neck and drag me somewhere.

"What do you think I bought," M shouted as he opened the door. Such an innocent face. He produced a sword from behind his back. A plastic sword but rather finely made.

"Lovely, isn't it?"

"Lovely indeed. Where did you get the money?"

"It makes a sound too."

He struck the sword on the floor. There was a sharp ringing sound, the ring of steel on steel. M went around the room striking various items. The desk rang out, the bikini wardrobe rang out, the computer keyboard rang out. It was like listening to the sound track of a war film. He struck me and I rang out.

"Did you buy the *ramyŏn?*"

"Oh, I forgot. I went to buy *ramyŏn*, didn't I? Anyway there's money left over."

"You need two swords for a sword fight."

"They're selling them at the intersection outside. Shall I buy another?"

"Forget it. Sword fights at our age? The rest of the money is for *ramyŏn.*"

"What's wrong with our age?"

I told M about the newspaper interview. He thought it was great. This was a bit unexpected. I thought he mightn't want to do an interview. M was excited. We need identical suits—uniforms!—he shouted, but we both were well aware that we didn't have that kind of money.

We went out to the intersection. Under the lurid lights there was a large display of toys: cars and trains; guns and arrows; and shields. Most were crudely made. I could see why M chose the sword. We bought another plastic sword. And we bought a transparent plastic shield. I thought at first it was made from glass—that it would break if you let it fall. You could see through it, but it wouldn't block an attack; and you'd have to clean it every day . . . That's what I thought. It was fun. But when I touched it, I knew it wasn't glass; it was transparent plastic. A shield that you could see through would have many advantages in a fight. Having bought the sword and shield, we had enough money left to buy about ten packets of *ramyŏn*. For a proper sword fight, we'd need two shields, but we had to leave some money for *ramyŏn*.

The shield gave off a ringing sound too. A ringing sword seemed fair enough, but the idea of a ringing shield was strange. If you bopped your head on the shield, it rang out; if you hit the shield with your fist, it rang out. And the sound of sword on shield was a double ring. A strange novelty item set.

"I don't want to do the job interview tomorrow," M said, banging his sword off the railing at the side of the road.

"Why," I asked, likewise striking the railing with my sword.

"I don't like the idea of a company that sells scales. How about you?"

"I don't like it much either."

"Let's give it a miss."

"Fine."

We banged our swords off the railing as we walked. People walking along the street stared at us. Still we kept striking the railing. Street noise tended to drown out the ringing of the swords on the railing. M struck the shield I was carrying.

"Why not try to be artists?" he said. "We seem to have what it takes. Let the interview tomorrow be our formal introduction into the world of art."

"Art isn't for everyone, is it? What do we know about art? Of course, if acting the fool can be construed as art, we're number one. . . . I don't really want to do the interview. Interviewing us for acting the fool is a bit of a joke, isn't it."

"But fun, surely?"

I couldn't see where the fun was. I hit the shield in my left hand with the sword in my right hand. I hit it hard, but the sound wasn't any louder. Traffic sounds and the radio in the cosmetics store drowned out the sound of our swords. We went home.

There were now five hundred comments tagged onto the photos. M sat in front of the monitor and absorbed himself in reading the comments. I was too tired. My mouth had a sandy taste: I was still feeling the effects of the beer.

Next day we slept in. We skipped the scales interview, had a late lunch, then put on our suits and headed for the Internet newspaper office. The prospect of the interview was a bit scary, but we were determined to enjoy ourselves. We took a deep breath and went into the office.

Our friend greeted us. "I know nothing about art," he said, "so I've arranged for an art professional to do the interview."

The art professional handed each of us his card. *Professional Art Reporter* was written on it. It was amazing that such a job existed, but since we were artists too, we made an effort to be very composed when we greeted him. We headed for the subway in the company of the professional art reporter and a photographer. "Today's photo concept is freedom," the photographer said. "Do you understand?" Of course we had no idea what a free photo was. We walked through the subway car carrying the blue yarn the art professional had given us. It was more like rope than yarn. He said it would have to be this thick to get it to come out clearly in a picture.

"There's nothing free about this. We're not exactly slaves in chains," M muttered. I felt the same way.

"Well then, feel free to do your own thing," the photographer said with a sigh. M took out the swords and shield and showed them to the professional art reporter. M had spent an hour shoving all sorts of things into his bag before we left home. You never know, he said, what they might need for the photographs.

"Why don't you photograph these?" M suggested. "Could be fun."

"What are you going to do with them?"

"Have a sword fight."

"That sounds a bit childish. Why not stick with the string?"

We ignored the professional and launched into a sword fight. I had shield and sword. M just had the sword. M rushed at me with a shout: "Fool, do you think you can block my sword with that silly shield?"

"Don't make me laugh," I roared. "Do you think you can break my glass shield with a plastic sword? I can see every move you make through the shield."

Our swords clashed. The ring of steel echoed through the car. The sound was much louder than I expected. The professional art reporter stared at us with an expression that said this isn't fun, it's ridiculously childish. But we continued the sword fight, each as if intent on killing his opponent. The photographer clicked the camera shutter industriously, but he didn't appear too happy.

Two small kids who had been sitting at a distance approached. The sight of two men in suits in a sword fight was special. The kids followed the fight closely. Two women who appeared to be the kids' mothers moved close. Two grandfathers intrigued by the clanging of the swords came up to us and two lovers also came up to us. The crowd gradually grew. We were sweating bricks in our attempts to exploit each other's defensive weaknesses, but our movements were so ridiculously slow that we didn't seem to be fighting at all. It was more like a dance. The two kids were pulling their mum's hands. "Buy me a sword, buy me a sword," each cried insistently. In the space of five minutes thirty people had gathered around. Their delight in the performance was written on their faces. The art professional brightened, the photographer's finger on the shutter speeded up. I tied M up with the blue yarn. Well, it was more like draping the yarn across him than tying him up. The train stopped in the station. We left the swords and shield in the car and stepped out on the platform. The swords and shield were presents for the two kids.

"That was fun, wasn't it?" M said proudly. The art professional laughed. We went to a coffee shop for the interview. As soon as we sat down, the art professional began to shower us with questions. We weren't able to answer too many. The questions were much too difficult.

"Bruce Nauman recorded his body language in picture form, the expression of an art concept. Have you been influenced by such art forms?"

"Bruce who?"

"Bruce Nauman. He said that the committed artist helps the world by illuminating the mystery of the real. What do you think is the meaning of what you do as artists?"

"We believe we're helping the world by illuminating everyday reality."

"And what is everyday reality?"

"Having fun, I suppose."

It was this kind of interview.

We made a joke of every answer. When asked how he intended to solve economic problems, M answered "Economically." When asked why we use yarn for our performance, I said we made a ball of mistakes in our lives and they seemed to spin off in yarn. The art professional found the interview increasingly tough going. He was primarily interested in our novelty performances at job interviews. We had so little to say that we had to sublimate what we did into art.

"We loved the fun of performing in the job interview space. We had no interest in getting jobs ourselves, but we did interviews regularly. We'd do a magic show for the interview panel or we'd put on a yarn event for them. Now that was fun."

"What was the yarn event?"

"We'd sit down the members of the interview panel and unravel tangled yarn. We were trying to see how long they'd put up with it, kind of an experiment in company patience."

"How did it work out?"

"Didn't last five minutes; they had no patience. If you're going to pick the right person for the job, you ought to be able to wait five minutes. Trying to evaluate someone in five minutes in an interview room is a bit of a joke, don't you think?"

"That's true. So you're actually making fun artistically of the rigidity of formal societal structures? How often have you done your job interview performance routine?"

"About thirty times, different routine every time, of course."

We were very happy to talk about the interviews. About interviews we had plenty to say. Having begun with the lie that we had no intention of taking a job anyway, we really had the feeling that we had been doing art.

Next day the article appeared in the Internet paper under the headline "Internet Pranksters Captivate a Society without Imagination." There was a photo of us sword fighting, one of me tying M up with the blue yarn, and one of the big crowd watching the sword fight. Most of the article covered our interviews.

"It's fair enough, isn't it?"

"Yeah, the professional touch is there. The article really makes us look like artists."

The article made us famous. Someone suggested that we make a documentary, *Street Artists*. There was a query from a university—could we teach a course titled Revolutionary Concepts? There were lots of requests for interviews. We rejected all offers except one, to join the panel of interviewers for an advertising company. Interviews were an area in which we felt we had competence. Of course, we weren't allowed to decide which candidates got the jobs. There were ten people on the panel. We were just excited to be interviewing anyone.

We discussed the interview over dinner the evening before. This was a new situation for us; the examinees were now the examiners. And yet nothing had changed. Our primary preoccupation was the same: how to make the interview fun. That was all we thought about.

"There's been another phone call asking us to take on job interviews."

"How many is that? We'll soon be professionals."

"Sounds good. Professional interviewers. That's for us."

There were lots of companies out there and companies regularly needed recruits. With a little more effort we'd be pros. At our preparatory meeting for the advertising company interview, we decided to make a firecracker. We let the firecracker off in the middle of the interview. *Poom!* With the explosion, colored thread showered the applicants. The others on the interview panel were equally in shock because we hadn't told them in advance what we planned to do. The applicants provided varied responses. One applicant shouted, another broke out in a cold sweat, still another fell backward over his chair. We had set the firecracker off to test their tension levels. We gave the highest marks to the fellow that burst out laughing when the firecracker went off. You can't do anything when you're tense.

"What's the next company on our list?"

"A securities company. What sort of event do you think would be appropriate?"

"Do you know anything about securities?"

"No, not a thing."

"Why not get the applicants to question the members of the board. They ask the questions; we give the answers. We know from experience that framing a good question is a skill."

"That sounds like fun."

The interviews were fun. And discussing the interviews beforehand was fun. True to our usual form, we staged a lot of novelty events. We let off firecrackers as in the advertising interview; we filled a box with odd items, got the applicant to pick one, and challenged him to make us laugh with the item selected; we got the applicants to compose cheerleader songs in support of their cause. M and I, of course, sang our cheerleader song. Many of the applicants liked our questions and our novelty event approach. We were more like people charged with making the interview a fun experience than actual members of the interview panel. If interviews had been conducted like this, I thought, we'd have got jobs too.

This, we thought, was our first experience of doing something meaningful. If you were to ask us what exactly we meant by *meaningful*, we wouldn't be able to answer. All we knew was that it was now the second half; we felt we were no longer on our own, asleep in the locker room. Fail-aholics ourselves for a time, we were now charged with giving encouragement to fail-aholics. We were delighted to be someone's shield. Even if the shield was only plastic or glass.

We had just completed our twentieth or twenty-first interview assignment. The interview had been for web designers. There had been so many applicants we were exhausted. We didn't feel like talking on the way home. We had to ask different questions to each applicant depending on personality and the answers each gave. And not everyone was able to adapt to the novelty event we had prepared. Bit by bit we reached the stage of exhaustion. We were running out of ideas and the process was becoming less and less fun. No fun after only twenty assignments. That was strange. We sat side by side in the back of the bus and looked out the window.

"Nothing's easy, is it?" M said, continuing to look out the window. The question seemed directed at himself rather than me.

"We'll have to go back to the beginning again," I said, also looking out the window. "This is not for us."

We were viewing the same scene.

"To the beginning? You mean back to doing interviews every day? That was fun all right, but this is better."

"No. Further back."

"Go to college again?"

"No, further."

M turned his head and smiled at me.

"You don't mean a suicide pact and meet again in our new life? Not that surely?"

"No."

"I'm not sure what you mean by 'the beginning.' We must have gotten here from some fork in the road."

"What was your dream?"

"Dream? Why suddenly ask about dreams? That's childish . . ." M turned toward the window. He said nothing more. He wasn't looking at the scene outside, he was trying to remember his dream. Once M told me he wanted to be a head gardener. He also said he'd like to travel and he'd like to be a zookeeper. M stuck his head out the window. We said nothing. I looked at M's profile. It occurred to me that this might be our last time in a bus together. We'd been sitting vacantly on a bus, we'd had a brief conversation, and now we'd passed a specific point. We had passed a fork in the road. He chose the left and I chose the right. I felt as if the ties that bound our ankles had been loosened without us even being aware of it. Tightly stretched electric wires showed where we had come from. I couldn't put a name on it, I couldn't date it precisely, but I felt that a phase of my life was ending.

Suggestions
for Further Reading

Collections

Land of Exile: Contemporary Korean Fiction. Revised and expanded
　　edition. Edited and translated by Marshall R. Pihl and Bruce
　　and Ju-Chan Fulton. Armonk, N.Y.: M. E. Sharpe, 2007.
Modern Korean Fiction: An Anthology. Edited by Bruce Fulton and
　　Youngmin Kwon. New York: Columbia University Press, 2005.
A Ready-Made Life: Early Masters of Modern Korean Fiction. Selected
　　and translated by Kim Chong-un and Bruce Fulton.
　　Honolulu: University of Hawai'i Press, 1998.
The Red Room: Stories of Trauma in Contemporary Korea. Translated
　　by Bruce and Ju-Chan Fulton. Honolulu: University of
　　Hawai'i Press, 2009.
Wayfarer: New Fiction by Korean Women. Edited and translated by
　　Bruce and Ju-Chan Fulton. Seattle: Women in Translation,
　　1997.
Words of Farewell: Stories by Korean Women Writers. Translated by
　　Bruce and Ju-Chan Fulton. Seattle: Seal Press, 1989.

Yi Hyosŏk

"Pig," 1970. Translated by E. Sang Yu. *Literature East and West* 14, no. 3 (September).

"When the Buckwheat Blooms," 1998. In *A Ready-Made Life*.

"City and Specter," 2007. Translated by Young-Ji Kang. *Acta Koreana* 10, no. 1 (January).

Ch'ae Manshik

Peace Under Heaven, 1993. Translated by Chun Kyung-Ja. Armonk, N.Y.: M. E. Sharpe.

"Mister Pang," 1997. Translated by Bruce and Ju-Chan Fulton. *Asian Pacific Quarterly* (winter).

"A Ready-Made Life," 1998. In *A Ready-Made Life*.

My Innocent Uncle, 2003. Translated by Bruce and Ju-Chan Fulton, Kim Chong-un, and Robert Armstrong. Edited by Bruce Fulton and Ross King. Seoul: Jimoondang. In addition to "My Innocent Uncle," this collection includes "A Ready-Made Life" and "Once Upon a Paddy."

"The Wife and Children," 2007. Translated by Bruce and Ju-Chan Fulton. In *Land of Exile*.

O Chŏnghŭi

"The Party," 1983. Translated by Sŏl Sun-bong. *Korea Journal* (October).

"The Toyshop Woman," 1989. Translated by Bruce and Ju-Chan Fulton. *Korea Times*, November 5, 7, and 8.

"Chinatown," 1989. In *Words of Farewell*.

"Evening Game," 1989. In *Words of Farewell*.

"Words of Farewell," 1989. In *Words of Farewell*.

"A Portrait of Magnolias," 1992. Translated by Bruce and Ju-Chan Fulton. *Koreana* (summer).

"Fireworks," 1993. Translated by Bruce and Ju-Chan Fulton. *Asian Pacific Quarterly* (winter).

"Morning Star," 1996. Translated by Bruce and Ju-Chan Fulton. In *Seeing the Invisible*, a special issue of *Manoa* (8, no. 2), on contemporary women's short fiction from South Korea.

"Wayfarer," 1997. In *Wayfarer*. Also in *Modern Korean Fiction*.

"Lake P'aro," 1998. Translated by Bruce and Ju-Chan Fulton. *Korean Literature Today* (winter).

"The Monument Intersection," 1998. Translated by Suh Ji-moon. In *The Golden Phoenix: Seven Contemporary Korean Short Stories*. Boulder: Lynne Rienner.

"The Release," 2003. Translated by Bruce and Ju-Chan Fulton. *Arirang* (summer).

The Bird, 2007. Translated by Jennifer Wang Medina. London: Telegram Books.

"The Bronze Mirror," 2007. Translated by Bruce and Ju-Chan Fulton. In *Land of Exile*.

"Spirit on the Wind," 2009. In *The Red Room*.

"The Face," 2009. Translated by John Holstein. In *A Moment's Grace: Stories from Korea in Transition*. Ithaca, N.Y.: Cornell University East Asia Program.

Pak Wansŏ

"The Good Luck Ritual," 1990. Translated by Stephen J. Epstein. *Korea Times*, November 1.

The Naked Tree, 1995. Translated by Yu Young-nan. Ithaca, N.Y.: Cornell University East Asia Program.

"Camera and Workboots," 1996. Translated by Bruce and Ju-Chan Fulton. *Koreana* (summer).

"Identical Apartments," 1997. In *Wayfarer*.

My Very Last Possession: And Other Stories by Pak Wansŏ, 1999. Edited
and translated by Kyung-Ja Chun. Armonk, N.Y.: M. E. Sharpe.

"Misty Rain, Departing Rain," 2004. Translated by Don Mee Choi.
Acta Koreana 7, no. 2 (July).

"Mother's Hitching Post," 2005. Translated by Kim Miza and
Suzanne Crowder Han in *Modern Korean Fiction*. The second
of three stories thus titled.

"Invitation," 2007. Translated by Jessica Ji Eun Lee. *Acta Koreana* 10,
no. 2 (July).

"Winter Outing," 2007. Translated by Marshall R. Pihl. In *Land of
Exile*.

"In the Realm of the Buddha," 2009. In *The Red Room*.

Who Ate Up All the Shinga? An Autobiographical Novel, 2009.
Translated by Yu Young-nan and Stephen J. Epstein. New
York: Columbia University Press.

Kim Wŏnil

Evening Glow, 2003. Translated by Agnita M. Tennant. Fremont,
Calif.: Asian Humanities Press.

Kim Yŏngha (Young-Ha Kim)

Photo Shop Murder, 2003. Translated by Jason Rhodes. Seoul:
Jimoondang.

"The Man Who Sold His Shadow," 2004. Translated by Dafna Zur.
Korean Literature Today (fall–winter).

"Lizard," 2004. Translated by Dafna Zur. In *Jungle Planet*, a special
issue of *Manoa* (16, no. 2). Also in *Modern Korean Fiction*.

"Moving," 2006. Translated by Jennifer Wang Medina. *Acta Koreana*
9, no. 2 (July).

I Have the Right to Destroy Myself, 2007. Translated by Chi-young
    Kim. Orlando: Harcourt.

"My Brother's Back," 2007. Translated by Kyong-Mi Kwon. *Azalea* 1.

"Their Last Visitor," 2007. Translated by Dafna Zur. *xchanges*
    (spring): http://www.uiowa.edu/~xchanges/spring2007/
    contents.html. Also in *Azalea* 1.

"This Tree of Yours," 2007. Translated by Dafna Zur, *Azalea* 1.

Your Republic Is Calling You, 2010. Translated by Chi-Young Kim.
    Boston: Houghton Mifflin Harcourt, 2010.

Ha Sŏngnan

"The Woman Next Door," 2006. Translated by Janet Hong. *Koreana*
    (winter).

"Blooms of Mold," 2007. Translated by Janet Hong. *Azalea* 1.

"Banner," 2008. Translated by Janet Hong. *Acta Koreana* 11, no. 1
    (January).

P'yŏn Hyeyŏng

"To the Kennels," 2008. Translated by Yoosup Chang and Heinz
    Insu Fenkl. *Azalea* 2.

"Mallow Gardens," 2009. Translated by Cindy Chen. *Acta Koreana*
    12, no. 1 (June).

"The First Anniversary," 2010. Translated by Cindy Chen. *Azalea* 3.

Kim Chunghyŏk

"Inuk the Inventor," 2007. Translated by Jennifer Wang Medina,
    Azalea 1.

About the Contributors

Cindy Chen is a graduate of the University of British Columbia and a law student at Boston University. Her translations of other stories by P'yŏn Hyeyŏng appear in *Acta Koreana* 12, no. 1, and *Azalea* 3.

Michael Finch is an associate professor in the Department of Korean Studies, Keimyung University. He is the author of *Min Yŏng-hwan: A Political Biography* (University of Hawai'i Press, 2002)and the translator of several books, including *Min Yŏnghwan: The Selected Writings of a Late Chosŏn Diplomat* (University of California Press, 2008) and *Korean Perceptions of the United States: A History of Their Origins and Formation* (Jimoondang, 2006).

Bruce Fulton teaches Korean literature and literary translation in the Department of Asian Studies, University of British Columbia. He and Ju-Chan Fulton have translated numerous works of modern Korean fiction, most recently *The Red Room: Stories of Trauma in Contemporary Korea* (University of Hawai'i Press, 2009) and *Lost Souls: Stories*, by Hwang Sunwŏn (Columbia University Press, 2009).

Janet Hong is a writer and translator living in Toronto. She won the Grand Prize in the 32nd *Korea Times* Modern Korean Literature Translation Awards competition for her translation of Ha Sŏngnan's "The Woman Next Door." She has received an International Communication Foundation Translation Fellowship and recently completed an M.F.A. in creative writing.

Miseli Jeon received her M.A. from the Graduate School of Simultaneous Translation and Interpretation, Han'guk University of Foreign Studies, Seoul, and her M.L.S. (School of Library and Archival Science), M.A. (Asian Studies), and Ph.D. (Programme in Comparative Literature) from the University of British Columbia. She was awarded a Korea Foundation Fellowship for Graduate Studies and a post-doctoral fellowship from the Social Sciences and Humanities Research Council of Canada.

Young-Ji Kang is a graduate of the University of British Columbia. She is currently translating fiction by Yi Hyosŏk and Kim Namch'ŏn.

Teresa Kim is a graduate of the University of British Columbia (English Literature). For "We Teach Shame!" she was co-recipient of the Grand Prize in the 4th Undergraduate Translation Workshop at the University of British Columbia in 2006.

Kevin O'Rourke, Professor Emeritus (Kyunghee University), is an Irish priest (Columban Fathers) who has lived in Korea since 1964. He has published many translations of classical and contemporary fiction and poetry including Yi Munyol's *Our Twisted Hero* (Hyperion, 2001), *The Book of Korean Shijo* (Harvard University Press, 2002), and *The Book of Korean Poetry: Songs of Shilla and Koryo* (University of Iowa Press, 2006).

Joel Stevenson graduated from Brigham Young University with a B.A. in Asian Studies in 1988. In 1999 he received an M.A. in Asian Studies from the University of British Columbia, where he translated "Constable Maeng" as part of his thesis project. He now resides with his family in Whitefish, Montana.

Dafna Zur is a doctoral candidate at the University of British Columbia, where she is completing her dissertation on the construction of the child in Korean children's magazines from 1908 to 1950. Her translations have appeared in *Modern Korean Fiction* (Columbia University Press, 2005) and in journals such as *Azalea*.